Praise for the w

A Message in Blood

Her characters are well-developed, even the bad guys. Chiara's PTSD and her sexual orientation are integral to the person she is, not just a quick paint job to make her more relevant.

The LGBTQ community seems to recognize her skills; she has been nominated for at least two Lambda awards. While NYC is an iconic place to set a mystery, especially a police procedural, it is also a place the author obviously is comfortable in and can write about with authenticity. It is obvious fairly early that the bad guys are well-connected; what is not obvious…is where all the strings are connected. That was a pleasant surprise…

-reviewingtheevidence.com

This is such an excellent mystery series! It's really well done and each book is better than the last. This is the third and possibly final book in the series and I could not stop reading it.

The mystery is all contained in this one book so you could start the series here if you really wanted to. I would recommend starting at book one, *A Matter of Blood* or at least I would suggest reading book two, *The Blood Runs Cold*, first. The main character Corelli has had some incredible growth in this series. I like my detectives flawed and a bit moody so I always enjoyed her character but it's still great seeing the new person she is becoming. Anyway, there is the growth in Corelli, the experience and backbone her partner grew, and just other relationships that you would miss out on if you didn't start reading this series at book one…If you could not guess by my glowing review, I would absolutely recommend this series to all mystery fans.

-Lex Kent's Reviews, *goodreads*

This is a dark and intense book that shows some of the worst sides of humanity—but it also shows good winning over evil. The characters feel real, and the mystery is filled with twists and turns—I never saw the end coming. If you enjoy a well-written dark mystery, I would recommend checking out *A Message in Blood*.

-KRL News & Reviews

I love a good lesbian detective novel and this one is an excellent example as to why, there is nothing more satisfying as reading about a network of strong women, mostly queer who work together to find justice for women and girls. Fantasy? Maybe but a good one. In this book the author wanted to shine a light on the horror of child sex trafficking and I think she did an excellent job…There is a lot in this book which really shows the power of a good crime novel especially with a network of kick-ass, mostly female, mostly queer people determined to do what they can in a corrupt society.

-Claire E., *NetGalley*

Matters of the Heart

Matters of the Heart is a lesbian medical romance where a doctor and patient find love together. I don't know how Catherine Maiorisi did it….I recommend *Matters of the Heart* to anyone who's looking for a solid, traditional romance.

-The Lesbian Review

I'm a sucker for a slow-burning romance, and this one nicely hit that spot. As is made clear in the introduction, it's Maiorisi's first attempt at a full-length romance—previously she has been known for murder mysteries. If she wants to continue in this genre, she's off to a great start.

-Rainbow Book Reviews

A Matter of Blood

This is an excellent mystery and whodunit with well-developed characters, an interesting backstory and great potential. The action is fast-paced but nicely interspersed with moments of stillness and humanity....Well written, enjoyable reading. I literally can't wait for the next one to see where Ms. Maiorisi takes us with both the crime-fighting team and the prospective romance.

-Lesbian Reading Room

This book was a long time in the pipeline for Catherine Maiorisi, and it shows. The pacing is perfect, and there has clearly been a lot of work done over a long period on making sure that everything is just right. As a result, this is a really easy read that will hold your interest until the final page.

-The Lesbian Review

The Blood Runs Cold

While I did not read the first book in Catherine Maiorisi's Chiara Corelli series, this did not prevent me from thoroughly enjoying *The Blood Runs Cold.* Maiorisi populates her story with some much-needed diversity, but never strays into exhortative territory: these characters feel like individuals rather than stereotypes intended to fill a role (or purpose). The mystery is suitably complex, sure to keep readers guessing until late in the game.

-The Bolo Books Review

In most cases, I will say readers can start with the current book and not miss anything. With Chiara ostracized by other members of the department, readers should start with *A Matter of Blood* to get the full effect and the background of Chiara and PJ working together. Both books are fast-paced thrillers, where every minute could be their last, with no one to trust and nowhere to hide....Love page-turner thrillers? Pick these books up—then try to keep up with Chiara. It'll be a breathtaking ride.

-Kings River Life Magazine

An excellent police procedural with twists, turns and surprises. Looking forward to other mysteries featuring Chiara Corelli.

-Map Your Mystery

the Disappearance of Lindy James

Other Bella books by Catherine Maiorisi

Matters of the Heart
No One But You
Ready for Love
Taking a Chance on Love

The Chiara Corelli Mystery Series
A Matter of Blood
A Message in Blood
The Blood Runs Cold

About the Author

Catherine Maiorisi lives in New York City with her wife, Sherry.

Before the pandemic she wrote in cafés in her Upper West Side neighborhood. Now she writes in their apartment and sometimes in their house in the Catskills.

When she's not writing, Catherine is reading. She loves well-written WLW books and reads most genres including romance, mystery, sci-fi, and paranormal. She also reads mainstream mysteries. If she's not reading or writing, she's cooking. Italian is her favorite but she's always on the lookout for good recipes in any cuisine.

Catherine has published four romances—*Matters of the Heart*, *No One But You*, *Ready for Love* and *Taking a Chance on Love*. Her romance short stories are included in three Bella Books' anthologies—*Happily Ever After*, *Conference Call*, *and In This Together*. "Come as You Want to Be" and "The Fan Club" are standalones available on the Bella website.

Catherine is also the author of the NYPD Detective Chiara Corelli Mystery series: *A Matter of Blood*—a 2019 Lambda Literary Award Finalist, *The Blood Runs Cold*—a 2020 Lambda Literary Award Finalist and *A Message in Blood*. *Legacy in the Blood* will be published in February 2022.

Though Catherine considers *The Disappearance of Lindy James* a family drama, it is her first general fiction book.

the Disappearance of Lindy James

Catherine Maiorisi

2021

Bella Books, Inc.
P.O. Box 10543
Tallahassee, FL 32302

Printed in the United States of America on acid-free paper.

First Edition - 2021

Editor: Ann Roberts
Cover Designer: Heather Honeywell

ISBN: 978-1-64247-131-1

PUBLISHER'S NOTE

Acknowledgment

The Disappearance of Lindy James started with an image of Quincy meeting Megan, a child about the same age as her missing daughter Emma. As I started writing their story it became clear that I didn't know important things, that I needed to learn what came before that meeting, that I needed to go back to the beginning.

When I completed the full story, I wasn't sure it was publishable. But not ready to give up on the book, I studied the manuscript and realized I'd mashed together stories about two different times in the lives of the same characters. So I separated and rewrote the two parts and ended up with two books. The romance, *Taking a Chance on Love*, was published in July 2020. *The Disappearance of Lindy James* revisits Quincy and Lindy, six years after their happily ever after. The books can be read independently.

Thank you, as always, to Jessica, Linda, and the Bella Books staff for all you do. I especially appreciate the support provided on Disappearance—reading and offering a critique and publishing a book that is outside the usual lesbian fiction genres. I think of it as a family drama.

Thanks, also, to my editor Ann Roberts, for identifying places that needed shoring up and, as usual, trying to improve my use of the comma.

And much appreciation to my friend Judy Levitz, a psychotherapist, who read and offered helpful comments.

Religion plays a big role in the story. And while the characters see the three religious ladies and the haven in Arizona negatively, they do recognize that Dorothy's religion, her church, and pastor are welcoming, caring, and loving.

In the effort to get it right, I did a lot of reading about and research on postpartum psychosis. I hope I've presented an accurate picture of the illness, but any errors are mine.

Finally, thank you readers, for buying my books, reviewing them, recommending them to friends, and commenting on social media. You may not realize it but receiving a note or seeing a comment on social media about how you feel about my books is a gift and always makes my day.

Disappearance is not an easy read. The journey for both characters is painful but the message of enduring love is positive. And in the end, Quincy and Lindy reclaim their happily ever after. What could be better.

Message me on my website: http://www.catherinemaiorisi.com or on Facebook at Catherine Maiorisi.

Dedication

For all those living with a mental illness. And the spouses, partners, parents, children, and friends who love them.

And, as always, for Sherry. Your love and support make everything possible.

CHAPTER ONE

Lindy

What's happening to me? I can't eat. I can't sleep. I'm exhausted. I'm in a rage all the time, tossing pots and pans, slamming things around. And my poor innocent babies are bearing the brunt of it. If I keep moving I can control it some, but I can see the girls are terrified. Poor Michaela, sometimes she's trembling when I put her to my breast. I hope my milk isn't sour. And Emma, my brave, big girl backs away when I come close, but she always keeps Michaela behind her, trying to shield her sister from me. Protective. Just like Quincy. Quincy the hero. Quincy my love. Quincy my wife. No. No. No. My head hurts when I think about her.

I pushed Michaela, or maybe it was Emma, out of the car when I was driving to Shop Rite a couple of days ago, but when I pulled over, they were both in their car seats. Did I do it? Or did I imagine it? Now I'm afraid to drive. Afraid I might do it again. I can't tell Quincy. She would be angry if I hurt the girls.

The rage erupts like a geyser shooting to the sky. I don't know why I'm so angry, why I can't stop crying. I swore I'd never be like my mother, that I'd never hurt my children. But I'm a horrible mother. I'm afraid I'll hurt them.

So many bad things are happening in the world. Accidents. Hurricanes. Earthquakes. Shootings. Men spouting hate on TV. We could all die in an instant. In a head-on collision like Sarah, the mother who found me. Or shot in the head, like John, Quincy's partner. The other night, after Letitia told me Quincy is the devil, I was sure Quincy would shoot me in the head when she got home. I hid in the bathtub until Sarah reassured me from the showerhead that Quincy would never hurt me. Sarah also said she'll always be my mom and she'll love me forever, but I should be careful because people would be upset to find out she talks to me. I felt better after talking to Sarah but now I don't know who to trust, who to tell about what's happening. Should I tell Babs? Will she think I'm crazy? Am I crazy? She's my best friend and she keeps asking me what's wrong. She even showed up here last week without calling. I asked her to leave but she insisted on feeding and putting the girls down for a nap first. I had to make up a story to get her to go and I've been putting her off ever since. And just this morning John warned me that, like him, Quincy could die in an instant while waiting in the car for lunch. Something bad is going to happen. I know it. I'm helpless, like I'm caught in a whirlpool being pulled deeper into the darkness with every day that passes. Every breath is a struggle.

Then there's this scary guy who comes into our apartment at night and sneaks around in the shadows. A couple of nights ago he threw Michaela against the wall because she wouldn't go to sleep. He must have picked her up because she was okay when I checked her in her crib. Another time he threw her down and stomped on her until she was flattened and dead and no longer screaming. But when I looked, she was sleeping on the floor. Should I tell Quincy about him? One of these days he's going to really hurt one of the children. Is he another one of Quincy's lovers? I know she's having affairs with all our friends and Mrs. Wysocki our elderly neighbor...but a man? I thought she was a lesbian. I'm not a lesbian. Quincy is the lesbian. Letitia says I've been seduced by the devil.

I stare at the knife in my hand. I can't remember what I was going to do with it. I stab it into the counter. I can't use it on myself. I'm a sinner. If I kill myself, I'll be condemned to hell for eternity. If I continue to live this life, I'll still be condemned to hell. Unless I repent. I must fall to my knees and beg God to forgive me. The girls are innocents who will suffer in hell for eternity through no fault of their own. And killing them won't save them from that fate. It's up to me to save them, to help them live a Christian life. It's up to me save them from…her.

Wait, what's that noise? Her car. What's she doing home so early? I force myself to stop pacing as I watch her park the car, but the girls are both sobbing. Will she use this as the proof that I'm a bad mom so she can take my daughters away from me to live with her in hell? I've tried so hard to hide it from her until I have a plan. But she knows. It must be the cameras she has watching me twenty-four hours a day. Or does Satan see all?

CHAPTER TWO

Quincy

Quincy looked up from the fairy tale she was reading to her daughters and listened for the squeak of the loose floorboard in the living room. Lindy was still pacing. She'd been at it since Quincy arrived home unexpectedly. Now she seemed to be having a heated conversation with someone. But she was alone in the living room.

Quincy silently berated herself. She'd been feeling something was off with Lindy for a while now but working two full-time jobs had kept her out of the house from six thirty in the morning until after midnight. And since Lindy stopped getting up with her in the morning and waiting up for her at night, they rarely saw each other. But three times last night the girls woke up screaming and each time she got out of bed to comfort them Lindy was pacing in the living room. Lindy *always* rushed to comfort the girls and thoughts of her ignoring their distress had played in Quincy's head throughout the day. The feeling that something was terribly wrong had brought her home early tonight. And now that she'd witnessed Lindy's agitation again, she understood the girls' behavior, understood this was not a one-time thing. But what was wrong with Lindy?

Emma had run into her arms, sobbing when she'd walked into the kitchen. She picked her up, scooped Michaela off the floor and soothed them while they cried their little hearts out. Lindy's hands covered her mouth as she watched the three of them, wide-eyed, from the kitchen. After they quieted, she approached Lindy and kissed her cheek. "Hi, honey, looks like the girls are having a hard time today."

Lindy nodded. Her eyes shifted from Quincy's face to something behind her. Quincy turned to see what she was looking at. The sight of the chef's knife with its point buried in the countertop chilled her. She turned back to Lindy, but she'd moved into the living room and was pacing and mumbling. She sat Emma on the counter, pulled the knife out and put it in the drawer. She picked up Emma and followed Lindy. "I'm going to play with the girls for a while before we feed them. Okay?" She waited but Lindy didn't acknowledge her, so she took the girls into their room. While her mind raced, trying to figure out what to do, how to handle Lindy, she tickled her daughters, twirled them around, then played a couple of games with Emma while teasing Michaela with one of her stuffed animals. Almost an hour later, when she brought the girls into the kitchen, Lindy was sitting calmly in a chair. She extended her arms.

The baby whimpered and turned her face into Quincy's shoulder.

Lindy flushed. "Come on, baby."

Quincy kissed Michaela's head. "Go to Mommy, sweetie, she's going to feed you." She placed the girl in Lindy's arms. Michaela squirmed and pushed away. It took a minute of coaxing, but she accepted the breast. Mother and baby relaxed.

Quincy made Emma's favorite cheese omelet and toast, then poured her a glass of milk. She watched her daughter eat as if she was starving and wondered if Lindy had taken her to nursery school where she usually ate lunch. Maybe they could talk over dinner. She smiled at Lindy. "I can't remember the last time we ate together, Linds. How about once the girls are asleep I make an omelet for us or, if you prefer, I'll order a pizza."

Lindy hesitated, then smiled. "I'd really like an omelet, sweetie." Her smile was faint but her husky voice murmuring the endearment warmed Quincy.

Thankfully, by the time Quincy took them into their bedroom the girls had settled enough that six-month-old Michaela dropped off almost immediately and Emma was yawning. Quincy had to dig deep in the drawer to find clean pajamas for Emma. They were a little short but fit okay so she put them on and sat on Emma's bed to read to her. Worrying about Lindy made it hard to focus and hearing her talk to some phantom was freaking Quincy out. She kept stopping to be sure she was hearing what she thought she was hearing.

Emma snuggled closer and pulled on Quincy's sleeve. "Read, Mama."

She kissed Emma's forehead. "Sorry, baby."

"Michaela's a baby. I'm almost four."

"You are right, Emma, my love, almost four is a big girl."

Quincy picked up the story where she'd left off. It was another half hour and two stories later before Emma fell asleep. Quincy sat with her daughters for a few minutes, listening to their breathing, watching them sleep, before gathering the dirty clothing scattered around the room, and tiptoeing out.

She closed the door behind her quietly and stood in the doorway. Lindy marched from the kitchen to the living room and back. It seemed like months since Quincy had really looked at her wife. The vivacious and playful Lindy, her joyful Lindy, had been replaced with an agitated, tense, and unsmiling Lindy. When had she gotten so thin? And her hair looked like it hadn't been washed in a while. During the six years since they'd met, she'd often watched Lindy move gracefully by herself either to music in her head or on her iPod, while cooking, cleaning, soothing one of their daughters or standing lost in thought, and always when their eyes met their connection flared. But tonight her wife wasn't dancing to what she was hearing in her head, and she either didn't see Quincy or was choosing to ignore her. Neither was comforting.

Quincy went into the small laundry room, threw the dirty clothing into the washer, and started the cycle. She was perplexed and angry at herself.

Lindy was the cheerful one, the serene one. Something was definitely wrong. And she'd stupidly let her exhaustion blind her to the truth. In the last few weeks she'd often found Lindy up in the middle of the night, but each time she'd tried to talk about it, Lindy insisted she was fine, just tired, or she'd snapped at Quincy, which was completely out of character. Now, it seemed, she was having a conversation with someone only she could see. And hear.

She swallowed hard. Lindy was having a breakdown. The image of the knife stuck in the kitchen counter flashed in her mind. Was Lindy capable of hurting their children? The thought blasted shards of anxiety through Quincy. It was unthinkable. But she was a detective and she'd seen the worst of people. She knew it happened, mothers drowning, beating, stabbing their children to death. Did Lindy know the code to her gun safe? Just to be sure, she would change it tonight.

She returned to the living room.

"Lindy?"

The pacing and the mumbling continued.

"Lindy, honey, can we talk?" Quincy touched her arm gently as she sped past.

Lindy pulled her arm away as if the touch burned. She stopped but kept her back to Quincy. "About what."

"You seem, um, upset, unhappy. What's wrong, sweetie?" Quincy wrapped her arms around Lindy from behind, thinking it would calm her. Lindy relaxed into her arms, leaned her head against Quincy's shoulder, then shivered and pulled away. "No. I can't. It's wrong." She turned but avoided Quincy's eyes.

"What's wrong? Let me help you."

"Nothing's wrong. I just…it's…I got my period and really bad cramps and the kids were a handful today so I'm kind of frazzled." She managed a weak smile. "Why are you home so early?"

Quincy flinched at the accusatory tone but went with her instinct to soothe Lindy. "I feel bad about leaving you alone with the kids all the time. Things were quiet so I left early. I was thinking of taking some time off so we could go away for a couple of days, just the two of us."

When was the last time they'd made love? In their six years together, they'd had stretches where, for one reason or another, they didn't make love but even then they'd slept close, and Lindy had always reached for Quincy, rolled into her arms, whatever time she'd gotten into bed. But lately Lindy kept to her side of the bed and stiffened if Quincy got close or touched her. Damn, she should have challenged Lindy sooner. But she was rarely awake when Quincy was home. And in the middle of the night when Lindy was awake, Quincy was too exhausted to have any conversation, forget pressing Lindy about her state of mind.

The decision that Quincy should work all the overtime she could get, and take on a second job so they could accumulate money quickly for the down payment on the house they loved, made sense three months ago, but now she wondered about the stress on Lindy, home alone day and night with two little girls.

"What do you think, Lindy, honey? Would you like a couple of days, just the two of us?"

Lindy didn't answer. Instead she turned and started pacing again, mumbling to herself. When she stopped, Quincy noticed she was clutching a gold chain hanging around her neck. She reached for it but Lindy stepped back. "No, don't touch it."

"Sorry, I didn't mean to be invasive. I was just wondering what it was."

"It's…one of the women in the group I've been going to gave it to me." She showed Quincy the small gold cross. "Yes, Quincy." She smiled, but the smile was too bright, her eyes filled with pain. "I'd like to go away for the weekend. Not tomorrow, though. My women's group meets on Thursdays and I don't want to miss it. How about Friday? You decide where we go. Surprise me." She hugged Quincy briefly then pulled away. "I'm still feeling bad so I'm going to bed now."

"What about dinner?"

Lindy stopped, her back to Quincy. "I'm not hungry."

Her anxiety spinning out of control, Quincy stared after her wife. Thin as she was and breastfeeding, how could she not be hungry? And that cross. Lindy detested anything to do with organized religion. Could she be having an affair? Come to think of it, a lot of this strange behavior started not long after Lindy joined that women's group at the library. Maybe she'd met someone there.

Well, she was hungry. Lindy hadn't cooked in days and as Quincy realized when she tried to figure out what to feed Emma, she hadn't shopped either. They had some peanut butter, cereal, a few eggs, milk, bread and a little cheese but not much else. She made a list of things they needed so she could shop on the way home tomorrow. But a peanut butter sandwich would suffice for tonight's dinner. While she ate her sandwich, she considered the best way to deal with Lindy. And realized she needed an objective opinion to see whether she was exaggerating things. She speed-dialed Lindy's best friend. Babs also had two young children and she and Lindy often spent the day together at the park or at one of their houses.

Babs picked up immediately. "Quincy, great to hear from you. How's my Lindy? I haven't seen her in a while."

Quincy explained why she'd called. Babs gasped. "Damn, I was afraid something was wrong. She's been brushing me off, saying she didn't feel well or she was busy. I dropped in around noon about a week ago to try to find out what was going on. I've never seen her so…so upset. She actually screamed at Michaela and Emma."

Quincy's antenna went up. "Emma was home? Not at nursery school?"

"I was surprised too but Lindy said she didn't feel well enough to drive her to school in the morning."

Quincy's stomach lurched. "I'm going to check in the morning, but I suspect she's stopped taking Emma to nursery school and Emma isn't getting lunch."

"Shit. No wonder she ate like she was starving. It took me a while but I was able to calm her and Michaela, then get them fed and into bed for a nap, but I couldn't get Lindy to talk about what was bothering her. She denied being angry at me but basically threw me out of the house. I almost called you because she said she thought she had postpartum depression. Then I remembered she'd been depressed after Emma and had pulled out of it. And though her doctor accused her of being lazy and looking for drugs, she did go to see him so I felt she was taking care of herself."

"I saw on the calendar that she had an appointment with her gynecologist but I haven't been able to talk to her about it, or about anything really. She insists she's fine. But tonight when I was reading to Emma, she was talking to someone in the living room but no one was there. Was she doing that when you saw her?"

"Not that I noticed, but I was focused on getting Emma fed and getting Lindy to nurse Michaela. You know breastfeeding always calms Lindy."

"Jesus, Babs, she's coiled so tight she could snap. I'm really worried about her and the girls."

"Yeah, I'm worried too. Maybe you should talk to her gynecologist tomorrow. I'll come over around noon after I do my shift at the boys' nursery school, see if I can get through to her."

"Good idea. She has her women's group in the morning. I'm coming home early but it would be great if you could show up when she gets back from the group. She hasn't shopped in a while so would you bring lunch for her and Emma? She's agreed to go away with me on Friday and I'm hoping I can get through to her, maybe get her into therapy."

Talking to Babs hadn't eased her worry and after they hung up Quincy stared at her phone for a moment. Though she was afraid to hear what her best friend Amelia, a psychiatric social worker would say, she called her. Amelia listened without comment while Quincy described Lindy's behavior, Emma and Michaela's distress, then expressed her fears. "I agree, something is seriously wrong. It could be postpartum depression but it sounds more serious, like she's having a breakdown. Why don't you put the kids in the car and bring them to my house right now? Or I can come and get them. Depending on how she is tomorrow, you can try to get her to the hospital or to a therapist, but at least you'll know the girls are safe."

"I'm afraid it will put her over the edge if she wakes up and the kids aren't here. She seemed calmer after agreeing to go away for a few days."

"Are you sure, Quince? It sounds as if she's hallucinating and that worries me."

"I can't just steal the kids, Meelie. She's already shaky and I think it would devastate her." Hearing herself use her childhood friend Amelia's nickname made her realize just how anxious she was. And she knew Amelia wouldn't have missed it. "I'll be here all night and I'll come home early tomorrow. Babs is going to stop in tomorrow afternoon. Lindy has her women's group at ten thirty so she'll be out for a couple of hours. Could you drop in around nine tomorrow morning to see if everything is okay? Between you and Babs and her group, she'll only be alone with the girls for a few hours." She took a deep breath. "I truly believe she'd never hurt them, but just to be sure, I'll take the knives to work with me."

"I trust your judgment, Q. I'll definitely go by in the morning and hang out with her a bit."

"Thanks, Meelie. I'll bring the girls over to your house Friday morning before we leave."

"Mia and Lara will be over the moon to have Emma here for the weekend." Amelia's voice was gentle. "And, Quincy, if Lindy doesn't seem better by the end of the weekend, you may have to hospitalize her."

Quincy flinched. She knew this was serious, but deep inside she'd hoped Amelia would tell her not to worry, Lindy would be all right. "I know."

She sat up thinking about things until midnight, the time she would usually be getting home. Lindy and the girls were her life. Just a couple more weeks and they'd have enough money for the down payment and legal fees but working a second job was no longer an option. If the house was sold before they had the money they needed, so be it. She changed the code on her gun safe, packed the knives, forks and scissors and went to bed.

Up at five thirty a.m. as usual, Quincy marveled that for the first time in months, Lindy had slept in her arms. Maybe she just needed contact and support. As she brushed her teeth she stepped to the door and peered into the bedroom. Lindy was still asleep. Though Lindy had stopped getting up with her to have coffee months ago, Quincy was hopeful she would join her today. When that didn't happen, she considered taking the day off to keep an eye on Lindy and the girls, but she had the day covered and it would be best to keep things as normal as possible until the weekend.

At six thirty, Quincy put a note on the kitchen table and left for work.

CHAPTER THREE

Lindy

As soon as I heard Quincy leave, I got out of bed. She was so tender and loving with the girls and with me last night, I wanted to tell her everything, to let her take care of me. When she got into bed I couldn't help myself. I gave in to the yearning for her touch and the desire for her to hold me. As usual, being in her arms soothed me and made me feel safe. I slept for five consecutive hours for the first time in a while. But this morning I realized she knows I know she's Satan. Her loving and caring and understanding are just pretenses to lure me back to her unchristian, sinful life. She's so powerful, so irresistible. I can't fight her. But if I stay, our unnatural love will condemn me to burn in hell for eternity. And our innocent girls who didn't choose to be born into this sinful life will burn with me. It's too dangerous for us to stay. Letitia, Lauren, and Joanna have offered to help me save myself and the girls.

Those three think I don't know what they're doing. They offered to help me get away from Quincy and they've been pressuring me to leave. They think they can control me, but I refuse to let them, or anyone, decide what I do or when I do it. God was angry with me this morning. He warned me to be wary of Quincy, her warmth and her loving tenderness are meant to lure me to hell with her. God said it's good that I'm stubborn, but I must leave. Today.

The coffee she made is still warm and I sip while I read the note she left for me.

Sweetheart:

I loved holding you last night, it's been too long. The girls didn't wake up overnight and neither did you so it seems we all slept well.

I'll be home early again tonight. Don't worry, I'll take care of dinner.

I've arranged for Amelia and Jackson to take the girls so we can go away as planned Friday morning.

I'm really looking forward to some quiet time together.

Love you more than ever.

Quincy

Is it the coffee that's burning my stomach or feeling Quincy's love come through in the note? She knows how to get to me. Love should be good and healing and wonderful but Satan's love is false and evil and poisonous, meant to lure me into eternal hell. The note confirms what God said. I have to leave. She's trying to trick me into staying. She knows I can't resist when she's close. I must go. Now is the time.

The girls are fed and dressed. I've packed just a few necessities for each of us, leaving the devil's things with the devil. Now a note for Quincy. How much can I tell her? How can I make her understand why I must take the girls away from our sinful lifestyle? It will be hard on her because she truly loves our daughters. But she is the devil. Can the devil really love? "It's okay, God. Please stop yelling at me. I'm leaving. I'm writing the note. I know I can't tell Quincy or the three bitches that you told me to leave. Yes, yes, I know you don't speak to everyone. Please just let me have a few minutes of peace."

Finally. The note is on the table. My heart is breaking. How can I leave the one I love? Loving Quincy even though I know she's Satan is a terrible sin. How can I love Satan and still love God? "I'm sorry, God. Yes, I'm leaving." I put my keys next to the note.

Ah, the doorbell. Letitia has come to drive us to a safe place. Letitia who looks fifty but is only in her thirties, is the leader of the pack, probably because her husband is the pastor at their pathetic church. "But it is pathetic, God. Yes, I know they're helping me so I should be nice. Okay, I'll stop calling them bitches." I clamp my mouth shut and try to relax before letting her in, no need to give her more ammunition to attack me.

I swing the door open and Letitia is tapping her foot as if she has a job to go to or something important to do. Her limp red hair, the pale, freckled face that always looks like she's just sucked a case of lemons, and the dowdy cotton dress make her look as if she's from another century. Maybe she is. She's not the kind, warm, and caring person one would expect of someone so religious. But I should know about that, shouldn't I?

"Ready?" She smiles but it's fake and doesn't fool me. "You should skip our women's meeting today in case...she comes looking for you." I know Letitia's support is not about me; it's about her. She lusts to win one for her church by getting me to leave. Maybe she gets points for each convert.

"Thank you. I'll think about your advice." Maybe she's right. I hand her the suitcase, pick up Michaela. "Come, Emma." As I pull the door closed, I feel panicky. I don't want to go.

Lauren, the warmer, kinder, and more caring one of the three seems to sense my reluctance and puts her arm around me. "We need to go in case she comes back." With her dark hair and dark eyes, Lauren is pretty but she seems flattened out, as if all the praying has taken her spirit away. I will not let that happen to me. Emma takes my hand as Lauren steers me to the car. I look back at the apartment. I've been happy here, maybe I shouldn't—

"YOU MUST GO NOW." God's voice blasts at me through the car radio. I jump but I manage not to respond. I can't let them know God talks to me. I see Letitia watching me in the rearview mirror. Did she hear? No, God was very clear that I'm special, that I'm the only one he talks to but maybe she suspects. I force a smile. "Shall we go?"

CHAPTER FOUR

Quincy

Quincy glanced at the time when her phone rang. Nine-ten a.m. "Quincy?" Amelia sounded distraught. "I'm at your apartment. Lindy's car is here but she's not answering the door or the phone. I think you should come right away."

Quincy got a black and white to drive her home with the siren blasting. She jumped out, signaled Amelia to stand back, and ran up the steps to unlock the door. Her heart threatening to break through the wall of her chest, she walked into the silent house. Weapons in hand, the uniforms followed. "Lindy. Lindy, honey, I'm home. Are you here?" She crept from room to room, relieved to find the apartment empty. "Thanks, guys, I guess it was a false alarm."

"No problem, Quince." Officer Gina Lawson, one of Quincy's closest friends, hugged her. As they turned to leave, Gina pointed to the kitchen table. "Quincy, there's an envelope with your name on the table." She looked at her partner and tilted her head toward the door. "Why don't you wait outside, Jimmy."

Quincy turned on the light. The envelope was leaning against a bottle of Dr. Pepper, Lindy's drink of choice. Lindy's keys lay next to it. She sat and stared at the envelope and the keys, afraid of what they meant. The envelope had her name on it but the writing was a far cry from Lindy's usually neat script.

She didn't hear Amelia come in, just felt her hands on her shoulders. "Open it, Quincy."

"I…" She turned to look at Amelia.

Amelia nodded. "Open it, honey."

She carefully opened the envelope and unfolded the letter.

Dear Quincy,

I'm sorry that I wasn't brave enough to tell you last night that I've recently come to realize we are living in sin, that we have conceived our children in sin and that they and we are doomed to eternal hell if we don't repent and denounce our lesbian lifestyle.

I know you won't agree with me and I'm really not strong enough to fight to convince you. The best I can do is take the girls and myself away someplace where we can live as good Christians, without the taint of lesbianism. It was you and I who sinned, not the children, and I will pray to the Lord for forgiveness for myself – and I will pray that someday you will see His light as well. But if I don't take our children away from our sinful life, and away from you, a sinner, then I will be responsible for them burning in hell. I know you don't want that for the girls. But maybe when you realize that I'm taking them away from you, you'll wish me to burn in hell for eternity.

I thought what I felt for you was love, Quincy, I truly did. But I know now that Satan had me in his grip and he led me to lust for you in an unnatural and sinful way. I'm sorry that I didn't realize this before we had two children in sin, but they are innocents and can be saved.

I pray we all can be saved – you too.

Please forgive me.

Lindy

Quincy handed the letter to Amelia and began to pace. "After all the horror stories she told me about growing up in that kind of an environment, how can she think of dragging our daughters through that hell. I've got to find my girls. Where would she go?" She rubbed her forehead, trying to erase the throbbing. "She left her car so she couldn't have gone too far. The cross. I should have known when I saw the cross. A woman in that group gave her the cross. I need to go to the library to get the names of the women in the group."

Amelia handed Gina the letter. "Give me a minute to make arrangements for someone to pick up my kids and I'll drive you there, Quince."

Gina paled and her hand shook as she read the letter. She folded it, hugged Quincy, and gave it to her. "We'll get her back. Jimmy and I will cruise the neighborhood and hopefully I'll spot her."

Quincy nodded. "Can we keep this between the three of us for now?"

"You bet."

The three of them left together.

The librarian stood behind the desk. "I'm sorry. I don't know anything about their members. They're not associated with the library. They just rent space for their meetings."

Quincy flashed her badge. "Are they here now?"

"They meet upstairs at ten thirty." She glanced at the clock. "It's almost eleven. They usually finish between eleven thirty and twelve. You can sit in the reading room until they're done."

"I can't wait." Quincy started up the stairs.

Amelia followed. "Stay calm, Quincy. Remember your objective is to bring Lindy and the children home."

Quincy and Amelia walked into the meeting and all eyes turned to them. Two of the twelve or thirteen women tensed visibly.

"I'm looking for my wife, Lindy James Adams."

The women murmured to each other. A washed-out redhead stepped forward. "She didn't come to the meeting today."

"Is she the only one who didn't come today?"

The same woman answered. "No, one other didn't make it. What is this about?"

Quincy scanned the group. The woman who had answered and an equally drab-looking, sandy-haired woman standing next to her were the only ones wearing crosses. "She met a woman here. Do any of you know who she is? Someone religious?"

Eyes swung to the two wearing crosses but no one said anything.

"I think Lindy is having a breakdown. I need to talk to her. I'd like the names and addresses of everyone in the group."

"We can't give you that information," the woman said, "it's private. And if Lindy wanted to speak to you she wouldn't have left—" Realizing what she had given away, the woman stopped. Quincy moved in front of her, invading her personal space and forcing her to look up. "How about you tell me where she is, Ms.?" She didn't attempt to hide her rage.

The woman tried to step back but a chair was behind her. "It's Mrs. Charles Leswick." She emphasized *Charles* as if to drive home that she was married to a man.

"Where is Lindy?"

She avoided Quincy's eyes and shuffled around her. "Let's end early today, ladies." Her voice was shaky.

Quincy and Amelia watched them file out silently under the watchful eye of the spokeswoman. "I could follow that bitch home but she's probably with the one who didn't show today."

"I'll catch up. I forgot my knitting." The voice from the stairwell preceded a chunky blonde who dashed in, grabbed a bag off the floor and as she walked past Quincy slipped a small piece of paper into her hand.

"Don't look at that now," Amelia said softly as she led Quincy out of the library, "you might tip the leader off."

They got into the car. Quincy opened the slip of paper. She read it to Amelia. "Call me. Ellen. 201-555-0170."

Amelia started the car. "Let's go for coffee. We can figure out how to approach her and other things you should be doing."

They found a table by the window in a nearby Starbucks. Amelia got a latte for herself and a black coffee for Quincy.

Quincy removed the cover and blew on the hot coffee before taking a sip. "When she joined the group, she said it was for neighborhood women with small children. She's probably staying with one of them. If I walk around, I might spot her on the street."

"You might, Quince, but there are legal things you should do right away, before you call that woman and before you make contact." She grabbed Quincy's hand to turn her attention away from the window. "You and Lindy both have legal rights to both kids, right?"

"No problem there. It's complicated so we had papers drawn up to protect us and the kids."

"These arrangements were done by a lesbian lawyer, I assume. Is she your friend or Lindy's?"

"Shayne Elliot did all the papers. She's our attorney but neither of us is friends with her. Why?"

"You need to contact her right now to discuss what's happening and work out a strategy for getting the girls back or at the very least shared custody."

Quincy dropped her head into her hands. "Oh, God, why didn't I see this coming? I should have listened to you last night and brought Michaela and Emma to you."

"Don't beat yourself up. You love Lindy and you were trying to take care of her and the girls. Who could predict she would go off the deep end like this?"

"I should have known."

"Should haves are meaningless. It's what you do now that matters. Pull yourself together and call your attorney."

After hearing the short version of events, Shayne Elliot instructed Quincy to come to her office so she could file papers immediately to keep Lindy from fleeing with the kids.

When Quincy and Amelia arrived they were shown right into the attorney's office. She waved them to the chairs in front of her desk.

"This is my friend Amelia Sinclair, she's a social worker. Amelia, my attorney, Shayne Elliot."

Elliot smiled. "You were smart to come right away." She opened a file folder that was in front of her. "Before we proceed, I want to review what I have on file. Correct me if I'm wrong or if something has changed. Emma is your daughter. Lindy James Adams acted as surrogate for you, carrying your egg fertilized by Eduardo Marcanti's sperm." The attorney looked up.

"Yes."

The attorney made a note before continuing. "Michaela is Lindy's daughter. Her egg fertilized by Eduardo's sperm and carried by her."

The attorney could see Quincy getting agitated. "Bear with me, Quincy, I need to do this." She looked at Quincy again. "Eduardo Marcanti gave up all parental rights to both children?"

"Correct."

"And, finally, you each adopted the other's child so you both have parental rights to both girls?"

"Yes."

Elliot made a note. "Have you married?"

"Originally, we did the civil marriage thing, then when gay marriage became legal, we married."

"Good. I'll immediately file an OTSC, that's an Order to Show Cause, with a petition for an emergency hearing to get you visiting rights. I'll argue that by unilaterally removing the girls from their home, Lindy interfered with your parental rights and caused you irreparable harm. That should get the judge to sign."

"So I'll have visiting rights but not custody?"

Amelia cleared her throat. "Quincy, tell Ms. Elliot about Lindy's mental state. Show her the letter. It might change things."

"What about her mental state?" Elliot was on it in a second.

Quincy stared at her hands. As much as she loved Lindy and wanted to spare her the embarrassment of being seen as crazy, it was more important to protect her daughters from harm. She looked up. Shayne Elliot was gazing at her with compassion. She took a deep breath, handed her the letter and launched into the story.

"Well, that changes things. If you're willing to attest to this in court I believe we can win full custody for you, at least while Lindy undergoes a psychiatric evaluation."

Amelia squeezed Quincy's hand. Amelia's support encouraged her to do what she had to do. "I'll do whatever is necessary to keep my girls safe."

Elliot nodded and made a note. "Okay, I'll file the OTSC with a petition for an emergency hearing. I'll also request a temporary restraining order to keep Lindy in New Jersey until the matter is resolved. And, based on what you described, and the religious tone of the note Lindy left, I'll file a complaint requesting permanent custody because she's a flight risk, citing the case of Lisa Miller, the lesbian who the Mennonites helped flee to Nicaragua to prevent her ex-lover getting visiting rights for their daughter. Hopefully, the judge will agree to the psychiatric evaluation of Lindy. How does that sound?"

Quincy took a deep breath. "This is moving too fast for me." Amelia squeezed her hand again. "But if this is necessary to ensure I don't lose my girls I'm all in."

Elliot leaned back. "Call that woman and find out where Lindy is staying if you can. Tell her you just want to make sure Lindy and the girls are all right. But don't go there. I'll need the address to serve her." She glanced at her watch. "In about an hour, I'll file the papers with the court. Then assuming the judge signs the OTSC, a first hearing will be set within a few days and you and Lindy will appear before a judge."

Quincy nodded.

"She may contact you after she's served and try to talk you out of going to court. Don't fall for it. If you eventually work things out, we can clear the court thing, but if it was me and my kids at risk, I'd wait until I was absolutely sure there's no threat. And, Quincy, I know it'll be hard to not go to wherever she's staying but it's better to wait. If you need confirmation, I have a PI on staff who can verify that Lindy and the girls are there and are all right."

"If I can't go myself, I definitely need confirmation. Can she get some pictures?"

"She'll try. Call me as soon as you have an address. Also, it would help to have a picture of Lindy so the PI and the process server get it right."

Quincy pulled out her wallet and handed Elliot a picture of the four of them in happier times. "I'd like that back."

Elliot took her hand. "You're doing the right thing, Quincy."

Outside, Amelia hugged Quincy. "Why don't you come home with me? You can call from there."

"I need to be home in case she changes her mind and comes back. But thanks. Your support means a lot."

"Hey, you're not getting rid of me so fast. I'm calling Jackson as soon as we get to your place. He'll be fine with the kids."

As soon as they walked into her apartment, Quincy punched in the telephone number. "Ellen? This is Quincy Adams, Lindy's wife. You asked me to call. I think Lindy is in trouble. She took our girls and left me a note filled with religious gibberish. I need to know where she is so I can be sure my daughters are safe."

The woman on the other end took a deep breath. "When Lindy joined the group, I warned her that they proselytize everyone. Lindy thanked me, said, 'been there done that' and laughed. Once they realized Lindy was in a lesbian relationship they went all out to convert her but she laughed and went head-to-head with them on religion. At first, she only saw them in the meetings. But after a while she seemed to get depressed. She talked about losing some people she was close to and said she thought she was suffering from postpartum depression. As soon as they sensed her defenses were down, they were all over her like flies on honey. She started hanging out with them after our meetings. Lately, she'd been acting strangely, muttering during meetings, getting up and pacing around while others were talking. I tried to find out what was wrong, asked if she needed help, but she insisted she was fine, just restless."

"Do you know where she's staying?"

"Probably with Lauren King, the only one of the religious trio that wasn't there today. She lives at 245 West Park Street. Letitia is the one who did the talking today so let me give you her address and Joanna's, as well."

Quincy wrote the information down. "Thank you. I…would you call me if you hear anything?"

"Definitely. I have your number in my cell now. I'm so sorry I never thought to try to contact you when I saw she was in trouble. Good luck."

While Amelia prepped lunch, Quincy called Elliot's office and gave her assistant the addresses where Lindy was most likely staying. It was one thirty in the afternoon and there was nothing she could do to bring her family home. The shock of Lindy leaving was easing but her anger was rising. How could Lindy take the girls from her? How could she destroy their marriage?

She couldn't sit still. In the living room she picked up each of the framed pictures on the faux mantel. Her hands shook as she lifted the one taken right after Michaela was born. Patsy, their photographer friend, had managed to capture a beautiful moment. The four of them were sitting on the couch, a radiant Lindy holding Michaela, and an equally joyful Quincy with Emma in her lap and her arm around Lindy. They stared into each other's eyes, still in love after more than six years together. Angry tears prickled her eyes. She put the picture down and moved to the doorway of the girls' room and did a quick scan. Her heart clutched. A part of her expected to see Emma and Michaela playing, to hear their giggles, and their absence seemed to echo in the emptiness.

She blinked, trying to focus. The room looked normal, toys neatly piled with a few stragglers on the bed and in the crib, books in the bookcase under the window, diapers stacked neatly on a shelf, a dirty diaper on the changing table. Her gaze lingered on the dirty diaper. Her anxiety amped up. Lindy must have been in a great hurry if she left a dirty diaper lying around. She took a deep breath and continued her scrutiny until her eyes fell on the empty space above Michaela's changing table where Lindy kept the breast pump. Somehow Lindy taking the breast pump with her made it real, made it clear she and the girls were not coming home tonight. Maybe never. Quincy's knees gave way. She curled into a ball, moaning in despair. Within seconds, Amelia was behind her on the floor. She wrapped her arms around Quincy and held her while she cried out her pain. When

Quincy's sobs turned to an occasional sniffle, Amelia pulled her into a sitting position, handed her a tissue, and continued to hold her from behind. "I'm glad you were able to release some of that tension, Q."

They'd been best friends since the second grade and early on Amelia had discovered it was easier for Quincy to speak from the heart if there wasn't eye contact, so over the years their most intimate and painful talks occurred when walking side by side or sitting like this with Amelia holding her from behind. Quincy leaned into the comfort of her friend.

"Want to talk about it?"

Quincy shrugged. Amelia waited.

"I was angry but when I saw she took the breast pump I felt as if someone had stuck a knife in my heart, twisted it, and then cut out my guts. I feel hollow. What if I never see my daughters or Lindy again? How will I live? I feel betrayed. How could she do this to me, to us, to our girls?" She took a deep breath. "But mainly I'm worried about her harming Michaela and Emma. And herself. This isn't her, Meelie. I told you about the knife stuck in the counter. Something or someone has her in its grip, and I don't know how to fight whatever it is from a distance."

"I know you can't help worrying but try," Amelia said. "We're pretty sure she's got people around her and that's good. Plus, we don't know how this will play out in court. Maybe you'll get custody. Maybe Lindy will be open to counseling. You need to focus on fighting for the girls."

Quincy leaned back into Amelia. "You're right, I'm getting ahead of myself."

Amelia tightened her arms. "You know I'm not saying you don't have good reason to worry, don't you?"

"Yeah. I can't promise to stop worrying but I'll try to contain it." Quincy stood and pulled Amelia up into hug. "Thanks. I was going to see what Lindy took for the girls." She moved into the room, ran her hands over the stuffed animals in Michaela's crib and on Emma's bed, sat the dolls on their shelf, and tossed the loose toys into their proper basket.

Michaela's favorite blanket and her stuffed bunny and Emma's tattered stuffed froggie were gone. It was harder to tell about the clothing but she thought Lindy had taken only a few items. The cloth diapers were in a neat pile but the emergency pack of disposable diapers was gone. Lindy was so committed to the environment that leaving the cloth diapers behind could mean she only intended to stay away a short time, but taking the pump indicated the opposite. Next she checked the closet and the drawers in her and Lindy's bedroom. Lindy mostly wore jeans, tees, and sweaters, so it was hard to say if any of those things were gone, but the dressier clothing and jewelry that Quincy had given her, things she'd loved, were all there. She turned to Amelia. "Maybe she was thinking of this as temporary?"

"Either that, or she was traveling light for a fast getaway."

Quincy sighed. "The note didn't sound temporary. I wonder if she left anything behind that would show what she's planning." She went into the living room and rifled through the desk but came up empty-handed except for the folder with ideas for decorating the house they planned to buy. Her first instinct was to shred it. *Damn, Lindy.* Quincy had worked sixteen-hour days for three months so they could have this house, and now when they were so close, she was gone. But Lindy wasn't herself and it was possible she'd rethink this decision after a couple of days. She closed the folder and put it back in the drawer.

Gina came over at the end of her shift with Chinese food for the three of them. Quincy had no appetite and was relieved that neither Amelia nor Gina commented on the fact that she basically pushed the food around on her plate. Babs showed up around seven after Danni came home to be with their boys. As the four of them talked and speculated about what had prompted Lindy to run away, they moved in and out of anger and sadness. At eleven o'clock, after Quincy reassured them she would be okay, her three friends left. Alone for the first time all day, Quincy reread the note and tried to recall any events of the last few months that might have triggered Lindy's abandonment. But her brain refused to cooperate and she could only obsess about the fact that Lindy was gone. Finally, her eyes heavy, unable to make sense of anything, she fell into bed about three a.m. Still, sleep eluded her and her anxiety-fueled imagination conjured heartbreaking images causing an eruption of sobs. Was Lindy in danger? Were the girls?

CHAPTER FIVE

Lindy

I made it. I escaped with my daughters. So why don't I feel safe? Why do I feel so alone? Why do I keep thinking about how much I hurt Quincy? And why do I feel like dead meat with three vultures circling, waiting for a chunk of my flesh?

But I'm unkind. They offered to help and I accepted. Lauren is the nicest of the three. She's warm and friendly, not so predatory, and she seems to sense that I want to be alone. I sit on the bed in her guest bedroom watching her nine-year-old daughter on the floor with the girls quietly reading them a religious story. I appreciate the peace, grateful for some time to think. Other than meals, I only see Lauren when the other two show up and Letitia starts nagging. I think Lauren is sympathetic and is trying to give me the space to figure out what I want. She doesn't seem as fanatical as Letitia and Joanna, who constantly pressure me to take the girls to a Christian safe haven they know, somewhere Quincy won't find us. I tune them out when they talk. They, especially Letitia, think they're in control of me but I'll do what I want. I don't see why I have to run away.

This morning, Letitia said Quincy came looking for me at the meeting yesterday and once again she brought up the safe haven. I knew Quincy would search everywhere for the girls so I'm not running until I decide I need to go. But I'm glad I didn't have to see her.

"What did Quincy say?" I know this can't be easy for her.

Joanna, Letitia's toady, pipes up. "She threatened poor Letitia. I thought she was going to hurt her." I fight to keep the smile from my lips. I'm sure she did. Too bad I missed it. At almost six feet Quincy can be imposing and frightening but she's not a violent person. Up against Letitia's five feet, two inches, I'm sure her goal was to scare the information out of her, rather than physically harm her.

"Don't exaggerate, Joanna. I was never in danger from the evil one after she saw my cross." While she pooh-poohs Joanna, Letitia eyes me, looking for a reaction. "It's time for you to meet the other women at the church, Lindy. You must come to church with us tonight after the girls are asleep."

She's not fooling me. I know Quincy is not afraid of the cross. I stop at that thought. Does that mean she's not the devil? God screams from the radiator, "She's so strong it doesn't affect her." I want to ask him if she's stronger than him but if I do they'll know he talks to me. I stare at the radiator hoping God will say more. When Lauren touches my shoulder, I look up blankly. They're all looking at me and I remember they are waiting for my answer about tonight. I don't think it's a good idea. I want to stay in for a few more days until Quincy gets used to us being gone. But I realize I'm dependent on them and I have to give a little if I want their support. So I agree.

It's eight p.m. when we step out of the house. I'm anxious. I don't want to leave the girls. I don't want to go to their church. As I walk to Letitia's car, I search for an excuse to stay here.

"Lindy James Adams?"

I whirl toward the voice. "Yes." I hear several clicks.

A woman shoves a paper in my hand. "You're served."

"Get away from her," Letitia screams. "You have no right to take our pictures."

I'm stunned. Two women jump into a car and pull away, tires screeching. I stare dumbly at the paper in my hand while Letitia yells at me for accepting it. I start to shake. Lauren puts her arm around me and leads me back into the house. She looks at the paper. "It's a summons to appear in court the day after tomorrow."

"Court?" It never entered my mind that court would be involved. God screams, "Quincy will win and you'll lose the girls to the devil!"

I cover my ears and curl into myself. I can't take all this screaming. I start to cry. I don't want to go to court. I want to go home to Quincy. She'll take care of me.

Lauren tries to comfort me. "Don't worry, we'll get a lawyer for you."

"But I don't have any money."

As always, Letitia takes charge. "We won't let you or your daughters burn in hell, Lindy. That woman can burn by herself."

Suddenly God's voice spews out of Letitia's mouth, reminding me Quincy is Satan.

I close my eyes and put my hands over my ears trying to shut them all out. I'm not aware that I'm screaming, "Get thee behind me, Satan," until I open my eyes and see the three of them wide-eyed and pale. Lauren waves the other two toward the door then puts her arms around me and tries to comfort me. I feel compelled to tell her that I will fight Satan until I face the judgment of Our Lord Savior. And I will fight Quincy in all the courts of this world.

CHAPTER SIX

Quincy

Quincy stood in the hall outside the courtroom with Shayne Elliot and two of her character witnesses, Amelia and Police Chief Connie Trubeck. Babs, her third character witness, was on the way. The hallway was filled with groups of people waiting to be called into one of the courtrooms and the noise level was high, but Quincy was barely aware of the conversations flowing around her. She'd been on an emotional roller coaster since Lindy left, one minute loving and missing her, the next minute hating and wanting to hurt her. Now waiting for her to appear, the anger was choking her. Her eyes flicked between the elevator and the stairwell, watching for her first sight of Lindy.

At last Lindy appeared. Despite the dreary-looking redhead with a proprietary hand on Lindy's arm and a mouth that never stopped moving, Lindy looked uncertain and alone as she exited the elevator with Michaela in her arms and Emma hanging on to her skirt. Her eyes swept the crowd, then locked onto Quincy's gaze.

Quincy's anger faded. Lindy looked so fragile and frightened. Quincy could feel her anguish and if it wasn't for Amelia's hand on her shoulder and her whispered, "No, Quincy," she would have bounded across the room and taken Lindy in her arms. They stared at each other until an overweight man in an ill-fitting suit joined Lindy and her friend. Letitia Leswick. She remembered the woman's name. He spoke and gestured toward the girls. Lindy shook her head vehemently. He appealed to the woman. She reached for Michaela. Lindy turned away. The woman's face twisted in anger and she seemed to be berating Lindy. Quincy recognized Lindy's stubborn face and knew she would not give an inch on whatever they were proposing. Lindy was near tears. Michaela started to cry. Quincy instinctively moved a little closer in case Lindy needed her.

In the middle of the struggle between the three adults, Emma spotted Quincy. "Mama."

She launched herself across the hall and Quincy swooped her up in her arms, near tears to be holding her daughter. She covered the girl with kisses and Emma giggled. "Where were you, Mama? I missed you."

Over Emma's shoulder, Quincy saw the anguished look on Lindy's face. Clearly this was difficult for her. Why was she putting all of them through this horror? She turned her attention back to Emma when the girl spoke. "Can I stay with you when they go in the room, Mama?"

Shayne Elliot was at her elbow. "The girls can't come in the courtroom. They'll have to stay out here."

So that's what Lindy was upset about. She looked around. Babs had just arrived and was watching along with Amelia and Connie. Babs pointed to herself. Quincy nodded. "How would you like to stay with Auntie Babs while Mommy and I go in that room?"

Babs came over and hugged Emma from behind. "Hey, sugarplum. You're going to be as big as me soon."

Emma twisted to look at Babs. "Are Daniel and Ben here?"

Babs kissed the girl's forehead. "They stayed home today, honey. Will you wait out here with me?"

Lindy approached but avoided Quincy's eyes. Michaela leaned toward her, Quincy shifted Emma and pulled Michaela to her chest. "Hey, baby girl." She kissed the baby's belly. "I miss you." Michaela giggled, latched onto Quincy's hair and rested her head on Quincy's chest. Quincy was overcome with sadness. Her family was broken and she had no idea how to fix it. She tightened her hold on the girls. But she would fight to protect her daughters.

Lindy stood by, stiff and pale. Emma swiveled in Quincy's arms to look at Lindy. "Can I stay with Auntie Babs?"

Lindy looked toward Babs but didn't meet her gaze. "Will you stay with them, Babs? They can't come in and I don't want to leave them with..."

Babs touched Lindy's face gently. "Of course, Lindy. Are you sure you still want to go through with this?"

Lindy glanced back at the glowering woman standing with the red-faced guy who must be her lawyer. Were they coercing her? Then she mumbled something that sounded like *temptation*.

Before Quincy could ask Lindy if she needed help, their case was called. Elliot signaled Quincy to follow and walked into the room.

Lindy kissed the girls. "Mommy will be back soon. Be good for Auntie Babs." She walked into the courtroom with her little group trailing behind.

Quincy lingered to hug and kiss both girls and reassure Emma she would see her later. Babs whispered, "My God, she looks awful." Quincy nodded, took a deep breath and entered the courtroom. Amelia and Connie followed.

It wasn't a formal courtroom but a room with three tables in a sort of pyramid arrangement with rows of chairs behind the two tables that formed the base. Quincy sat next to Shayne Elliot at one table and Lindy sat next to Mr. Huff and Puff at the other. Quincy turned when the door opened again and was surprised to see many friends and colleagues from work sitting behind her on a workday. As she turned back, her gaze fell on Lindy, sitting at the other table. She appeared to be paying no attention to the conversation between the two people with her and didn't seem to be aware of the whispered conversations of the large group of their friends in the room. Instead, her focus was on the painting of a stern-looking older man in the black robe of a judge on the wall to their right. She fingered the gold crucifix that seemed to be a fixture these days and her lips moved. It looked like she was speaking but maybe she was praying. The rush of anger roiled the bile in Quincy's stomach. Lindy who hated all organized religion, Lindy who had suffered at the hands of her ultra-religious parents, Lindy whose childhood was isolated and loveless and lacked the joy of books and music and art, now was fighting to bring her daughters up in that same environment. She poured herself a glass of water.

Judge Myra Fleming explained the legalities, then spoke to Quincy's attorney. "Ms. Elliot, I see as usual, everything is in order. I'm impressed by the number of character statements in support of Ms. Quincy Adam's request for custody."

Elliot stood. "Your Honor. Detective Adams is a well-respected member of the community and a true hero as attested to in some of those statements."

Judge Fleming turned her attention to Lindy's attorney. "Your paperwork, Mr. Krause, is not sufficient."

Krause stood. "My apologies, Your Honor. I'm a member of the church Ms. Lindy Adams attends. I do real estate, not family matters, and I didn't have time to get up to snuff on procedures since this hearing was scheduled so quickly."

"I see." She thumbed through the papers. "Ms. Lindy Adams, would you mind answering a few questions?"

Lindy tore her eyes from the painting and stood. "Of course not, Your Honor." She smiled and spoke in a soft but strong voice. "Please call me Lindy."

The judge smiled. "Come closer and tell me a little about yourself."

Lindy hesitated, stepped closer, then cleared her throat. "Well, there's not much to say. I'm not a hero like Quincy, Your Honor. I'm just a stay-at-home mom who loves our daughters and wants what's best for them."

"I notice you've only known your three character witnesses for a few months. Why is that? Do you not have connections in the community?"

"Most of my friends are also Quincy's friends, some from her job, and a lot of lesbians. And, um, I recently got back in touch with my religious beliefs and I now believe the lesbian lifestyle is not acceptable to God so I wouldn't ask lesbians to be character witnesses. Besides, I assume all our friends will side with Quincy."

"Why is that?"

Lindy shrugged. When the judge seemed to be waiting for an answer she glanced at Quincy and said, "Because they care about Quincy and about me and the girls. They would want us to be happy and stay together. But none of them are very religious and I don't believe they understand where I'm coming from."

"Have you always been religious?"

Lindy stiffened. "I grew up in a religious home but I never believed in organized religion. I always sort of believed in God but it's only recently that I truly began to believe and to realize how wrong my lifestyle is."

The judge glanced at her papers. "You've been together more than six years. Why did you leave now? Did Ms. Quincy Adams object to your turn to religion?"

"No. Quincy is a good, kind person, a loving wife and mother, and a good provider. It surprised her but she didn't object. At least she hadn't before I left." The gasp from behind her caused Lindy to swivel to look at the woman she'd come with. She abruptly turned to the painting hanging on the wall and frowned. She appeared to be listening, then she muttered something.

The judge frowned. "Who are you speaking to, Lindy?"

Lindy didn't respond but continued to stare at the wall.

"Lindy?"

Lindy turned to face the judge. "Sorry, what was the question?"

"You seem to be speaking to that painting. Are you feeling all right?"

Lindy hesitated. “I was speaking to you. Why would I speak to a painting?”

“That’s what I was wondering.” The judge glanced at the papers in front of her. “Have you been hallucinating or hearing voices recently?”

Mr. Huff and Puff struggled to his feet. “I’m not sure where you’re going with this, Your Honor. Ms. Adams is nervous, and rightly so since these proceedings will decide whether her daughters will grow up in a loving Christian home with her or in a sinful lesbian environment.”

“Thank you, Mr. Krause. Ms. Quincy Adams indicated she observed Ms. Lindy Adams having a conversation with someone in an empty room.” The audience gasped and whispered conversations broke out. Lindy stumbled back. She grabbed onto the table. “Quiet please or I’ll ask you all to leave.” The judge spoke to Krause. “So you can see why I’m concerned that your client appeared to be talking to that painting. Let’s continue.” She focused on Lindy. “Have you been hallucinating or hearing voices recently?”

Lindy started to turn toward the painting but caught herself and faced the judge. “I’m not sure how Quincy or you got that impression, but the answer is no. Mr. Krause is right. I’m worried about my daughters.” Her voice shook.

Quincy started to stand to object but Shayne Elliot grabbed her arm. “Don’t.”

The judge made a note. “Lindy, was Ms. Quincy Adams ever abusive to you or your daughters?”

Lindy didn’t hesitate. “No. She would never hurt me or our daughters. But, um, she’s a lesbian and I now think our lesbian relationship dooms us and our daughters to burn in hell. So I took our daughters away to save them.”

“Aren’t you a lesbian?”

“I was but I’m hoping through prayer I can save us. I left because I needed some time to figure things out.”

“So you took your daughters away from their other mother to save them from hell?”

“Yes.” Lindy seemed surprised to see the frown on the judge’s face. “Also to think about my relationship with Quincy and with God. And, uh, it made sense for me to take both the girls with me since I'm the one who is at home with them and takes care of them."

"How will you support yourself and the girls?"

"That's one of the things I need to figure out. I'm staying with…um, a friend for now."

"Do you have any objection to Michaela and Emma seeing Ms. Quincy Adams?"

Lindy lifted her fist to her mouth and seemed to gnaw on her knuckles. She turned so her back was to the painting. "That's the point of leaving, Your Honor. I'm trying to keep them away from her because of our sinful lifestyle." She glanced over her shoulder.

"Tell me what that painting means to you."

"What." She turned to the painting again. "Oh, the painting. Um, no significance. I, uh, as I said, I'm nervous."

"According to the papers filed by Ms. Quincy Adams, Michaela is your biological child and Emma is her biological child, but both are legally her daughters as well as yours. Therefore, she is entitled to a say in their upbringing and to spend time with them. In fact, she's petitioned for full custody. She claims you are currently mentally unstable and her attorney has petitioned the court to have you undergo a psychiatric evaluation."

"What?" Lindy shouted. She spun and glared at Quincy. "She'd say and do anything to get the children back." She turned to the judge. "I've been upset. Wouldn't you be, Your Honor, if you felt your lifestyle would hurt your children. And I've been depressed. It's not easy to leave the person you thought you loved, your friends, and everything important to you to protect your children." The fist was at her mouth again. She closed her eyes for a second, then faced the judge. "If it takes a psychiatric evaluation to prove that I am a loving, capable mother, I'll gladly agree to it. In the meantime, I guess it would be all right for them to see her while I figure things out. But I don't want them to be alone with her. I want to be with them."

"Has she molested the children or physically abused them?" The courtroom erupted. The judge used her gavel to silence the crowd. "Well, Lindy?"

Lindy turned to look at the women who'd accompanied her, then her head jerked toward the door at the faint sounds of Emma running and her laughter drifting in from the hall. Her eyes met Quincy's briefly, then she turned back to the judge.

"No, Your Honor, as I said, Quincy would never hurt them. I'm afraid she'll take them away and keep me from saving them."

"Do you have any plans to travel? Do you have a passport?"

Lindy smiled. "No, I don't have a passport and neither do the girls. Where would I go?"

"No family or friends you'd go to?"

"Quincy can confirm that I haven't spoken to anyone in my family since I was fourteen and I've never had any desire to see them."

"Ms. Adams?"

Quincy stood. "That's true, Your Honor, but her family is very religious and until recently she's been virulently anti-religion, so who knows?"

"Lindy speaks highly of you. Is she a good mother?"

Quincy stepped closer to Lindy. "Lindy has been a wonderful mother. I love her dearly but recently she's seemed…uh, unsettled and agitated. I believe she's having a breakdown. The other night I arrived home earlier than expected because Lindy ignored the girls when they woke up screaming several times overnight and I suspected she was doing the same during the day. Our daughters have been distraught and stressed, unable to sleep through the night. Lindy had stopped taking Emma to nursery school and failed to replace the lunch she usually ate there. Emma was starving when I made her dinner. And Michaela was so frightened of Lindy that I had to cajole her to take Lindy's breast."

Quincy glanced at Lindy standing next to her. She didn't want to hurt her but the stakes were too high. "Lindy spent most of the night pacing and talking to people who weren't there. I'm a detective. I've seen what mentally unstable people, mothers, are capable of. The night before Lindy left me, I found a large chef's knife stabbed into our kitchen counter. The danger was so clear to me that the next morning I made arrangements for friends to visit with her until I could return home and took all the knives, forks, and scissors to work with me. I believe Lindy is a danger to herself and the girls. I believe giving me full custody is in the best interest of Michaela and Emma."

The crowd went into an uproar.

The judge banged the gavel. "Quiet if you want to stay."

"Lindy?"

"Our marriage is a sin. Leaving them with her will put them in more danger than they already are. Schedule the psychiatric exam. If the psychiatrist thinks I'm a danger to the girls I'll gladly give them to Quincy. But I need to be with them to know they're safe and I need to be separate from Quincy to think clearly."

While the crowd whispered, the judge shuffled some papers, made more notes and turned to Lindy and Quincy. "Ms. Quincy Adams are you willing to continue to support Lindy and your daughters while we wait for the results of the psychiatric evaluation?"

"I am, Your Honor. I haven't changed anything since she left so she still has access to all our joint accounts, her phone, and her car if she wants it."

"All right, Mr. Krause, this needs to be done quickly. Schedule the exam for the earliest date possible, hopefully, tomorrow. Ms. Lindy Adams can take the children home tonight, but I'll communicate my temporary custody decision tomorrow morning. Once we have the psychiatric evaluation, I'll schedule a full hearing. Mr. Krause, I expect you to be up to snuff with the filing. If you can't handle it, the court will assign a lawyer with knowledge of the custody laws." Judge Fleming stood.

Shayne Elliot rose. "I object, Your Honor. Leaving the children with Lindy Adams puts them in real danger. I think the chef's knife stuck in the kitchen counter and, to be frank, her behavior in this courtroom with regard to that painting should be enough to award my client full custody until the psychiatric examination is completed and reviewed by the court."

The judge turned to Lindy's attorney. "Do you want to address that, Mr. Krause."

He hesitated. Lindy stepped forward. "Your Honor, I think I should answer since I'm the one being accused of being crazy. I put the knife down after chopping vegetables for dinner and it fell off the counter twice. I'll admit I was annoyed at myself because I hadn't put it back far enough from the edge. I stuck it in the wooden counter out of frustration and fear the girls would be hurt. Obviously, I didn't stab myself or the girls and I didn't attempt to hide what I did before Quincy came home. As for the painting, I'm really frightened that you'll give my daughters to someone I consider a sinner and I think it's kind of a nervous tick. Finally, before I left Quincy's house I was alone with the girls all day until late at night because Quincy was working two jobs. Now I'm staying with a friend who's in the house with me all day. I don't know where she keeps her knives and scissors but I'm only alone when I go to sleep so we're all perfectly safe. Your Honor, please let me keep the girls until I take the exam and prove my sanity."

The judge took a moment to consider the arguments. "My ruling stands. Ms. Lindy Adams will take the children home tonight and tomorrow I will issue my determination about ongoing custody when we have the results of the psychiatric evaluation. She banged the gavel and left the room.

As they turned to follow the crowd out of the room, Quincy took advantage of the opportunity to confront Lindy. "Don't do this to Emma and Michaela, Lindy. I love you. Come home with me. We can work this out."

"Why can't you understand that I have to go away to save Michaela and Emma and me?" Lindy closed her eyes. "You're trying to tempt me, to keep me living in sin to drag us all down to hell."

Quincy's anger flared but she managed to keep her voice gentle. "I don't understand, Lindy. How is telling you I love you and the girls trying to tempt you? And in your heart you know our love is not a sin. How could something so wonderful be a sin."

Lindy's anguish was palpable.

Quincy fought the impulse to take Lindy in her arms and comfort her. She spoke softly. "And how can you think I'm trying to drag you all down to hell? I'm the woman you swore to love till death do us part. And you said it yourself. I would never harm you or the girls." Quincy touched Lindy's cheek. "Let's go somewhere to talk, just the two of us."

Lindy turned her face and Quincy's fingers slid over her lips. Lindy trembled. "I—"

"Lindy?" Lindy's eyes flew open at the sound of her name. She looked from Quincy to Letitia and back to Quincy. "No." She backed away from Quincy. "You're the devil trying to trick me." Quincy stared at her wife's rigid back as she hurried out of the room. *Shit. Does she really believe I'm the devil? Why had she become religious now? Is there any hope we could reconcile?* She slowly followed Lindy out of the room, arriving in the hallway in time to see Lindy take both girls from Babs and rush to the elevator where the redheaded woman was holding the door. "Mama!" Emma screamed when she saw Quincy. She leaned out of Lindy's arms reaching for Quincy. Quincy reached them as the elevator door closed. She banged on the doors in frustration, then turned toward the stairs.

"Stop her." She didn't know whether it was Elliot or one of friends who issued the command but strong arms held her back. Jackson apologized and held her as she sobbed. When she looked up, she and Jackson were surrounded by her friends. She sniffed. "Thank you for being here." He handed her his handkerchief.

"Sorry, Quincy, I don't want to give them grounds to deny you visiting rights," Shayne Elliot said as she stepped into the circle. "We need to talk."

Her friends took the hint and took turns hugging her before leaving. When it was just Amelia and Quincy, Elliot led them down the street to a coffee shop. She waited until the waitress had deposited their drinks on the table before speaking. "Lindy must have been well rehearsed by that broken-down attorney of hers. She managed to project fragile strength and a sincere desire to protect the girls. She was quite effective. Judge Fleming can often be difficult but she was gentle with Lindy. I think she was taken with her."

Quincy shook her head. "I don't think she was rehearsed at all. That was the real Lindy. Right, Meelie?"

Amelia nodded. "That's why we love her. She's honest and forthright and gutsy." She looked at Quincy. "And loving. But I'm surprised the judge bought her story. Her attention kept going to that painting and she seemed to be listening. I'm pretty sure she's hallucinating, hearing voices. I think she even answered the voice at one point."

Quincy sat up straighter. "I thought it was the stress. You think it was voices? The last thing she said to me as we left the court was that she knew I was the devil trying to tempt her. Do you think she really believes I'm the devil?" She looked from Amelia to Elliot.

Amelia took Quincy's hand. "I believe she's having a nervous breakdown. But I have to admit, even I almost bought her final statement to the judge."

"She was right to the point, unlike her attorney." Elliot stirred her coffee. "Judge Fleming isn't seeing her as clearly as you, Amelia, and it's what the judge thinks about Lindy that counts." She put her spoon down. "Hopefully, Fleming will give Quincy temporary custody until the psych evaluation is complete. Based on what you've said and what we saw in court, I'm sure it will prove she's mentally unstable."

CHAPTER SEVEN

Quincy

Quincy and Amelia were in Shayne Elliot's office the next day when Judge Fleming called. Elliot put her on speakerphone. To everyone's surprise, the judge concluded Lindy was not a flight risk and though the first available slot for the psychiatric examination was in ten days rather than this morning, she awarded Lindy temporary custody and scheduled the hearing for a week after the exam. Quincy was given generous visitation rights, but she could only meet with the girls in a public place—a playground, a park, a McDonald's—selected by Lindy, who would call Quincy by ten in the morning to tell her where to meet them.

Quincy's face darkened. She stood, ready to do battle.

Shayne Elliot put her finger to her lips to silence Quincy, before challenging the judge. "With all due respect, Your Honor, it seemed pretty clear to me yesterday that Lindy is disturbed. Not only is she a flight risk *à la* Lisa Miller but given her state of mind I believe the girls are in danger if they remain in her care."

Judge Fleming made no effort to hide her annoyance. “Are you questioning my judgment, Ms. Elliot? In my opinion, the mental issue comes down to what Quincy claims, what Lindy says and what I saw in my courtroom. You are aware, of course, that I could have granted sole custody to Lindy, but I didn’t because I believe their daughters need both mothers. If you’d rather your client not see her children until we know the results of the psychiatric examination, continue to push, and I will change my ruling.”

“Sorry, Your Honor. I’ll inform my client.” Elliot hung up the phone. “Damn, I was afraid she’d be taken in by Lindy but I was sure she’d award you temporary custody.” She met the gaze of a white-faced Quincy sitting with Amelia in front of her desk. “I’m sorry, Quincy. I know this is a blow but believe me it will be worse if I continue to push the judge. I advise you to accept the arrangement, always take Amelia or another friend with you and engage with Lindy as little as possible to avoid problems. The last thing we want is to face the judge again before we have the exam results.”

Quincy took a deep breath. It wasn’t what she wanted but maybe it would work to her benefit. The court didn’t rule that Lindy had to be there, but maybe spending time with her and the girls would change Lindy’s mind.

Quincy switched to the night shift so she could spend Monday, Wednesday, Friday and Saturday afternoons with the girls, at least until the psych eval and their court appearance. At their first meeting, Quincy and Amelia watched Lindy enter the park carrying Michaela and holding Emma’s hand. Quincy watched them stroll toward her, her eyes flicking from the girls to Lindy and back. The woman walking next to Lindy, the redhead who’d accompanied her to court, didn’t stop talking but Lindy seemed oblivious. Her eyes never left Quincy’s face. Amelia squeezed Quincy’s arm. “Let them come to you, honey.”

“She looks upset.” Was Lindy upset because she thought Quincy was the devil or because she still loved her and wanted to come home? Or maybe that woman was saying something that upset her. “Maybe I should—”

"Don't jump to conclusions, Quince. Despite what she's saying and doing, it's clear she still loves you, so seeing you under these circumstances must be difficult for her."

Lindy leaned over and spoke to Emma. The girl dropped her mother's hand and dashed to Quincy. "Mama." She clutched Quincy's legs. "Can I come home, Mama, please?"

Quincy knelt and pulled her close, struggling to answer through the tears choking her. Then Michaela was leaning out of Amelia's arms to get to Quincy. Quincy stood with Emma in one arm, took Michaela in her other arm, and twirled the two of them to keep them from seeing her tears. The girls were giggling when she put them down on a bench, trying to catch her breath. Amelia pulled Michaela into her lap and hugged and kissed both girls, giving Quincy time to dry her eyes.

"Where are Lara and Mia?" Emma demanded. "I haven't played with them in a long time."

Amelia smiled and kissed Emma again. "The twins are in nursery school so they couldn't come today. They miss you, too. I'll try to bring them next time."

"I miss nursery school. Can I go again, Mama?"

Quincy raised her eyes to Lindy hoping their daughter's plea to come home and get back to her normal life would have an impact. Lindy looked away.

Not knowing what to say, she deflected. "Let's play."

"We aren't allowed to run or scream."

"Stay calm, Quincy, you could lose custody if you do what you're thinking." Only Amelia's calm voice kept Quincy from screaming at Lindy and punching the smirking redheaded bitch sitting next to her. She took a breath. "You can't run in the house but when you're outside with me, you can play games and run and scream." Though Quincy had brought some of their toys, they spent most of their three hours together with Quincy holding Michaela in her arms playing catch and chase and tag with Emma. Near the end of her time with them, Quincy opened their favorite fairy tale book to read a story to settle them. Emma glanced at Lindy, sitting on a bench a little way off. She whispered in Quincy's ear, "We don't read fairy tales anymore, Mama. We only read about baby Jesus now."

Quincy kissed both girls. “It’s okay to read fairy tales when you’re with me.”

Emma grinned. “Do you remember my birthday is coming soon?”

“Would I ever forget such an important day?”

The girl glanced at Lindy again. “Mommy says I can’t have a party but I can have presents, can’t I?”

“A birthday girl always has lots of presents.”

Lindy cleared her throat, then pointed to her wristwatch. Her time was up. “You have to go with Mommy so I can go to work.” She picked them both up and started toward Lindy. Emma whispered, “Can I have a book of fairy tales for a present?”

Quincy’s heart broke. She would buy one, but she knew it would be thrown out.

The first week of the arrangement seemed to work for the girls and Quincy loved spending so much time with them. Amelia brought Lara and Mia along twice. On the two days Amelia couldn’t make it, Gina, Quincy’s other close friend came in her place.

Working her two jobs to earn enough for the down payment on the house they loved, Quincy had barely seen Lindy and the girls so the intense contact that first week was wonderful. Sometimes she felt so happy playing with them that she’d turn to share a smile with Lindy. And remember. Lindy was trying to take their daughters away from her. The first day of the second week, three days before the scheduled psychiatric evaluation, was Emma’s birthday. Quincy arranged a party in the park with Amelia’s girls, Lara and Mia, and Babs’ sons, Daniel and Ben. Lindy knew Quincy had planned a party but she didn’t know her best friend Babs would be there. The pleasure on her face when she saw Babs standing with Quincy and Amelia turned to a look of pure panic, then settled into a mask of pain and sadness. She passed Michaela to Quincy as Emma ran to greet her friends. Her minder hadn’t come today and Lindy sat alone on a bench separate from the group but close enough to keep an eye on the girls.

Lindy's only contact with Babs since she'd left had been at the court hearing, so Quincy and Amelia encouraged Babs to try to connect and talk some sense into her. Once Quincy had engaged the children in games, Babs wandered over, kissed Lindy's cheek and sat next to her. She took Lindy's hand but watched Quincy and the children as Lindy continued to do. "How are you, my friend. I've missed you."

"Stressed but okay." She dropped Babs' hand to wipe her eyes. "Babs, I can't—"

"It's okay, Lindy. I just want you to know Danni and I are here for you if you need us, whether you go back to Quincy or not."

"Thank you." She glanced over her shoulder toward the entrance to the park. "I'm sorry for the hurt I'm causing everyone but it's best for the children to not be around sinners."

Babs swiveled to face her. "You mean lesbians? Have you forgotten the love we all share? We may all be sinners but being lesbians is not the sin. We may be sinners, but we all love and miss you, Lindy. Come back, let us help you."

She brushed her eyes again. "I'm so sorry. Please try to understand. I can't let my daughters burn in hell." Her voice was low and filled with pain. She got up, walked to another bench, and sat. Alone.

Babs sat for another minute, wiped her tears, then walked back to the party.

Quincy had gone all out with cake, ice cream, candy, balloons, and gifts for all of the kids. She'd bought Michaela and Emma gold lockets and put a picture of her with Emma in Emma's and her with Michaela in Michaela's. Hoping Lindy would let them keep the jewelry, she fastened the lockets around their necks so they'd have something of her with them all the time. She'd also bought them each a doll, age-appropriate books and educational toys, plus some new clothing in their favorite colors, pink for Michaela and purple for Emma. Emma's special gifts were a book of fairy tales and the purple big girl's two-wheeler she'd been wanting.

Amelia's husband, Jackson, picked up Lara and Mia after about an hour. A little later, Babs was leaving with her two boys and Daniel, the older one, broke away from her and threw himself into Lindy's arms. "Auntie Lindy." Ben followed his brother's lead.

Quincy watched Lindy hug Danny and Ben, say something, then gently push them toward Babs, without looking at her. Babs wiped her eyes, then herded her boys out of the park. Lindy sat and stared into space. Then her mouth started moving. Quincy and Amelia exchanged a glance.

Emma begged Quincy to remove the training wheels so she could ride like a big girl. For nearly an hour, Amelia held Michaela while Quincy ran behind Emma holding the bike until she learned to balance and was able to ride short distances alone. Quincy did a happy dance with Emma in her arms. Emma giggled and shouted to Lindy and Amelia that she could ride a big girl's bicycle.

Quincy was watching Emma ride solo when Lindy walked over. Most of the time Quincy had spent with the girls in the park, Lindy had sat with her "handler" as Quincy thought of her, and not said a word. Today the handler was nowhere to be seen.

"Quincy, I'll take the clothing but could you take all the toys home—I mean to your house. There really isn't room for them where we're staying. Maybe we'll come there next time, instead of the park."

"I miss you, Lindy. When are you coming home?"

"I can't."

"Can't or won't? Do you really think I'm evil? After loving me for more than six years?"

Lindy looked away. "I'm evil. I'm a sinner and I need to repent and find Christ again."

Quincy was perplexed. How did Lindy go from being anti-religion to becoming a believer? "I can't believe you really want the girls to grow up in a harsh, barren, unhappy Christian environment like you did."

"It won't be like that with me."

She tried to rein in her anger but the thought of her daughters living that kind of life horrified her. "Really? No fairy tales, no running, no screaming, no parties. And those are just the four forbidden things Emma mentioned. Is laughing allowed? Girls riding bicycles and playing catch? You'll find the lockets I gave them under their shirts. Will you let them keep them or will you throw them away?" She put her hand on Lindy's cheek and turned her so they were eye to eye. "I love you, Lindy, and I beg you to stay with me, but if you need to go, leave the girls with me." Her throat tightened. "Please."

"No. They need to be saved. You'll make sinners of them, like you."

"Your parents did everything possible to *save* you and look what happened. You became a lesbian and were never happier in your life. Or so you said."

Lindy was wringing her hands. "You'll never understand. Can't you do the right thing and let them go with me to live a good Christian life?"

"No, Lindy, I can't. I'll do whatever it takes to save them from you and the likes of your holier-than-thou friends who think God speaks only to them."

Lindy's eyes widened, and she jerked as if she'd received an electric shock. "God only speaks to—" She gazed up at a tree behind Quincy, nodded several times, then looked at Quincy again. "Say goodbye to the girls, Quincy. We're going now. Take the toys with you."

CHAPTER EIGHT

Lindy

Quincy had, as usual, gone all out to give Emma the birthday party she wanted and the gifts she coveted. Watching Quincy play with our daughters, seeing how much she loves them and they her, and seeing Babs, remembering the fun and friendship and love we'd all shared, I feel myself wavering in my resolve to save myself and my children from the sin of our lesbian lifestyle. The ways of Satan are devious, I remind myself. He shrouds evil in the cloak of love, but women loving women are an abomination and God damns lesbians and their spawn.

It helped to move away from Babs, away from the temptations of the devil. I'd flirted with the devil with Cora, the first woman to seduce me, then again with Melanie, but it was Quincy, the strong, vulnerable and loving Quincy, who had seemed to be a good, kind person who had sucked me down into the degradation I'd thought was love, had thought was heaven. I'd been taken in and had borne two children in sin, two innocents doomed to burn in hell unless I save them.

When Quincy touched my face and stared into my eyes, pleading with me to stay or at least let the children stay, I almost threw myself into her arms and begged her to take us home. But then she said she'd do whatever it takes to save the girls from me and I knew she would never let me have the peace to think and pray and repent or the space to raise the girls as good Christians. I knew Quincy would never stop fighting for the girls. It's getting harder and harder to ignore the voices. If I fail the psychiatric examination, I'll lose my daughters to Satan. They will suffer eternal damnation and so will I for bringing them into a sinful relationship and allowing them to live surrounded by sinners.

Hearing God's voice outside shocked me. Hearing God say, "Joanna and Lauren and Letitia are right," sort of annoyed me but suddenly I understood. I can't wait for the psychiatric evaluation. I must go to their safe haven, a place where Quincy will never find us. I must do this for my daughters. Carefully, so as not to warn her, I say farewell. "Say goodbye to the girls, Quincy. We're going now."

She hugs and kisses Michaela then hands her to me. Emma clings to her as if she senses this is the last time she'll ever see her Mama. Quincy kneels and hugs and kisses her. "Be good for Mommy. I'll bring your bicycle next time." Emma takes my hand and we walk out of the park. I'm crying, struggling to control my sobs, knowing this is the last time I'll see Quincy. I feel bad for hurting her and depriving our daughters of someone who truly loves them, but her false love will deprive all of us of heaven. I can't see any other way. I must go.

In the car, I remove the lockets and put them in the pocket of my jeans. I will decide what to do with them, not Joanna or Lauren or Letitia, though they seem to think they are in charge of my life. When I arrive back at Joanna's house, I don't give them a chance to begin their none-too-subtle pressure for me to leave with the girls. Instead, I tell them immediately that I've decided to accept their offer of help to get away from Quincy rather than chance losing my daughters. I almost change my mind when I see the sly smiles they exchange.

I didn't expect to leave that night, nor did I expect to feel like a fugitive. But I do. And I feel anxious and guilty and panicky about leaving. Am I doing the right thing for the girls? What about Quincy?

I'm folding the girls' clothing when Letitia barges in. Trying to control me as usual, she picks up my wallet and my cell phone from the bed, pulls out the credit cards and puts them and the wallet on the dresser. She hands me the battery from the cell. "Throw this out of the car window after you've driven a couple of hours." I nod. She thinks she's in charge of me but she's not. She places the phone on the dresser. "Tomorrow Lauren will get rid of your credit cards and your phone so Quincy can't trace you." When she walks out of the room, God speaks from the mirror on the dresser. "Don't be stupid, you might need those things." I toss the battery, the cards, my wallet and the phone in the suitcase and quickly cover them with my clothing. The charger was in the suitcase before she started ordering me around. I finish packing the girls' things and close the suitcase.

At midnight, Joanna carries my suitcase and the diaper bag, Lauren carries Michaela and I carry Emma out to a waiting car. Their car seats are still in my car at Quincy's apartment, so Letitia arranges three pillows and three blankets on the back seat. They introduce me to Wally, the man who will drive me on the first leg of the trip to the safe haven in Arizona, then I slide in and settle the sleeping girls on either side of me. Bossy to the last, Letitia tells Wally to remind me to throw the phone battery out of the car window later. Knowing that when I don't appear tomorrow, Quincy will do everything she can to find us, I'd left the battery loose in the suitcase with the phone and the charger.

After a few minutes of small talk, Wally and I are silent. I'm thankful for the quiet, thankful to be away from Letitia's constant chatter and their constant lecturing. I'm tired of hearing Letitia say that the Bible condemns lesbians, just as much as gay men. Tired of Letitia quoting Romans 1:26-27 to prove her point. "*Because of this, God gave them over to shameful lusts. Even their women exchanged natural relations for unnatural ones. In the same way the men also abandoned natural relations with women and were inflamed with lust for one another. Men committed indecent acts with other men and received in themselves the due penalty for their perversion."*

I close my eyes and lean back, letting my mind wander. Lying about the phone is kind of silly, but the lie formed without my intention. Quincy always laughs at how stubborn I get when I'm told what to do. That's probably why I did it. A couple of hours later, Wally's voice jolts me awake. "You should throw the battery away now."

I smile. "Thank you." I swivel away from him, pretend to take the battery out of my pocket, lower the window and fake tossing it out. Strange I don't feel bad about lying again.

"Would it be okay if I put the radio on? Not too loud so it wakes your children but loud enough to keep me awake."

"Sure." The last thing I want is for him to fall asleep at the wheel.

He snaps the radio on and Marvin Gaye's "Let's Get it On" comes on. It's one of my favorites. It was playing the night I met Quincy.

Lulled by the drone of the car whooshing through the night, I put my head back again and remember that night at Maggie's Bar. *A group of us were celebrating Babs and Danni's engagement. We were laughing and teasing and having a lot of fun. Babs and I were dancing to "Let's Get it On" when she nodded at the bar. "Someone can't take her eyes off you."*

"What?" I turned. A lone figure huddled at the bar amidst the exuberant Friday night crowd was watching us in the mirror over the bar. I was intrigued. The woman seemed damaged in some way and Maggie the owner/bartender was fluttering around her.

I yelled into Babs' ear, "I think she's watching you, sweetie, because you're positively glowing tonight."

Babs grinned and wiggled her hips, but now my eyes kept wandering toward the bar. As Danni stood to get another round, I put a hand on her shoulder. "Hey, you can't leave your sweetie all alone, I'll get this round." I danced over to the bar.

Waiting for Maggie to fill my order, my eyes kept flitting over to the woman at the end of the bar. Then Maggie nodded at the silent TV over the bar. "Her name is Quincy. She damn near got blown up pulling twelve people out of burning cars before help arrived. She needs a ride home."

"Shit. No wonder she looks wasted. I'll drive her if she wants." I delivered the drinks to my table and approached Quincy. "Hi, I'm Lindy James. Maggie says you need a ride home."

"Do you believe in God, Lindy?" Quincy asked above the racket of the music and laughter and conversations.

"When I look at the beauty in the world or think about things like the perfect complication of the human body, sugah, I believe there must be a higher power of some sort, but I don't believe in religion or any church. All we can do is lead the best life we can, being kind to others, doing what we can to make their lives better, loving and enjoying the beauty of life."

The music changes abruptly as Wally searches for something more to his liking. I cringe remembering how I'd answered her question about God. That night was the beginning for us. I believed what I said then. Was the devil already speaking through Quincy? I close my eyes feeling the pain of separation from her, from her gentleness, her love. I let the tears run.

Someone shaking my shoulder and calling my name wakes me. It takes a few minutes to remember Wally and then I notice we're parked in a driveway, next to a dilapidated house. "Wake your children and go inside. They'll give you breakfast and someone else will take you on the next leg of your trip."

I thank him but I'm wavering again. Do I really want to do this? I dreamed of Quincy and now I hear her voice begging me to come home. He hands me the diaper bag. As I walk to the house, I consider asking him to take us back with him but I know God will be angry if I do.

The woman who greets us seems anxious. She gives us a few minutes to use the bathroom then herds us into the kitchen where breakfast is on the table. The three of us are cranky and Emma is insisting on knowing when she will see her Mama again. I have to coax her to eat, and as usual, it takes Michaela a while to settle at my breast. I am conscious of the woman hovering behind me as I push my eggs around on my plate. I take a few bites to show my appreciation, then since Michaela has started eating a little solid food, I feed her bits of my eggs. Though I can tell the woman wants us gone, I take my time washing myself and the girls in the bathroom, knowing that a day confined in the car will be difficult for all of us.

We left our coats in New Jersey and it's chilly when we go outside so I hurry toward the car. But Emma has other plans. She digs in her heels and pulls me toward the swing set in the backyard. She begs me to let her play. I glance at the car and assume the man standing there is our new driver. He has the back door open and doesn't look happy at the delay. God screams from the swing that we are running away and there's no time for play. He also reminds me that I have no idea where I am or where I'm going, that I'm totally dependent on these strangers and shouldn't alienate them. Emma is sobbing as I drag her to the car. The man introduces himself as Luke. He takes the diaper bag from me, puts it with my suitcase on the front passenger seat and then helps me into the car for the next leg of our trip. I settle the girls on the blankets and pillows he's arranged for us on the back seat. Emma is inconsolable, crying to go home, crying for her Mama, and of course Michaela joins her. It seems like hours before they both fall asleep.

As I expected, the girls are cranky and mostly cry or sleep through the day and the night. When we pull off the highway at a rest stop to eat and use the bathroom, Emma is angry and resentful that she isn't allowed to run. I do my best to choose healthy food that she will eat but she's not used to fast food so it's hit or miss whether she's actually eating enough. Finding anything vegetarian for me is ridiculously difficult. This place doesn't even have the wilted salads or cold pizza I've eaten so far but since I'm breastfeeding, I force myself to eat the sad-looking grilled cheese even though it's been cooked on the grill used for hamburgers.

We are getting strange looks from the people around us. I wonder if I look as crazy as I'm feeling now. At each stop, I quickly change Michaela's diaper and sponge Emma in the bathroom, then eat fast and get back to the car. We change drivers frequently and I can't seem to hold the names of the recent ones in my head. I try to sleep, but what I'd said to Quincy about religion the night we met haunts my thoughts. And God keeps throwing it in my face as proof that Satan had pierced my heart from the moment I'd met Quincy.

CHAPTER NINE

Quincy

Quincy's eyes flicked to the clock so frequently that she stopped pacing to confirm it was working because the hands didn't seem to move at all. Lindy had said she might bring Emma and Michaela here today so maybe she thought she didn't have to call to confirm. But she should have been here already or called to arrange a different time and place for today's visit with the girls. Calls to her cell were going directly to voicemail. Quincy's stomach churned. Maybe the psychiatric evaluation was today. She called Shayne Elliot's office and her assistant confirmed that the psych eval was Wednesday, not today. Quincy swallowed, trying to push down the rising bile that came with the realization that Lindy wasn't coming. Amelia's call ten minutes later about where to meet them, spurred her into action. She drove to the house where Lindy and the girls were staying, but no one was home, so she went to the rundown storefront that served as a church for the group.

She knocked and walked in on eight women sitting in a circle chatting. Eight pairs of eyes settled on her, none of them the soft hazel ones she was looking for, none of them friendly. The group stared. No one spoke.

Quincy scanned the room to be sure Lindy wasn't there. "Can you tell me where I can find my wife, Lindy James Adams?"

Quincy heard the hushed repetition of the word wife, repeated around the circle.

Letitia the witch stood. Since their first meeting at the women's group, then again in court, and each time she'd sat next to Lindy during one of Quincy's visits with the girls, Quincy had felt as if she and Letitia were battling for Lindy and the girls. She suppressed the urge to punch Letitia's smug face. "Actually, we were wondering ourselves. She was staying with Lauren but she disappeared the other night." She turned to one of the other women. "Tell Quincy what happened, Lauren."

Lauren appeared nervous, not as self-assured as Letitia. "We talked some when she got back from Emma's birthday party. She was upset because Emma was inconsolable, wanting to go home with you and her bicycle. Anyway, we said goodnight about ten and when I got up around six thirty the next morning, she was gone." She sniffed. "She didn't even leave a note to thank me or to let me know where she was going." She maintained eye contact with Letitia, rather than looking at Quincy, as she spoke in a robot-like voice telling the story they'd obviously rehearsed.

Quincy pretended to believe her, hoping to get some information, any clue to Lindy's whereabouts. "Did she mention other friends she could have gone to or her family? Or any other arrangements?" Quincy tried but couldn't keep the fear out of her voice.

Letitia took control again. "Not to anyone in our group. We're all close and we would know. Maybe you should check the bus station."

"Did she mention taking a bus somewhere? Florida or Georgia?"

Letitia shook her head. "No. She seemed intent on staying and fighting for full custody of her daughters. I mention the bus because she didn't have a car."

Her head spinning, her stomach clenched, Quincy turned to leave. At the door, she glanced back and caught the triumphant smile on Letitia's face. She considered going back to pummel the woman but realized it would be a distraction and slammed the door behind her. She needed to concentrate on finding her family.

If she believed those religious bitches, which she didn't, no one had any idea Lindy was leaving or knew where she was headed. If Lindy had left during the night after Emma's birthday, she had almost a two-day head start. If Lindy had gone to any of their friends, surely they'd have called Quincy to let her know. Her family had disappeared. She stumbled to her car, called Amelia, and somehow drove home.

This was her fault. She knew Lindy was in trouble. She should have known she wouldn't consider giving up the girls just because a judge ordered it. She should have known that Lindy wouldn't hang around for the psychiatric evaluation and chance losing custody. Quincy sat at her kitchen table, head in her hands, sobbing. Her girls, her Lindy, her world had disappeared. In her panic this morning she'd dashed out, leaving the kitchen window wide open and now she couldn't stop shivering. The last time she'd felt this anguished, this helpless, this lost and this cold was the night she'd met Lindy.

She had just gone off-duty during an unexpected October blizzard when her radio ordered all available cars to the scene of a huge pileup on the highway. She was nearby and the department was overwhelmed with calls, so she went. And stumbled into hell. Bodies strewn around, people screaming for help. She was the only responder on the scene. The storm had surprised her and everyone else so she was wearing her winter uniform and standard shoes rather than heavy winter gear. She shivered as she surveyed the scene. Even in her shocked state she knew the people in the burning vehicles were the priority. She pulled a baby and five adults from three of the cars and dragged or carried them to safety. When she got to the fourth burning car, the smoke was thick, the flames were high and closing in on the gas tank. The driver was trapped and they both knew there was no hope of her getting out. "Please save my husband and children," she begged. Quincy carried all five to safety and then returned to the woman. There wasn't much time before the tank exploded. "Run. Save yourself," the brave woman screamed. Quincy couldn't leave her. She would save her or die doing so. She managed to put the fire out and save them both but not without flashing back to the horror of helplessly watching her lover burn in a firebombed SUV in Afghanistan.

When Quincy left the scene, she felt herself sinking into the familiar darkness of pain and memory. She drove to the light, to life, to Maggie's, her friend's lesbian bar. Cold and shivering, deep in despair and feeling hopeless, she stared into the mirror behind the bar. Her eyes widened, her spirits soared as a beautiful blonde brimming with light and joy and life, appeared in the mirror dancing alone. Lindy.

Now the light and joy were gone from her life. *Damn it, Lindy, how could you leave me and deprive me of our daughters?* If she had known it was the last time she would see her children or her wife, she might have done something different. Like take the girls and run or throw Lindy and the girls in the car and drive somewhere far away from the proselytizing harridans so she could pierce Lindy's brainwashed, bullshit-spouting brain and get down to the real Lindy. But she hadn't known. And she hadn't done any of those things. Instead she'd played by the rules, gone home loaded down with toys, happy she'd made her girls happy, looking forward to seeing them in two days, wondering if Lindy was starting to warm up to her, and hoping the results of the psych eval would force the judge to award her full custody. If only. If only.

Arms wrapped around her from behind. Amelia. She leaned back seeking comfort from her friend. "I can only try to imagine what you're feeling, Quincy, and I wish I could tell you everything was going to be all right, but I don't have a crystal ball. You have every right to scream and cry and rage, but beating yourself up with should haves won't bring them back."

"My heart feels as if someone has stabbed it with an ice pick, Meelie. I'm not sure I can go on without them."

Amelia tightened her arms and kissed the top of Quincy's head. "You can and you will. You are the strongest person I know, my friend."

Quincy closed her eyes.

CHAPTER TEN

Lindy

I've lost all sense of time. Sometimes the radio tells me what day it is but I feel like we've been driving for weeks. Maybe we have. God is complaining about it taking so long to get there. Since that first morning when we'd stopped at someone's house and I washed up before going on, our only stops have been grimy rest areas on the endless highway. I've given up trying to find something healthy for Emma to eat and for the first time in her four years she's eating french fries and burgers and drinking soda. Because I'm breastfeeding Michaela, I force myself to eat breakfast every day but I can't get anything else down. I wash the girls as best I can in the public bathrooms but there's no way I'm going to strip to wash myself. I smell rank, like a street person, and with the bad dye job and chopped off haircut Lauren gave me the night I left, I look like an escapee from a concentration camp.

Emma needs to exercise but the men who drive us are afraid to spend too much time in one place so they rush us back to the car. One of the men said we're fugitives and the police are looking for us so they are taking a roundabout route and are being careful to avoid being found. Lately, the men only let us go inside to use the bathroom. They buy the food and we eat in the car. The girls are crying constantly but it's the woman continuously screaming about Satan and lesbians and God that is getting to me. She used to go in fits and starts but recently she almost never stops.

We're locked in the car now. The driver is standing outside talking on his cell phone. The windows are partially down, I guess so we don't suffocate, and I hear bits and pieces of his conversation. He puts the phone through the window, then puts it to his ear. "Can you hear her? Yes, stark raving mad. That's the kids crying in the background. Making me crazy. I'm going to leave them here in the parking lot." He listens without speaking, then shrugs. "Two hours away? Okay. I'll need help when I get there." I catch a glimpse of myself in the rearview mirror. My mouth is wide open as if I'm the one screaming.

He starts the car and turns to face the back seat, though he doesn't really look at me. I see his mouth moving but I don't understand what he says because the girls are crying, the radio is yelling, and the screaming has started again. So many voices, from the radio and the keys and the mirror. And God is fed up. He's angry that it's taking so long to get there. Somewhere in all the noise I hear a calm voice. "The baby is hungry. Feed her, Lindy." I look around for Quincy. I don't see her but I feel calmer. I pull Michaela close and offer her my breast, for what it's worth these days. After a brief struggle, she grabs a handful of my hair, latches on, and begins to suck. I close my eyes and relax. I'm comforted by Quincy's voice, I feel safe. My mind fills with thoughts of Quincy, of the weekend we met when I helped her feel safe.

After rescuing twelve people from burning cars in a highway pileup during a surprise October snowstorm, Quincy had come to Maggie's seeking light and life. Soaked to the skin, exhausted and desolate, she sat at the bar staring in the mirror, watching me dance. Maggie noticed and asked me to talk to her and we'd connected. Quincy was in no shape to drive. I was so taken with the vulnerable, devastated hero that I volunteered to drive her home. When we arrived at her building, Quincy yawned and turned to me. "I think you should stay here tonight."

I stared into her eyes. "Because of the roads or because you'd like my company?"

Quincy took a few seconds before answering. "I think the roads are too dangerous to be out by yourself." Her smile was sad but it was the first I'd seen. "But the real reason is I don't want to be alone." She tore her eyes from me and stared straight ahead.

I studied Quincy, noted her flush, her nervous picking at her wet pants, and the sound of her rapid breathing. Then I made a decision. "Just so we're clear. I don't sleep with women I don't know. So sex is not included."

"Don't worry. Neither the mind nor the body could handle sex tonight. I need human contact."

We'd spent the entire weekend cooking and talking and walking, getting to know each other. We had lots of contact, physical and emotional, but nothing sexual. It was hard to leave Monday morning, but in fact, I'd run away, frightened by the strong connection, my strong feelings for Quincy.

My eyes pop open. And now I'm running again. But this is different. I didn't know Quincy was the devil then. Now I do and it was God who told me to leave to save myself and Michaela and Emma. I look down. Michaela is sleeping. Emma is awake, sucking her thumb. I want Quincy. And suddenly, the screaming starts again.

CHAPTER ELEVEN

Quincy

Acknowledging she'd get no work out of her distraught detective, the chief reluctantly assigned Quincy and her partner, Tony, to investigate the disappearance of Lindy, Emma, and Michaela. Judge Fleming didn't even have the grace to acknowledge that she was wrong about Lindy being a flight risk. And by the time she agreed that the girls had been kidnapped to avoid legal action, and Quincy was able to put out a nationwide BOLO for Lindy and the girls, the trail was cold.

Quincy and Tony went at it nonstop, going to the bus and the train stations at different times on different days, hoping they'd find someone who'd sold Lindy a ticket or saw her and the girls board a train or a bus. But either they hadn't traveled that way or they were in disguise. They interviewed everyone in Lindy's women's group several times and went back to the eight women in the church over and over, hoping one of them would let something slip, but they played innocent and stonewalled them. Quincy would have continued to show up at odd times, catching one or two of the women alone, but the minister complained of harassment to the chief and she was told to lay off.

She and Tony interviewed the neighbors who lived near the house Lindy and the girls were staying in. Although they found an elderly woman who said she saw a woman carry a child out to a car about midnight the day of Emma's birthday party, she couldn't say if the woman was Lauren. She described the car as dark, not too big, not too small, and no, she hadn't noticed the license plate. They tag-teamed Lauren for hours trying to break her, but she maintained her story. She said the woman must be mistaken, she'd gone to bed early that night. Maybe it was Lindy she saw. They re-interviewed all the neighbors trying to extract more information about the car but no one else had seen them leave. They had no leads.

With no money and no car Lindy had disappeared into thin air. She most probably had help from the religious women, but they appeared to have limited resources so she must have gone someplace where she wouldn't have to worry about food and a place to live. If Sarah was alive, Quincy knew Lindy would have run to her. But Sarah was dead and her daughters, Angela and Kelly, who lived in Florida, denied having heard from Lindy. It seemed highly unlikely she would run to her parents for help, but then again, it was even more unlikely Lindy would become a religious fanatic.

Unlikely or not, Quincy was desperate and that was the only scenario she could come up with. So, on the off-chance Lindy had gone back to her abusive, religious parents, Quincy asked for time off to fly to Georgia. Connie, her boss and friend, refused her request and insisted Tony go with her, that the visit be an official one.

A couple of days later, Quincy and Tony flew to Georgia, rented a car and drove to Newtown Springs where Lindy's parents apparently still lived. They walked around the small town, hoping for a sighting of Lindy or the girls, then went into the James General Store. Quincy assumed the nasty older man criticizing a younger man who resembled Lindy was Lindy's father and the younger man who snarled back was her brother Aaron.

The older man looked Quincy up and down. "Can I help you, *gentlemen*?"

The younger man snickered at the intended insult.

Quincy felt Tony tense and put a hand on his arm to silence him. "We're visiting from New Jersey. I was going to ask if you knew a good optometrist but now that I know you can't see, I'll ask someone else."

"What are you saying, lady?" Lindy's dad roared. He thrust his reddened face into her space trying to intimidate her, but she held her ground. She sniffed. "You know mouthwash and a shower could eliminate those smells, no pain involved, and it might help business."

"Get out of my store, heathen bitch," he snarled as he stepped back.

"I guess you see better than you let on, old man." Quincy's smile didn't reach her eyes.

"I see what you are and you disgust me. Get out. We don't like your kind around here."

The old man blanched as she moved toward him with fisted hands.

Tony grabbed her arm. "Don't waste your energy on this turd. Let's go. We'll get what we need elsewhere." They walked out. The younger man was right behind them.

When they were out of his father's sight, the blond man laughed. "You really zinged the old buzzard good."

Quincy laughed. "I did, didn't I?" She looked into hazel eyes that reminded her why they were here. "You know, you look just like a woman I met a while ago. Her name was, uh, Linda, no Lindy, and I think she said she was from around here. Know her?"

He looked back toward the store and lowered his voice. "My sister was called Lindy but she's been gone a long time. You meet her in Atlanta? Is she okay?"

Quincy studied him and decided he was sincere. "Yes, it was Atlanta. She was doing just fine."

He nodded. "She was the smart one, leaving here. If you see her again, tell her Aaron says…tell her I hope she's happy."

Head bowed, shoulders slumped, he followed a customer into the store.

They walked down the block to the only luncheonette in town and ordered pork sandwiches and coffee. The waitress took their orders to the kitchen and returned with their coffees. "Where y'all from?"

"We're just passing through from New Jersey. I'll bet you don't see many of us around here." Quincy hoped that would trigger some information about Lindy and the girls.

"None that I can recall." The sound of the bell from the kitchen got her attention and she turned away. A few minutes later the bell rang again and the waitress delivered their sandwiches.

"You know I met someone from here up in Jersey. What was her name, Tony?"

Tony squeezed his eyes shut as if trying to remember. "Lindy, I think."

"That's right, Lindy James. You know where she lives?" The waitress looked puzzled. "Never heard of a Lindy. Hope James is married to the preacher's son but she's never gone nowhere that I heard. You sure it was Newtown Springs?"

Quincy responded quickly to avoid tipping off the family. "Oh, you're right, her name wasn't James, it was Jamison. I didn't know her that well so I might be confused about the town too."

After paying the check, they drove out to the family place. They agreed on the direct approach with the mother but sat in the car and watched the house for almost an hour before ringing the bell.

The woman who opened the door had the same lanky body, coloring, and features as Lindy, but all the life had been beaten out of her, leaving the dry shell of a woman dressed in a too-large, gray sack of a dress. She looked as if she'd just sucked a dozen lemons.

Tony took the lead. "Mrs. James?"

She stared at him, then switched her hard eyes to Quincy.

"Who wants to know?" Her voice crackled with anger.

"I'm Detective Tony Marciano and this is Detective Quincy Adams. We're from New Jersey and we're looking for Lindy James."

She frowned and seemed to rummage in her mind to recall who they were talking about. It took a few seconds but there was no doubt the memory she dredged up about Lindy was bitter. Her already hard features flattened, and she hissed in an accent so thick it was difficult to understand her. "Lindy left this house more than twenty years ago to go to the devil and I hope she's suffering in the fires of hell." She slammed the door.

"Well, that went well." Quincy turned toward the car, thinking of Lindy growing up with this mother and the father they'd seen in the store, remembering the belt marks on her back. Quincy hoped Lindy wasn't sick enough or desperate enough to come back to them. "Let's go to her sister Hope's house. I'll take the lead this time."

Hope's house was a little less rundown than her parents' house. When the door opened, Quincy stumbled back from the shorter, thinner, joyless version of Lindy standing before her. She was Lindy without the sparkle. Lindy without the glow from within and the bubbly spirit. Lindy as she might have been had she stayed here. Actually, Hope was Lindy as she looked the last time Quincy saw her. "Yes? Are you lost or something?" Her voice was tight.

Quincy caught her breath. "Is Lindy here?"

Hope frowned. "Lindy?" She looked from one to the other of the detectives, then glanced back into the house. "What has she done?"

"Is she here?" Quincy stepped forward trying to see in the house. "Emma. Emma." She called her daughter, hoping if they were there she would run toward her voice.

"Well, sugah, Lindy hasn't been here for a lot of years. Who's Emma?"

"So you haven't seen Lindy recently?"

"No. And if I had I wouldn't..." She started to close the door but changed her mind. "Is Lindy in trouble?"

"No. I…we just need to talk to her." Quincy felt queasy staring into those hazel eyes so like Lindy's yet so unlike them.

"This is probably the very last place on earth Lindy would come. She'd know she wouldn't be welcome." Hope glanced over her shoulder, leaned in toward Quincy, and whispered. "Is she married?"

Tony opened his mouth to respond but Quincy elbowed him. She thought it better not to mention she was married to a woman, just in case she did show up here. "Yes, she's married and has two beautiful daughters. And you?"

"Yeah, I'm married but luckily no children." She glanced into the house again. "If you find her, tell her that her sister Hope misses her every single day." Her eyes filled.

"Do you need help to get away from here?" Quincy spoke softly.

Hope wrapped her arms around herself and looked down. "It's too late for that. What would I do? Just give her my message."

"Are you sure?"

Hope's smile was sad. "Yeah. I'm sure. Tell her…tell her I love her." She swiped a tear from her eye.

"I will." Quincy handed her a card. "If you ever change your mind, give me a call and I'll come for you."

Hope's mischievous grin pulled at Quincy's heart. There was her Lindy. She lightly punched Quincy's shoulder. "Fancy me, do you?" She tucked Quincy's card in her pocket. "Thanks."

As Tony drove away, Quincy looked back. Hope waved and Quincy could see her in the doorway, watching, until they turned a bend. When they were clear of Newtown Springs and well on the way to Atlanta, Tony cleared his throat. "It's hard to believe Lindy came from those parents, isn't it? I could see her in Aaron. And Hope is the spitting image of her but kinda worn and drab. So what would you have done with her if she wanted to come with us?"

"It's obvious she isn't happy and based on what Lindy told me about her husband, it's likely she's being abused. I think Lindy would have wanted me to help her so I would have taken her home with me if she wanted to come. But I didn't really think much beyond that."

Tony grinned. "Softie."

She shrugged. "At least where Lindy is concerned."

She leaned back and closed her eyes, remembering the first weekend she and Lindy had spent together, getting to know each other. It was intense. They'd gotten extremely close. Lindy had run away then too, taking a piece of her heart. But this time was worse. This time Lindy had stolen her life.

CHAPTER TWELVE

Quincy

Quincy refused to be discouraged. They'd exhausted all leads but she spent hours sifting through accident, robbery, and murder reports from around the country. She read every FBI report that mentioned children or a blond woman and searched online for anything that might lead her to her family. At night when the chief forced her to go home, she searched Lindy's clothes and books and papers, tore up carpeting, checked for loose floorboards, unzipped the covers on the sofa cushions and the bedroom pillows, and looked under every picture, every drawer and every piece of furniture in their apartment. Finally, hidden in a box of old clothing in Michaela's closet, she found a notebook. It didn't contain many entries but what was there was chilling.

Without dates it was hard to know exactly when Lindy had started writing, but Quincy guessed it was about four months after Michaela was born. The first entry mentioned Quincy's partner, John, being shot in the head while waiting in their car for Quincy to pick up lunch at the deli. Another entry discussed Sarah, who raised Lindy from the age of fourteen and was recently killed in a head-on crash. The last entry was probably right before Lindy left. In between the written entries were drawings and doodles, which toward the end, consisted of devils, lots of flames, red tears dripping like blood, and words like Satan, eternal damnation, sin, sinner, lesbian, and Satan's spawn written in huge caps. Some of the drawings were small, some a whole page. It was all so nightmarish, she hesitated to read it, but she needed to understand.

Funeral today for Quincy's partner, John. What if it was her? What if she was the one sitting in the car while he went in to pick up lunch and the guy with the gun shot her in the head instead of him? I could lose her at any time. What would I do without her AND Sarah?

Five times today I called Sarah. I know she'll understand. She'll help me, but then I remember she's gone. Too many random deaths. What if she hadn't gone to help Kelly with the kids and hadn't been on the highway when the drunken driver swerved into oncoming traffic? Someone else would have died, not my beloved Sarah. I miss her so much. Did she die because she loved me, a sinner?

Not eating, not sleeping, anxious all the time, afraid to drive with the girls in the car, getting harder and harder to leave the house, crying constantly for no reason.

I didn't expect a second child to be so overwhelming. I feel hopeless, everything is so difficult.

Saw Dr. today. He pooh-poohed my suggestion that I have postpartum depression. He says it comes days and weeks after delivery, not almost 5 months. He told me to stop feeling sorry for myself and gave me prescriptions for sleeping pills and Valium. But I'm breastfeeding Michaela and I don't want to fill her with drugs. What's wrong with me? I feel like I'M GOING CRAZY!!!

I can't read. Words are all mixed up!! And TV and radio announcers are speaking strange languages.

Sarah spoke to me from the radio today. She said I should talk to Quincy. But Quincy is working two jobs. Why??? I don't want to be any more of a burden than I already am.

Caught myself in the mirror this morning. I look like shit. No wonder Quincy is never home. I think she's having an affair, not working overtime.

The announcer on the radio confirmed that Quincy is having an affair with Gina. And also, Grace.

Almost talked to Babs today but how do you tell your best friend you're going crazy? Better not to see her until this passes. If I could only get some sleep.

Quincy said I should stop breastfeeding so she can feed Michaela while I sleep!! But breastfeeding is when I feel connected. I think Q wants to separate me from the baby so she can steal her when she leaves to be with her girlfriends!!

Cameras everywhere so she can spy on me.

I tell Quincy I'm fine. She wants me to get together with friends so I'm not alone with the girls all day but What if I slip and mention THE VOICES?

Totally out of baby food so I forced myself to walk to the market. Other than my women's group that meets at the library twice a week to talk about mothers' issues, I don't go out anymore. The group is safe because the library is only two blocks away and they have childcare.

Eleven women in the group. Three of them somehow always bring the discussion around to God and religion. Ellen, one of the other women, warned me they would try to convert me. No hope of that.

But I'm afraid to talk about my feelings, about the voices.

Feeling so alone and sad. I miss Sarah. I can't talk to Gloria because I might slip and tell her how happy I am that John was murdered, not Quincy. I miss Quincy. Can't stop crying.

The three religious women get that I'm a lesbian and are pressing me to change. I've started having coffee with them after our meetings. Maybe GOD is the answer. They say being a LESBIAN!!! is the problem.

Today a woman screamed at me from the toaster and said I'm sleeping with the devil. That I'm evil and dirty and I, and my daughters, will burn in hell. The voices are getting louder. I can't sleep more than twenty minutes without them ranting at me.

Letitia, Lauren, and Joanna SAY Quincy is THE DEVIL!!! if I stay with her, I and Michaela and Emma are condemned to burn in hell.

Is Quincy devil? Who can I tell the voices I'm crazy put me away can't leave Emma and Michaela!!!!! Or Quincy!! Does she want me put away so she can sleep with all her lovers?

Quincy is worried. Wants to cut back on her hours so she can help me with the girls. NO NO NO!!! She can't be around. What if she notices? I tell her I'm fine, that I can't wait for the new house. She believes me. Is the devil so trusting???

Joanna gave me a cross today. She and Lauren and Letitia are praying that I REPENT AND LEAVE THIS SINFUL LIFE to save myself and the girls.

JOANNA AND LAUREN AND LETITIA SAY I AM A SINNER!!! I AM A LESBIAN. MY DAUGHTERS WILL BURN IN HELL BECAUSE THEY WERE CONCEIVED IN SIN!!!!

GOD SPOKE TO ME TONIGHT I PROMISED NOT TO TELL HE WILL PUNISH ME. HE SAID I WILL SUFFER ETERNAL DAMNATION IF I DON'T REPENT AND SAVE MY DAUGHTERS. I THINK I'M GOING CRAZY. IS GOD REAL!!!! AM I REAL????

Oh, MOMMA. YOU AND DADDY WERE RIGHT. I AM GOING STRAIGHT TO HELL AND SO ARE MY BABIES UNLESS I REPENT. I SHOULD HAVE STAYED AND MARRIED JEDIAH. OUR BABIES WOULD HAVE BEEN SAFE.

I AM EVIL. I LOVE SATAN. I AM LIVING WITH THE DEVIL. MICHAELA AND EMMA ARE THE SPAWN OF THE DEVIL!!! AND THEY WILL PAY FOR MY SINS.

WHAT KIND OF MOTHER AM I?

Thoughts of killing my daughters and committing suicide but if I kill them they would be doomed to burn for eternity. If I kill myself and leave them with Quincy then they would still be doomed to burn for eternity.

QUINCY KNOWS. SHE CAME HOME EARLY LAST NIGHT BECAUSE SHE KNOWS SOMETHING

> *IS GOING ON. AND SHE SAW THE KNIFE STUCK IN THE COUNTER!!! I DON'T WANT TO LEAVE BUT SHE IS THE DEVIL!!! SHE MAKES ME FEEL SAFE AND LOVED AND IT'S WRONG, IT'S SINFUL!!!! THE GIRLS AND I WILL BURN IN HELL WITH HER IF I DON'T GO. TODAY.*

Quincy rubbed her eyes. She was stunned. Lindy had suffered a breakdown right in front of her and she had believed her denials. Worse yet, Lindy didn't feel she could ask her for help. Poor Lindy, so alone. No wonder their daughters were so agitated. Quincy swallowed, pushing the bile down. This was her fault. Being tired was no excuse. She'd gone about her business while Lindy lost weight, while she didn't sleep, while she spoke to imaginary people, while she no longer touched Quincy, and while she lied about feeling good. She'd believed Lindy because it was easier not to think about the alternative. She'd gone about her business never considering that her daughters weren't being cared for properly, that Emma missed nursery school and wasn't getting lunch, that Michaela was rejecting Lindy's breast, that her babies were frightened of their mommy. And now she'd allowed Lindy to take them away. And maybe harm them. Whatever harm came to Michaela and Emma was on her. All on her. There was no one else to blame. She ran to the bathroom, vomited into the toilet, crouched on her knees with her arms around the cool porcelain, and sobbed.

She woke in the middle of the night, stiff and cold, her head still on the rim of the toilet bowel. Her mouth tasted vile, her knees fought being straightened, and her neck throbbed. She pulled herself up, and fully clothed, tumbled onto the bed.

When her alarm went off, she showered and dressed and then went to Amelia's house.

Amelia took one look and pulled her into a hug. "Do you have news? Are they okay?"

"No news." Quincy lifted the notebook she was holding. "I found something of Lindy's that I want you to see."

Amelia handed her a cup of coffee, they sat at the table and Quincy pushed Lindy's notebook over to Amelia. She'd read it again this morning and she was still stunned. Amelia read it, and except for an occasional gasp she didn't comment. When she closed the book, she opened her mouth but closed it again without speaking. She reached for Quincy's hand and shook her head. They sat for a long time in silence.

"What are you going to do with it?"

Quincy shrugged. "What can I do with it? I'll keep it until I find her, then I'll either use it to get custody of the girls or give it to her therapist or both. I pray she doesn't hurt herself or the girls." She broke down, sobbing. Amelia held her until she calmed down, then handed her a napkin. She dried her face. "I have to find them."

"I know, honey."

CHAPTER THIRTEEN

Lindy

I wake with a start. Where am I? Where are my daughters? "Quincy?" I try to sit up but two women are pressing on my shoulders. One looks like a dried stick and seems angry, the other looks like a loving grandmother and seems happy to see me. I focus on her warm brown eyes and try to figure out if I know her. She tells prune face she can go. When we are alone, she takes my hand. I'm lulled for a minute by the contact and her kindness but then I panic again. "Who are you? Where am I?"

"I'm Dr. Baumann. You're in a religious community in Arizona." She leans in close to my ear and whispers, "Did you come here willingly?"

Did I? I close my eyes, searching through the fog. "Be careful," the doctor's wristwatch warns me. I stare at it but it doesn't say anything else so I go back to trying to remember. It's all fuzzy. Then images flash as though I'm scrolling through my memory bank. Quincy. Satan. Letitia. Driving. "Yes. I ran away from Quincy." *No, from Satan.*

I bolt upright. "Where are my daughters?" I try to get out of bed but I'm so weak the doctor easily pins me down.

"Shush. They're fine. Look." Dr. Baumann tips her head toward the open door to my left. Michaela and Emma are sitting on a mattress in the hallway and a girl is reading to them. Ms. Dry Stick is perched on a chair watching me like a hawk. "Who is that? Why is she staring at me?"

"That's Hannah. She's here to ensure you don't hurt yourself or your daughters. She and other community women will take turns watching you day and night until you're feeling better and we're sure it's safe for you to be alone with your daughters."

"What do you mean safe?"

She ignores my question. "Jemma, please bring the girls in here." The doctor's voice is gentle but commanding.

"Mommy." Emma climbs on the bed and the doctor moves back to allow me to hold her. Hannah hands Michaela to me. I clutch the girls and my tears overflow. "Are you and Michaela all right, Emma?"

"Jemma reads to us and we color. She sleeps with us too. Are you all better? Can we go home now? I miss Mama."

I kiss them. "Yes, baby, I'm feeling better." I glance at the doctor. "We have to stay here, Emma. We can't see Mama now."

"I want to go home. I don't like it here." Emma sobs and Michaela joins her. I kiss their heads and rock the two of them until they doze off. Hannah and the doctor carry the girls to the mattress in the hall. I take this unobserved moment to scan the small room trying to scope out an escape route if I need one. Only the one door, a single bed, a small dresser, a night table with a lamp, and a small window. The walls are bare. The doctor sits on the bed again.

"Why are my daughters on the floor in the hall?"

"If they don't see you, they get hysterical. I think the trip here traumatized them."

I don't understand but she seems willing to answer my questions so I tamp down my rising panic. I need information. "Where is here exactly."

The doctor takes my hand in both hers. "You're in a Christian community just outside of Chino Valley in the Arizona desert. Do you know why you're here?"

Christian community…so it should be safe to tell her. "I… my daughters are in danger of burning in hell because I gave birth to them in a lesbian relationship. I came here to save them, to keep my wife, Quincy, who loves them but is still a lesbian, from getting custody." *And because Quincy is Satan.* "Are you the doctor here?"

"I treat the women who live here but I'm not part of the community. I live and practice medicine in Chino Valley, about twenty minutes from here. They asked me to be here when you arrived yesterday because your driver called ahead to say you were acting…strange."

I close my eyes trying to remember what was strange about my behavior but nothing comes to mind. "What was I doing?"

"You were screaming. You were delusional, raving about God bringing you to the desert, talking to God, alternately cursing him and begging him to let you go home. You seemed to think you and your daughters were in danger from…us, the people who were waiting to help you. You were sure if you got out of the car we would murder you so you fought hard to stay there. You begged Quincy to come and save you and you said you didn't care if she was Satan. You loved her anyway. You were out of control and your girls were petrified. And so was the man who brought you here. He said you'd been raving constantly for nearly a day and he almost left the three of you at a rest stop but he felt sorry for the girls."

"Oh, God, what have I done to Emma and Michaela? My poor babies."

"While you were distracted by the men trying to pull you out of the car, I got the girls out. It took six men to remove you from the car and drag you into this room in the dormitory for single women."

"I don't remember. When was this?"

"Yesterday." She glanced at her watch. "I gave you a shot to calm you about thirty hours ago and you've been asleep since.

I've been told you were in the car for nine days, without a break. That must have been horrible for you and your daughters."

"What's wrong with me?"

"You've had a psychotic break. Has anyone in your family been diagnosed with a mental illness like bipolar disorder or schizophrenia?"

"Not that I know. But I left home at fourteen and haven't had any contact since. I've often thought my parents were crazy but I think it was more religious fanaticism than mental illness."

Dr. Baumann nods. "What about you? Have you ever been diagnosed or have you ever had a similar episode?"

"Never."

"What about drugs? Are you taking any prescription drugs or have you used any hallucinatory drugs like LSD or others?"

"Neither. I smoked marijuana a couple of times when I was younger but that's the extent of my drug use."

"How long have you had these symptoms?"

"What symptoms?"

The doctor's gentle brown eyes pierce me. She's not going to let me evade this discussion. I sigh. "What is today's date?" She tells me. I take a few minutes to consider. "Michaela is almost six months old. I'm kind of foggy about events but I believe I got depressed a little while after she was born." *Should I tell her about the fantasies of dropping her or accidently hurting her? About the constant crying and sadness?* "The last month was the hardest."

"I gather your parents were very religious. Have you always been religious or is this relatively recent?"

I anguish about how much to say. Her wristwatch is screaming but it's God's voice this time and he says I should tell her everything.

Then I hear Quincy's voice. *I can't believe you really want the girls to grow up in a harsh, barren, unhappy Christian environment like you did.*

"Obviously I wasn't religious when I was a lesbian and had two daughters with the…Quincy. It wasn't until the last month or so that I realized the sinfulness of my life and burden of sin on my daughters because of it."

"When you got here you were calling for Quincy to save you and your daughters. Yet you think she's Satan. Did you love your wife in the years before you realized you needed to save your daughters from her?"

I pick at the blanket. Was it love or lust or had Satan seduced me? "In the six years we were together I thought I loved her. But that was before I realized she's Satan. Besides she was cheating on me with everyone and had planted cameras around the apartment."

Dr. Baumann lets go of my hand to write something in a pad she pulled out of her pocket.

Had I said something I shouldn't have?

"When you arrived, I was told that you hardly slept during the nine days of the drive. Were you sleeping okay at home?"

"No. Except for the last night when I slept with Quincy."

"Were you able to enjoy reading and watching TV?"

"I used to love to read. Then Quincy made the words hard to understand. And she mixed up all the words on the TV shows too."

Dr. Baumann nods as if she understands everything. "When you arrived, you said God was talking to you. I notice you staring at my wristwatch and listening intently. Are you hearing voices now, Lindy?"

I glance around the room. No way to escape with the girls. Is it safe to tell her? But she already knows, doesn't she? "Yes."

"Have you ever thought about hurting yourself or Michaela and Emma?"

I go still. Then I understand this is what she meant when she said they would watch me until they were sure it was safe to leave me alone with the girls. I swallow and pray she won't commit me. "Yes. For a minute. But killing us would condemn the three of us to burn in hell for eternity and I was trying to save us all from that fate, so I ruled it out." I tense waiting for the verdict.

Dr. Baumann smiles as if she's happy with my answer, makes more notes and then looks me in the eye. "I believe you're suffering from postpartum psychosis. I've seen it a few times in my practice and in this community."

Is she trying to trick me? "My obstetrician told me Michaela was too old for me to have postpartum depression. He said I was imagining things, that I was just feeling sorry for myself."

"I treat a lot of women and based on my experience I would say he doesn't know what he's talking about. Postpartum psychosis is not depression. It's different, more severe, but it can be treated. I'd like to prescribe medication that I believe will help."

"And if it's not that?"

"Then we'll try another medication."

She reaches for my hand but I tuck my hands under my arms. "No medication. I'm breastfeeding Michaela and I won't endanger her."

"Michaela is doing fine. She's accepted the formula and the cereal we've given her. Believe me, your being out of control around her like you were before I gave you that shot is much more harmful than stopping breastfeeding."

"Absolutely no drugs." My desire to protect my daughter, to give her the best shot at a healthy life, fuels my stubbornness. I'll fight this.

Dr. Baumann stands and closes the door, then sits again. She looks me in the eye. "I'm jeopardizing my ability to treat the women in this community by saying this, Lindy, so I'm not going to repeat it and I'll deny it if you do. This community will not tolerate women with mental issues, so if you get out of control again, which you will without medication, they won't hesitate to ship you off to a state mental hospital. And that would mean leaving your daughters here to be raised by strangers. It seems to me that in trying to protect your girls from your wife, whom you say loves them, you will be sentencing them to live alone in this community, to a, perhaps, loveless life, a life much different than I think you want for them."

I gasp. What have I done? Can I trust her? The wristwatch chimes in again. "Maybe she's the devil." We stare at each other for a few minutes. Dr. Baumann puts her hand on my thigh. "Look, Lindy, I have no pony in this race. I'm not part of this community. I'm the only woman doctor in the area willing to come here. As a physician, I want to do what's best for you and for your daughters. And I honestly believe the best choice for you, and for them, is for you to take the medication."

I would sooner send my daughters back to Quincy than leave them alone here or anywhere. If I believe Dr. Baumann, the next time I freak out they would probably commit me and keep my daughters. I'd slept for more than a day after being injected with something, so they could easily do that again and lock me in a hospital somewhere. Could I risk that? "Would you be willing to call Quincy to come and get the girls?"

Dr. Baumann walks to the window. "Am I right that you ran away from her because she's a lesbian and you believe staying with her condemns you and the girls to hell?"

"Yes."

"So sending them back to Quincy means they won't be left alone here but it also means they'll be back in the situation you rescued them from *and* you won't be breastfeeding Michaela. Doesn't it make more sense to just stop the breastfeeding and keep the girls here with you?"

The voice coming from the doctor's wristwatch warns me the devil is trying to confuse me. "How do I know you're not the devil?"

The doctor tilts her head forward. "Feel my head. No horns."

I rub the doctor's head. No horns. "Quincy doesn't have horns either. At least I never noticed any."

The doctor looks at me. "Are you sure Quincy is Satan?"

The question stuns me. I am sure. Or am I? "God told me. It's confusing, though, because she's good and kind and loving and I swear she would never hurt me or the girls. But God should know. Right?" I chew my thumbnail and wonder why God talks to me of all people. Then I know what she's doing. "You're trying to trick me. To make me take drugs."

Shaking her head, Dr. Baumann sits on the bed again and picks up my hand. "I know you're afraid, Lindy. But I believe your condition is caused by a chemical imbalance that the medication will correct. If you decide not to take the medication so you can continue to breastfeed, you chance losing everything.

It seems to me stopping the breastfeeding is a small price to pay to protect your sanity and the future of your daughters. What do you say?" Dr. Baumann gently rubs my hand. "You can always stop the meds and go back to breastfeeding."

It sounds logical. And, for some reason, I trust Dr. Baumann. I fill my lungs and belly with air, listen for objecting voices, and hearing none, I slowly exhale.

I jump as God's voice reverberates in the small room. "Do it."

So he trusts her too. "Okay."

Dr. Baumann smiles and pats my hand. "Good girl. I'll start you with a light dose that you'll take after Michaela's last feeding at night. That will minimize the amount, if any, that she gets. Once she's weaned, I'll adjust the medications. I'll fill the prescriptions later and come back with the pills so you can start tonight. I'll come by frequently to check on your progress. How does that sound?"

"It sounds good but I don't have money to pay you. And if I use Quincy's insurance she'll be able to find me."

"Don't worry, the community will take care of everything."

Community. I frown. I hadn't given much thought to where the terrible threesome, Letitia, Joanna, and Lauren, were sending me so I know absolutely nothing about this place. And I'd been whisked away so quickly that I hadn't had time to think about money or how I would support myself and the girls. What was expected of me?

Dr. Baumann interprets my frown correctly. "Try not to worry." She squeezes my hand. "Right now your job is to focus on getting well. I'm sure Joel, the leader of the community, will meet with you as soon as you're feeling better and explain everything."

Arizona is far from New Jersey in more than distance. It's dry and hot and dusty and the asthma I'd had as a kid is back. The inhaler Dr. Baumann gave me helps but sometimes I think I might die for lack of air, even though I sleep with the window open. Maybe that's the problem but I have no choice since we're in the desert with no air-conditioning and no fan. The door is open, of course, so my watchers can be sure I'm not killing myself or my daughters in the middle of the night. I resent them but they also make me feel safe from the man who used to come in at night to hurt Michaela. Most nights in the single bed with the wriggling girls, pretending the women are not there staring at me, hoping the light snores of Emma and Michaela will still my thoughts and lull me to sleep, I do drop off and sleep until dawn. I wonder whether Dr. Baumann has included a sleeping pill along with the antipsychotics.

Michaela takes to the bottle faster than expected and within two weeks she is totally on formula and solid food. Dr. Baumann says the drugs will take a while to kick in but even with the low dose she starts me on life slows down and seems easier. She visits three times a week and after she checks me out physically, we talk. Or more correctly, I talk. And since the doctor wants me to exercise, we usually walk, trailed by my two watchers of the day and Jemma pulling the girls in a wagon.

Whether it is the medications, my talks with the doctor, the fact that there is nothing I have to do, no decisions I have to make, or the fact that I feel safe away from my fear of Quincy and the pressure being brought to bear by Joanna and Lauren and Letitia, the community begins to feel like a sanctuary.

After a month I'm calm and appear to be in control. The good news is the watcher brigade is retired and I am allowed to be alone with my daughters. The bad news is Dr. Baumann cuts back to once-a-week visits, though sometimes when she's called in to see a sick woman, we talk a few minutes. She tells me I'm still fragile and must avoid stress. But counter to her recommendation, Jemma is sent back to school, leaving me to care for Emma and Michaela. They are miserable, especially Emma who misses Quincy terribly and is angry and irritable at not being able to run and play. I'm not sure where this falls on the good/bad spectrum but I brought them here so it's only right that I deal with their unhappiness.

I'm haunted by Quincy's accusing and angry voice yelling about bringing the girls into a situation similar to the one I'd hated growing up, so every day after breakfast and again after lunch, I carry Michaela and Emma walks with me to burn off energy. I'm limited to the area within the walls surrounding the community, but I've discovered a spot with a few trees far enough away from the living area that I feel safe letting Emma run and Michaela crawl. I play tag and Simon Says with them. When they seem calm, we go to the chapel for a while so I can pray, and then we return to our room where they nap or draw or color in books the doctor brings. I lie with them. Sometimes I sleep, sometimes I pray again. We also walk after dinner and before returning to our room, we go to the chapel so I can pray some more. By that time Emma and Michaela are tired, and while I am on my knees they drop off to sleep. I dedicate myself to praying and repenting. I *will* save Michaela and Emma.

But I'm lonely. My only interactions with the members of the community are during the three times a day I go to the communal dining room and the rare occasion I bump into a member of the community in the shared bathrooms or the hallway of our dormitory. I'm not sure whether it's the difference in our schedules or whether the others consciously avoid the sinning lesbian. Do they feel the fox has been invited into the chicken coop? If they knew I barely see them, that it's Quincy I think and dream about, that even with her it's not the sex but her love and compassion and strength that I desire, would they feel safer?

From time to time a man or several men eat in the dining room, but for the most part it's a community of women. I feel estranged from the others. Many of them are older, many look worn out, and almost all appear depressed. What could we possibly have in common? I think they must feel the same about me, because though some of them acknowledge me with a nod or a slight smile in the dining room, no one speaks to me. I wonder what stories they've heard about the crazy lesbian lady.

Dr. Baumann's visits are the highlight of my week. When I ask her about this place, she always answers that I need to concentrate on getting better. God continues to speak to me during the day and at night when I'm trying to sleep, but he is no longer angry. Instead he just points out things I hadn't noticed, like all the women and the girls wear the same drab, shapeless, unflattering dresses. Pants are not allowed here so the girls and I were each given two identical shapeless cotton dresses, several pairs of cotton grandma bloomers and two equally unattractive cotton nightgowns when we arrived. I don't mind. It's one less decision to make every day. And best of all, at the end of the day I dump the clothing we wore into a bin on our floor and someone washes, folds, and returns it to our room by late afternoon.

I enjoy the peace and quiet and the simplicity of the life here. I enjoy time to myself. A weight has been lifted off my shoulders and I begin to decompress and think. But thinking is the problem. I pray and pray and though I know it is Satan baiting me, I miss Quincy, miss her loving presence, miss the safety I'd always felt in her arms. I speak to Dr. Baumann about God and Quincy and she tells me to be patient and to keep praying. She increased my medication again two weeks ago and she promises that once it fully kicks in, things will look brighter. I'm not exactly sure what she means but I trust her.

Tomorrow will start my eighth week here and at dinner tonight, Hannah told me the girls will start school in the morning and I've been given a work assignment. In fact two assignments. To ease the transition for the girls I'll work in their classrooms in the mornings, then after lunch I'll work in the kitchen. I'm ready, I think.

When I return from the chapel, I put the girls to bed and decide to reorganize our dresser. As I move the clothes we were wearing when we arrived from the top drawer to the bottom drawer, I hear something fall. It's the lockets Quincy gave the girls. I'd shoved them in my pocket the day of Emma's birthday party knowing Letitia would tell me they were the devil's baubles and I should throw them away. Then, in the rush to get away, I forgot about them. I stare at the photos, remembering that day in the park. *Remembering Quincy asking whether I would let Michaela and Emma keep the lockets she'd put under their shirts, or would I throw them away? I remember Quincy's hand gently touching my cheek. I hear her saying, "I love you, Lindy, and I beg you to stay with me."*

No. I open my eyes. I won't go there. Satan is putting these thoughts in my mind. I throw the lockets in the bag I use for garbage and fall to my knees to pray. I wake to the morning gong signaling breakfast in a half hour. I'd slept on my knees, pitched forward onto the bed I share with the girls. Despite the pain in my knees I pull myself to my feet and stare at the lockets nestled in the bag, unsure what to do. God is unusually quiet, leaving this decision to me. The lockets aren't evil in and of themselves, and as long as they're hidden they can't hurt the girls. I've deprived the girls of their mama and someday they, especially Emma who is Quincy's biological child, might want to know about Quincy. I retrieve the lockets from the garbage, slip them back into the pocket of my jeans and shove the jeans back in the bottom drawer. I wake the girls and our day starts.

I'm feeling melancholy but with work and prayer I'll forget the past. Today things will be better.

CHAPTER FOURTEEN

Quincy

Quincy came to consciousness slowly. Damn she ached all over. She must have fallen asleep over her computer again. But how did she end up on her back with her hands pinned? She panicked. Was she a prisoner? While she struggled to open her eyes her senses took in the cool room, silent except for the rhythmic pinging sound and a faint medicinal smell. A hospital? Her eyes popped open. Amelia and Gina were slumped in chairs on either side of the bed, each holding her hand tightly, as if trying to tether her to this world. The good news was she wasn't a prisoner. The bad news was she was in the hospital and her best friends looked distraught. "Meelie?"

Amelia's eyes widened. She jumped up and leaned over her, tears in her eyes. "Quincy, thank God you're awake." She kissed her forehead.

Gina squeezed her hand. "You scared the shit out of us."

"What happened?"

Amelia touched her face as if to reassure herself that she was alive. "You collapsed at work and were rushed to the hospital.

Since I'm listed as your emergency contact, the chief called me. It happened in the middle of the night, two nights ago."

Lying on her back looking up at Amelia and Gina made her feel helpless or maybe it reminded her that she was helpless. "Um, I feel at a disadvantage here. Could you raise the bed so I'm sitting? And give me some water."

Gina laughed. "Ah, she commands. You must be feeling better." She used the remote control to bring Quincy to a sitting position, then handed her the remote.

While Gina helped Quincy drink a little water, Amelia fixed the pillows behind Quincy. "By the time I got here you were sedated and hooked up to IVs and heart monitors. You were bloodless, lying so still that if I hadn't seen and heard the monitors registering your vitals, I would have assumed you were dead." Amelia sniffed and held Quincy's hand to her heart. "The ER doctor said you were dangerously dehydrated and anemic, that your blood sugar, potassium, and salt were also perilously low." Amelia fought for control. "If you hadn't been at the stationhouse with people nearby, you might have died, Quincy." She pushed the words out through her sobs. "Killing yourself won't bring Lindy and the girls back. Not eating, not sleeping, focusing totally on finding them is draining the life out of you right in front of our eyes. And we feel helpless to stop you from committing suicide."

Quincy flinched. Amelia's whispered words felt like an accusation. But she knew it was her anger speaking. Was she trying to commit suicide? Maybe. Without Lindy and the girls her life seemed meaningless. In the four months since Chief Trubeck had reluctantly put the search for Lindy on the back burner, she'd continued to work her job and spent every waking minute on the desperate search to find her girls. Most nights she only slept a few hours when she dropped off over her computer.

Amelia's husband, Jackson, built her a database to keep track of leads. He also set up a search program that would alert her if Lindy's name, social security number, credit cards, or bank accounts were found. She read every report that came into the station and anything she could find on the internet that might lead her to Lindy. Tracking down sightings took her to Canada, Mexico, California, Massachusetts, Florida, Kansas, and Missouri. No joy with any of it. Her hope and determination had given way again to feelings of helplessness, hopelessness, and despair. She couldn't hold anything down. She avoided mirrors rather than face her sunken and shadowed eyes. She yawned constantly and had trouble concentrating. Her friends, one after another, tried to get her to take a break. She always said she would, but she never stopped the relentless search. She looked at her two distressed friends. "I'm sorry." The sobs she'd been holding back since Lindy disappeared because they meant admitting defeat, erupted and her body convulsed. "I don't know how to live without her."

Amelia, Gina, and Grace, her other close friend, took turns staying with her until she was released from the hospital three days later. Amelia didn't ask. She took Quincy home with her and settled her in their guest room where she could make sure Quincy slept and ate and had enough fluids. Two days later Quincy was feeling better and talking about going home to her apartment, but Amelia insisted she stay another night.

After dinner that night, Quincy's closest friends arrived, one after the other in a steady stream. Quincy was surprised but it felt good to be surrounded by people who cared about her.

When the last guest, someone Quincy didn't know, arrived, Amelia stood in the middle of the room and asked for quiet. "We're all here tonight because we care about our friend Quincy who is extremely distressed about losing Emma, Michaela, and Lindy. I believe it's clear to everyone in this room that if Quincy continues the way she has for the last four months, she will kill herself."

Quincy stood, her face an angry red. It was one thing to say that when it was just Amelia and Gina but not everyone here was as close as the two of them. "What the hell, Amelia?"

Amelia took Quincy's hand and looked up into her eyes. "Honey, I'm not saying you don't have good reason. I'm not saying you're committing suicide. I'm saying you're killing yourself and you came pretty damn close to succeeding this week. I invited Dr. Denise Singer, a psychotherapist, to meet with you and the people who love you, Quincy, to help you and us figure out how to get through this."

"I don't need—"

"But you do need. You can walk out right now, but we're here because we love you. Give us a chance to help."

Quincy looked into Amelia's eyes and saw the love and the concern. Then she looked around the room, saw the love in everyone's eyes. Her eyes filled. She sat.

By the end of the hour-and-a-half session everyone had cried with and for Quincy, and she had agreed to six concrete measures. First, she reluctantly agreed, she would step back from the search and let Connie use the resources of the department, as she would for any kidnapping, to follow up on local leads. Second, she would accept Grace and Mike's offer to hire a private detective to follow up on sightings and any other things the department couldn't handle. Third, she would see Dr. Singer regularly starting tomorrow. Fourth, she would go back to running and exercising at the gym. Fifth, she would eat regular and healthy meals. Finally, she agreed to spend evenings and weekends with friends in order to get back to a more normal, healthy life.

CHAPTER FIFTEEN

Quincy

Three months later, Quincy had regained her equilibrium. She mourned the loss of her wife and children every day and stayed on top of the search, but with the help of her friends and twice-a-week sessions with Dr. Singer, she'd mostly stuck to the plan laid out that night.

Today, taking another step toward restarting her life, she was moving from the apartment she'd shared with Lindy and the girls, into the house she and Lindy had set their sights on more than a year ago. The house had been sold right after Lindy fled but had come back on the market recently because the new owner was being transferred to California. When the broker called, she'd immediately put a binder on it. Now it belonged to her, and the bank, of course, and she hoped one day her family would join her there.

Not all her friends could make it, but there were more than enough hands and backs to make loading the truck at the apartment and unloading it at the house go smoothly. Every box was labeled with the room it belonged in and Quincy played traffic cop, directing the placement of the furniture and other items in the house, basement or shed. There were so many helpers and she was so organized that the move went faster than expected. By six in the evening everything was in place, all the pizza and most of the beer had been consumed, the truck was on its way back to the rental site, and everyone but Amelia had left.

Though Amelia had seen the house right after Quincy signed the papers, she hadn't been back since it was painted so Quincy did a walk through, commenting on the new colors and pointing out the things that had drawn her and Lindy to it—the size of the rooms, the beautiful woodwork throughout, the window seats and small alcoves, the huge modern kitchen, and the large windows that brightened the house and gave it an open airy feeling.

Amelia hugged her. "I'm so happy for you, Q. It's such a lovely house. I hope Lindy and the girls join you here someday but whatever happens, I know you'll be happy here."

"Thanks. I wasn't sure when the realtor called me but now I'm positive I made the right decision. It feels like home." Quincy led Amelia to the sofa in the living room. They sat and rehashed the day, talked about their plans for the next few days, then slipped into a comfortable silence, each lost in her own thoughts. After a few minutes, Quincy reached for Amelia's hand. "Thank you for rescuing me, Meelie. I don't think I would have survived without you."

"Another installment on payback for saving me in second grade and then protecting me until we graduated high school." Amelia brought Quincy's hand to her heart. "I'm ready to head out unless you'd like me to stay with you tonight."

Quincy stood. "You're the best, but I have to sleep here alone sometime, so I might as well start tonight. Besides, I'm going to change into pj's and get into bed with the mystery I'm reading. I'll probably be asleep by eight." She slipped her arm through Amelia's and walked her to the door. They hugged and Amelia dashed down the steps to her car. As she drove away, Quincy turned to face the empty house, much too big for one person, perfect for a family. She ran her fingers through her hair as she moved through the downstairs rooms. All the furniture and big items were in place, all the boxes were stacked in the rooms where they belonged, and thanks to Gina, the refrigerator was stocked with eggs, bread, butter, and milk for breakfast, a healthy chicken salad for lunch and the sauce for a pasta dinner. She wouldn't have to think about food tomorrow. She could just focus on unpacking.

Suddenly exhausted, she walked upstairs to the bedroom, regretting telling Gina and Amelia she would make the bed and they should just throw all her clothing on it. Now she'd have to hang up her clothes, unpack the boxes with bed linens, towels, bathroom stuff, and pajamas before taking her first shower in her new home. Maybe she'd just sleep in her clothes on the bare mattress.

Tears filled her eyes when she walked into the master bedroom. She was one lucky woman. Her friends had made her bed and hung not only her clothing, but Lindy's as well. Amelia or Gina had dug a pair of pj's out of one of the boxes and put them on the bed along with a towel, face cloth, and bathmat. She looked in the bathroom and smiled. Her toothpaste and toothbrush, the soap, shampoo, conditioner, and powder she would need to shower and wash her hair were neatly lined up on the vanity.

If by some chance there is a God and he or she considers me an evil sinning lesbian, why would I have so many generous, kind, loving friends who care so deeply about me?

As she showered, her thoughts turned to Lindy and the girls, wondering as she did a hundred times a day, where they were, were they okay, did they miss her? Ironic that she was here in their dream house without Lindy. She remembered the day they'd seen the open house sign in front of the house they'd admired for years. They'd slowly walked through it, picturing where they would place their furniture, what they'd need to buy and what colors they would paint each room. Lindy had been her vibrant, beautiful self then as they chatted with the real estate agent about the cost and the down payment needed. Later, after the girls were asleep, Lindy set up a "House" folder with all the information the agent had provided plus their ideas and dreams for the house. Then Quincy got silly and challenged Lindy's choice of colors, suggesting things like orange and fuchsia and they'd laughed and argued until she agreed to Lindy's choices which she actually loved. Quincy was touched when Lindy spoke longingly of wanting a screened porch, and she silently vowed to make it happen. They'd spent part of the evening discussing the options for coming up with the down payment. Quincy taking the lucrative second job she'd been offered, protecting headliners who performed at the New Jersey Arts Center, had seemed like a good idea at the time. With hindsight she wondered if leaving Lindy totally on her own with a new baby and a three-and-a-half-year-old had caused her breakdown. But she'd learned enough in therapy to know that what was done was done and you can only focus on what was ahead.

She put on her pj's and picked up the family photo her friends had thoughtfully placed on the night table. She still occasionally felt angry with Lindy, but mostly she felt sad that she'd not taken better care of her and the girls. And tonight, in bed alone in the house that was meant to be theirs, she was overcome with sadness. Curled into the fetal position, longing for what couldn't be, and holding her love for Lindy, Emma, and Michaela close, Quincy slept.

CHAPTER SIXTEEN

Lindy

Try as I might, I can't get Quincy out of my thoughts. I spend hours every day on my knees in the chapel praying to forget but memories of Quincy and longing for her gnaw like a low-grade toothache.

Partly I'm feeling guilty. As Quincy had predicted, this religious community, like the one I'd grown up in, works hard to suppress the individuality of girls and mold them into obedient, docile daughters, wives and mothers submissive to their fathers, husbands and sons. Every day at school with the girls I'm forced to witness and participate in the snuffing out of the light in the eyes of these beautiful youngsters. It's not so bad for Michaela and the other little ones because playing and running and being noisy in class and outside during recess are still acceptable behaviors. But it's horrendous for Emma and the girls in her age group, who must sit with hands folded, repeating the alphabet after the teacher, learning to read religious stories or listening to stories that teach them the place of women in this world. The only play allowed focuses on being a proper wife and mother. Even on breaks outside, girls Emma's age and older are only allowed to walk around and take a turn on the swing. No running, no climbing, no screaming, and no throwing balls for girls. Only boys are allowed to do those things.

And school is a misnomer, since the girls are not exposed to history or literature or science. They just learn basic skills—to read simple religious books, to do basic arithmetic, to spell a limited list of words and to print their names and addresses. Once the girls turn fourteen, school ends. I decide they probably only do the minimum required to conform to state law.

Emma is constantly reprimanded for talking or moving and naturally looks to me to protect her. I try and often go head-to-head with the teacher. One evening after a particularly harsh confrontation, Hannah informs me that I am no longer assigned to the school, that starting tomorrow I will work full-time in the kitchen. I'm angry and frustrated and worried about Emma but I'm dependent on these people and have no choice but to cooperate. Lying in bed that night comforting a tearful Emma, I realize I can't stay, that I will have to pay attention and find a way to leave. If only I could be as brave as Quincy.

Several days later, while I'm chopping vegetables for lunch, God speaks to me for the first time in weeks. "Be careful, this is a polygamist group."

Shocked, I look up. "What?" My voice seems to echo in the silence. None of the five women working in the kitchen respond, but all eyes turn to me. I realize they hadn't heard God speak. "Sorry, I thought someone said something." I lower my eyes and continue chopping, but my mind is racing. Polygamist? I'm almost certain polygamy isn't legal. Yet God said it so it must be true. I'd been so focused on myself and the girls that I hadn't paid much attention to what was going on around me, hadn't listened to what little conversation there was as we prepped for meals. Now, it's as if I've woken from a long sleep and my eyes are open physically and emotionally. I begin to surreptitiously watch everyone and listen intently.

Within a few days I've confirmed God's statement but I don't understand the part about being careful. I make a conscious attempt to relate to the twenty-plus women I cook and eat meals with, listening to their conversations, being more upbeat and friendly, and when it seems safe, asking questions. It turns out most of the women are here because their husbands rejected them. In some cases, it was because they didn't get pregnant, in others they hadn't been able to get along with their husband's other wives. Sometimes they weren't obedient enough to suit him. A few of the women are outsiders like me, drawn to the community for whatever reason. Whether never married or married before, they all seem content to work here and, I gather from their giddy gossip about the men who occasionally eat dinner in the communal dining room, wait for Prince Charming to select them. No one ever mentions leaving.

I begin to pay attention to the men and surmise they are there to look over the stock, to pick up a wife. Or two. I avoid looking directly at them, tend to my daughters, and as soon as I can without calling attention to myself, wash our dishes and leave for our nightly walk and my nightly visit to the chapel. By this time I've given up lying to myself about going there to pray. Instead, my thoughts always turn to Quincy, our friends, our life together, and what I've done to our daughters. I puzzle over why I, of all people, turned to religion. And the only thing I've come up with was that I was crazy. After all, what sane person thinks inanimate objects and God talk to them? And thinking about God, I realize in the four or five weeks since announcing that this was a polygamist religion, God hasn't spoken to me. And it comes to me that maybe the voice of God was really me expressing my fears and my take on what was going on, what was important.

I worry about my future and the future of the girls in this religious, polygamist community. I understand now why the sole goal of the so-called school is to train the girls to be obedient wives. This is not the life I want for my daughters. Or, for myself. I'm married to a woman I love and I have no interest in being married to anyone else, certainly not a man. So my thoughts once again turn to leaving.

One day I'm alone in the kitchen with Abby, a woman about my age and the closest thing I have to a friend. Abby didn't get along with her husband's other wives and her parents refused to take her back so she and her daughter have been living here for a year waiting to be chosen again. I take a chance. "Can you leave here if you want? And how would you do it?"

Abby gasps. "You want to leave?"

I hasten to reassure her. "No, I'm just curious. It looks like some of the women have been here forever waiting for a husband and I wondered if anyone ever gave up and went somewhere outside. And that made me realize I'd never seen a bus or a taxi pick anyone up. In fact, since I've been here, I don't know of anyone leaving."

Abby nods. "I could leave but I have no money and no job skills so I don't know where I'd go or what I'd do. Besides, I'm sure Tiffany's dad would insist she stay in school here. And I won't leave her."

It's scary that Abby is so matter-of-fact about them keeping her daughter here if she left. I shiver thinking of Emma and Michaela. "There's no transportation so how would you leave?"

"Oh, I guess Joel or one of the men would drive me into Chino Valley."

"I see. It makes perfect sense." I smile to signal that I get it. Wanting to divert Abby, I ask about the two men who'd come for dinner last night. While Abby launches into a comparison of the men, number of wives, financial status, and good and bad qualities, I think about leaving. Would Joel or one of the men drive me and the girls into Chino Valley? I'm not sure why I feel uneasy, but I'll think carefully about this before asking.

Maybe I can steal a car. There aren't many since only the men have cars and very few, other than Joel and the ones who come to look over the women, spend time here. But I only need someone to forget once so I will keep my eyes open for keys left in the ignition, grab the girls from school and run. That's the only option I can see. Except stealing a cell phone. Damn Letitia. I wish I had mine. Is there even a signal in this godforsaken place? But even if I could call a taxi, I don't have any money.

As I chop, the diamonds in my engagement ring catch the sunlight and flash rainbow sparks. They'd taken my rings off when I first arrived but last week I found them in the back of a drawer and I'd started wearing them at night. As I removed my wedding band this morning, Emma started fussing about school and I turned to comfort her, forgetting totally about the engagement ring. Now that I'm aware of it, I slip it into the pocket of my dress and go back to chopping. I can't help smiling at the memory that floods me. *The candlelight restaurant was so romantic. And the electricity between us felt physical. Once we ordered, I was practically levitating. "I want to give you my Valentine's Day gift now."*

Quincy, grinning like the proverbial cat that ate the canary, said, "Let's exchange gifts at the same time."

I nodded and slipped off my chair to one knee. When I looked up, Quincy was also down on one knee. Eyes huge, we stared at each other, realizing what was happening. Holy smokes we were both proposing. Then, as if we'd rehearsed it, we spoke simultaneously.

"Lindy, will you marry me?"

"Quincy, will you marry me?"

Oh, my God. We fell into each other's arms. "Yes, yes." We spoke in concert again, then kissed. The couples in the small restaurant broke out into applause as we exchanged rings.

Slightly embarrassed at the attention, we waved and mouthed thank you. We sat and grinned at each other.

I held out my hand to admire the delicate, old-fashioned setting. The diamond sparkled in the candlelight and cast rainbows in the air. "I love my ring." It was perfect, so me.

My gaze shifted to her. "We never talked about marriage. I was so afraid you would say no."

"I felt the same. I didn't know what I would do if you rejected me but I want you with me forever and I had to risk it."

Forever. I almost chopped a finger off when Abby interrupted my thoughts by touching my arm. "Oh, sorry, I must have been daydreaming. What did you say?"

"I asked if you noticed Efraim Fieldstone watching you at dinner last night?" Abby sounded breathless.

"Um, no. Why?" I deliberately avoided looking at the men who showed up for dinner, but I'd sensed something like that was happening because of the flurry of excitement of the women near me. I'd kept my eyes on Emma and Michaela.

Abby leaned in close and whispered, "Everybody noticed. He's interested in you."

My heart fell. "But I'm already married. And you're much prettier."

"I don't think that kind of marriage counts here." Abby's eyes widened and she slapped a hand over her mouth. "Sorry."

I'd wondered how much of my story was public knowledge here and now I knew. Gossip existed everywhere. "Does everyone know I'm married to a woman?"

Abby blushed. "It's common knowledge. Everyone heard you screaming it to the high heavens when they brought you in." She cleared her throat. "Bearing children and getting along are more important than being pretty for a wife. Besides, you pray a lot, which is good, and though you're kind of thin and seem down a lot, anyone can see your natural beauty."

I don't get it. The last time I'd caught my reflection in a window the raccoon eyes that stared back were as lifeless as my hair, my shoulders slumped, I was thinner than I'd ever been, my hair was half brassy orange and half blond and looked as if someone had chewed it off. I was tanned, though, from all the walking outside. How could anyone think this was natural beauty? "My marriage doesn't count?"

Abby shrugged. "Not in the eyes of God."

Or men. "Well, I'm still healing and praying for God's forgiveness so I'm a long way from being ready to marry." *That's my story and I'm sticking to it.*

CHAPTER SEVENTEEN

Quincy

To her surprise, Quincy slept soundly the first night in her new house but she woke at six o'clock as usual. She unpacked most of the kitchen boxes then made herself scrambled eggs and toast. It was a beautiful June morning so she carried her breakfast and coffee out to the front porch where she could check out life in the neighborhood. She retrieved the newspaper that had been tossed near the front steps and read while she ate.

Her attention was jerked from the story she was reading by the slamming of the screen door at her neighbor's house—unlikely behavior from the older woman who lived there alone. Quincy turned to make sure there wasn't a problem and was surprised to see a five- or six-year-old child staring at her. "Hi." Quincy smiled and waved.

The girl ran down the steps and stood at the property line. "Hi, I'm Megan. Can your children come out to play?"

The child had unintentionally landed a sucker punch. When she'd finally signed the papers to buy her and Lindy's dream house, Quincy had imagined Emma and Michaela making friends with neighborhood children and playing in the large backyard. If only her daughters were here, if only she could call them to come out and play with the neighbor. It had been a while since she'd cried but ready tears rushed to her eyes. She struggled to catch her breath and right her world.

She looked up at the sound of the screen door opening again. A thin gray-haired woman came out of the house. Her gaze found Megan, then moved to Quincy. "Good morning." Her eyes widened, then her smile dimmed. Had she noticed Quincy's distress and thought Megan was annoying her? Or did she somehow know Quincy was a lesbian and didn't want the girl talking to her? "Stop bothering our new neighbor, sweetie. Come and read your book." The girl threw Quincy a hopeful glance, then trudged back to the porch, shoulders drooping. The woman sat in a rocking chair.

A few seconds later Quincy had recovered her equilibrium. She dried her eyes and walked over to the steps of her neighbor's porch. Up close the woman's kind blue eyes looked tired and her body seemed to sag. Quincy estimated she was somewhere in her sixties. "Hi, I'm Quincy Adams."

"Nice to meet you. I'm Dorothy Wilson and this is my granddaughter, Megan. Welcome to the neighborhood."

"Thank you." She turned to the girl. "I'm sorry, Megan. My children don't live here but I'm sure they would love to play with you if they did." Quincy frowned. "How did you know I have children?"

Dorothy leaned forward. "We watched you move in yesterday and Megan was thrilled to see the two-wheeler and all the other toys. I guess she assumed your children lived with you." Dorothy glanced at Megan. "She's lonely. She's only been with me five months and the friends she's made in the neighborhood and in school all left for camp or somewhere else right after school ended."

Quincy's eyes shifted to Megan, slumped in the chair next to her grandmother and clearly near tears. The girl's distress pained her. "If it's all right with you, Dorothy, I'd love to play catch with Megan later." Without waiting for an answer, she added, "And I'd love Megan's help with some things in the backyard. I have a table and chairs out there so you could watch us and get some fresh air."

Dorothy nodded. "That would be nice. I'll bring some lemonade for you working girls."

"So, Megan, first we work, then we play catch. Do you have a mitt?"

Grinning, Megan jumped up. "I'm strong." She displayed her bicep. "I can be a big help." She glanced at her grandmother and shifted from foot to foot. "I'm a good catcher too, but I don't have a mitt, um, Mrs.?"

"Call me Quincy. I have a mitt you can use. Give me about an hour and I'll come and get you." Quincy hadn't intended to do anything in the yard until she finished inside but she felt a tug toward this little girl and knew she had to build some trust with Dorothy before she could be alone with Megan in her house. She whistled as she went inside to unpack a few boxes of books and locate Emma's mitt.

At the end of the afternoon, after bouts of playing catch, hide-and-seek, and tag, a sweaty Quincy dropped into a chair next to Dorothy while the exhausted Megan sat under the tree reading her book.

"You're wonderful with her. She's been depressed. I've been worried but I don't have the energy to run and play the way she needs. Thank you for taking the time. I know you must have lots to do in your house."

"You're welcome. I enjoyed it too. I love kids. I hope you'll let me play with her again."

"Are you free to join us for supper tonight? Nothing fancy, just chicken cutlets, mashed potatoes, broccoli, and a salad, Megan's favorite meal. We'd both enjoy it."

Quincy eyed the older woman and decided she wasn't just being polite. "I'd love to. How about I bring some ice cream for dessert? What flavor suits you both?"

Dorothy smiled. "We're easy. Vanilla for me, chocolate for Megan. We eat at six."

Dorothy stood. "Come inside with me, Megan. I'm sure Quincy would enjoy a little peace and quiet. Besides, she's coming to supper tonight and I need your help."

"Oh, boy, can we play a game after dinner, Quincy? Can we?"

Quincy laughed. "Sure, I'd love to."

After they left, Quincy went into the house and unpacked several more boxes of books, showered, and called Amelia. Playing with Megan brought back vivid memories of her last few weeks with Emma and Michaela and the feeling of loss gnawed at her stomach. Could they run and play? Were they happy? Did they miss her? Did Lindy miss her? Amelia reminded her to focus on what she could control. Since it sounded like playing with Megan made her feel good and was fun for Megan, why not focus on that?

Dinner was delicious and Quincy needn't have worried about the conversation flagging because Megan was so excited she couldn't stop talking. It was as if she had to tell Quincy everything about her life. She also kept excusing herself to get things to share with Quincy, her mom's picture, her favorite books, her favorite doll and her favorite soldier figures.

With her eyes on her ice cream, Megan asked, "Quincy, would you read me a story when I go to bed? Please." Quincy's heart skipped a beat. She glanced at Dorothy for permission.

Dorothy nodded.

"I'd love to, Megan."

"Could we play a game first?"

This time Dorothy looked to Quincy for permission.

Quincy nodded.

"Quincy can play one game and read one story. Finish your ice cream, then go wash and put on your pajamas."

"Yippee." Megan started shoveling in her ice cream. When she finished she put her dish in the sink and ran upstairs.

While Quincy was helping Dorothy clean up, she said, "I'm curious. The realtor said you lived alone. Was I misinformed?"

"No, the realtor probably didn't know Megan had moved in with me. As Megan said, her mother, my daughter Kaitlyn, is a captain in the army. She deployed to Afghanistan about five months ago. It's her third time there."

"Is her dad a soldier, as well?"

"He was. They'd worked it out so one of them would be home with Megan while the other was deployed. During Kaitlyn's first tour in Afghanistan when Megan was eleven months old, he was home with her. Kaitlyn's tour ended when Megan was two and a half, and not long after, Jared went to Afghanistan. And died there. So Megan has been with me during Kaitlyn's last two deployments. I'm hoping Kaitlyn will retire after this tour."

"That's tough on all of you. How does she do it?"

"She's a West Point graduate. The army is her career but she's riddled with guilt about leaving Megan. Her job involves secret missions and is dangerous. I worry about her all the time. And I worry about Megan. I'm not in great health. What if something happens to Kaitlyn?" Tears filled Dorothy's eyes.

Struck by the sacrifices military families make while the rest of Americans go blithely about their lives, Quincy hugged her. "Anything I can do to help, just ask."

"Playing with Megan today was a big help, Quincy, but I don't want to impose. I know you have your own problems."

"How did—"

"When I was cooking, I remembered your name and your face from stories in the newspaper. And our pastor includes you and your family in the prayers we offer for people in distress as part of our service. I'm sorry for your loss."

Stunned, Quincy sat. "I didn't know. What church do you belong to?"

"Our Lord of Mercy. Nina Mayfair is our pastor." Dorothy put a hand on her shoulder. "Maybe I shouldn't have brought it up."

Quincy covered Dorothy's hand with her much bigger one. "No, no, it's okay. I'm just surprised that any church would pray for my family. So I guess you know I'm a lesbian. Do you have a problem with me spending time with Megan?"

"I have absolutely no problem with you spending time with Megan." Dorothy smiled. "Actually, I suspect Kaitlyn is bisexual. I just worry about the demands Megan is likely to make on you if you don't set limits."

"Megan isn't an imposition. She's a gift. Spending time with her today gave me a lot of pleasure. As for limits, I'm a mother, and I have no problem setting them. I hope you'll allow me into both your lives."

"Quincy, I'm ready," Megan called from upstairs.

"You're being paged." Dorothy smiled. "I think I speak for Megan when I say we'd both love to have you in our lives, Quincy."

"Good, then you'll come to my barbeque Saturday? Just a small get-together for my friends and there'll be real kids there for Megan to play with."

"May I bring some potato salad?"

"That would be great."

Quincy kissed Dorothy's cheek and went upstairs to play.

CHAPTER EIGHTEEN

Quincy

Monday morning, Quincy took her coffee out to the porch. Megan was sitting on Dorothy's porch ostensibly reading, but Quincy could see she was actually watching for her. Quincy headed over to her. "Good morning, Megan."

"Morning, Quincy." Her smile was shy. "Can we play today?"

"Sure." Quincy ruffled her hair as she knocked on Dorothy's door.

Dorothy appeared at the screen door. "Oh, Quincy, I thought you'd be at work today."

"I'm on nights, eleven to seven, Monday through Friday. I'm thinking of going over to the public pool for a couple of hours. Would you two like to join me?" Behind Quincy, Megan drew a quick breath, then chanted under her breath, "Please say yes, please say yes."

"Is there a shady place where I can sit and crotchet or read?"

"Yes. There are some trees and I'll bring a chair for you."

Dorothy grinned at Quincy. "So what do you think, Megan? Should we go to the pool with Quincy, or would you rather stay home?"

Megan jumped. "Pool, pool, let's go to the pool."

"I'll make sandwiches so after Megan and I swim, the three of us can have a picnic lunch."

"No, no, let me make lunch. I have some chicken cutlets left over from last night or I can do tuna or egg salad, if you prefer."

"Surprise me."

"What else will we need?"

"Just bathing suits and towels. I plan to be back by two so I can sleep a couple of hours this afternoon. If we leave by ten, we should have plenty of time."

As Quincy turned to go home, Megan pulled on her shirt. "I don't know how to swim, Quincy."

"Well, it's time you learned. Don't worry. I'll teach you."

Quincy unpacked a few more boxes before changing into her bathing suit. Then she dug out Emma's water wings, packed a blanket and a couple of towels, and filled the cooler with juice and water.

At ten, the three of them piled into her car and she drove to the public pool. She settled Dorothy in the shade, put the water wings on Megan and walked to the steps at the shallow end. She sat in the water with Megan on her lap for a few minutes before carrying her into the deeper water. At first, Megan's arms were tight around Quincy's neck and her body was rigid but after a while Megan loosened her grip and seemed relaxed about being in the water and Quincy took them back to the shallow end of the pool. She started by making a game of putting their faces in the water. Another half hour and Megan was lifting her legs and using the water wings to float. Then, she showed her how to use her arms to do the doggy paddle.

After a few minutes, Megan shouted, "Grandma, look at me. I'm swimming."

At some point, Dorothy had moved her chair closer and was watching them with a huge smile. She clapped. "Look at you, swimming like a fish."

Quincy let her swim for a few minutes then scooped her up. "Now, it's time for lunch."

"Can I swim again, please, Quincy."

"We'll see after a little rest."

Megan swam again before it was time to leave. All the activity wore her out and she fell asleep in the car. Quincy carried her into the house for Dorothy. "There's a new animated movie in town. Would you and Megan like to go to a matinee tomorrow?"

"Are you sure you don't have things to do around the house?"

"I'm slowly unpacking the boxes so I'm good. Movie tomorrow, then Wednesday I need to shop for the barbeque so I'll be busy unless you need to shop. Then we can all go together."

"Yes to both. Do you want to stay for dinner?"

"No thanks. My friend Gina is coming over to help me hang some pictures and she's bringing dinner."

After they'd eaten the Mexican food Gina provided, they cleaned up and turned their attention to the pile of pictures Quincy had set out for a family photo gallery on the staircase wall. Standing on the landing at the top of the staircase, Quincy held up the two photographs taken about fourteen hours after she'd met Lindy. She smiled at the memory. Lindy had held and comforted her all night and then accompanied her to the hospital to meet the strangers whose lives she'd saved.

After the emotional visits and an almost equally emotional press conference, they'd snuck down to the emergency room to get something to treat Quincy's hands and feet, which had come close to being frostbitten during the rescue. Waiting for the nurse to gather what they needed, Quincy had an arm on Lindy's shoulder and Lindy looked into Quincy's eyes, listening as Quincy thanked her for helping her through her trauma last night and the afternoon's stressful meetings. Two flashes jolted them apart. Patsy McKenzie, a young photographer, now one of their close friends, had captured that intimate moment. It was obvious in the photos that they were already falling in love but neither knew it.

Gina pointed to the picture in Quincy's left hand, but Quincy looked from one to the other, unsure of which to choose. Both were lovely. "I've never been able to decide which of these I like better so I'm going to hang both. They hung them and continued down the stairs with the others: Quincy in uniform receiving the medal for saving all those people and another of her surrounded by the people she'd saved, Quincy receiving the Silver Foundation's Award for Bravery, the two of them the night of their engagement, several pictures of them the day they were married, Lindy with Sarah, pictures with their friends, Lindy pregnant with Emma, then pictures of them with Emma, Lindy pregnant with Michaela and pictures of them with Michaela and Emma. When they finished, she hugged Gina. "Thanks. I couldn't have done it alone."

"I'm glad you asked." She surveyed their work. "It looks great but are you sure it's not too morbid?"

Quincy walked to the top of the stairs, then down, stopping at each photograph. At the bottom, she smiled at Gina. "It's the opposite of morbid. Lindy and the girls are always in my heart and in my thoughts, and these pictures mark the happy times in our lives. They remind me of the strength of the love Lindy and I share. They give me hope."

CHAPTER NINETEEN

Quincy

Quincy woke early Saturday, July 4th. It was a glorious day, sunny, in the eighties with low humidity, perfect for a barbeque. She set up lawn chairs and the table in the yard, then moved on to preparing the food. She'd made hamburger patties, a quinoa salad, a pasta salad, and coleslaw. She'd prepped the steaks, marinated the chicken, the shrimp and slices of tofu, sweet potato, onion, mushroom, zucchini, and red pepper for the vegetarian skewers. Lindy always complained that people never gave vegetarians a thought, that she was often left to eat salad or the side vegetable when they were invited to dinner. Tears prickled Quincy's eyes. Lindy loved barbecues, loved to eat outside, and until the last few months, loved to entertain. Memories flooded in and her brain switched to a familiar track. Were Lindy and the girls happy? Did they miss her the way she missed them? Did Lindy still love her? Would they ever come home?

"Hey, Quincy, how come you're crying?"

Megan was standing in the doorway. Quincy hadn't heard her come up the back steps.

Damn. The kid didn't need to deal with this. "I always cry when I slice onions." She wiped her eyes on her arm, planted a smile on her face, then looked up. Dorothy was standing behind Megan with a large bowl in her hands.

"I hope we're not intruding. We came to help." Dorothy studied her for a second and her eyes slid from Quincy's face to the pile of unpeeled onions on the counter. Dorothy tilted her head toward the onions and tomatoes. "Perhaps I could take care of those for you. Do you want slices?"

"Yes, slices." She sniffed and offered a weak smile. "Please come in. I'll just be a minute." She left them there and went into the bathroom to wash her face and blow her nose. When she returned, Dorothy had deposited the bowl of potato salad on the table and was peeling onions.

Quincy made room for the potato salad in the refrigerator. Megan pulled on Quincy's shirt. "What can I do?"

"Come outside. You can put the beer and soda and water in the coolers. Then when you're done, we'll add ice." They went out to the deck and Quincy showed Megan what she wanted her to do and returned to the kitchen.

Dorothy touched her shoulder. "Are you okay?"

"Sorry. Sometimes the memories—"

"No need to apologize. I was about to move on to slicing the tomatoes. Do you have another plate?"

With Quincy directing, the three of them worked steadily. They were just cleaning the kitchen when Amelia and Jackson arrived. Quincy, Dorothy, and Megan went outside and Quincy introduced everyone. Jackson set up the playpen for Alexander while Quincy and Amelia spent some time with Amelia's twins, Lara and Mia. Megan was beside herself to meet two girls her age. Quincy had asked Megan to select some toys from the shed so the children would have things to play with besides the wading pool she'd filled. The three girls immediately started playing.

Amelia stood with her hands on her hips, watching. "The twins can sometimes lock out other kids but they seem to be into Megan." She dropped into a chair next to Dorothy.

Quincy smiled. "If they continue to get along, I might have to borrow them or drop Megan off at your house because right now I'm her only playmate. I don't mind but she really needs other children."

"How do you two know each other?" Dorothy asked.

Amelia grinned. "We love to tell this story."

Quincy lightly punched Amelia's shoulder. "You're the one who loves it, so start."

"My first day of second grade in a new school, Fairmount Elementary, and I was standing on the playground when five white boys cornered me. They were about to beat me up when this huge white kid stepped between me and them. 'She's my best friend. Leave her alone.' The tall kid moved toward the boys and they ran off."

Quincy smiled. "Well, I was the tallest kid in the second grade. But instead of thanking me, she got attitude, put her hands on her hips and gave me the evil eye. 'I don't even know your name. How can I be your best friend?'"

"Even then she had that special Quincy swagger and self-confidence." Amelia laughed. "'My name is Quincy. You will be my best friend. What's your name?' Then I realized she was a girl and I couldn't stop giggling."

Quincy threw her arm over Amelia's shoulder. "And we've been attached at the hip ever since, the giant white girl with blue eyes and the petite brown girl with chocolate eyes."

"And we always will be." Amelia patted Quincy's cheek. "So that's how we met, Dorothy."

Dorothy smiled. "What a lovely story."

Quincy excused herself to greet newly arrived guests while Amelia and Dorothy compared notes on the girls.

Guests continued to stream in carrying drinks and food. Everyone pitched in and the grill was going all day and into the evening. As Quincy circulated, she noted Dorothy chatting easily with her other guests, straight and gay, and she assumed they were all giving Dorothy character references.

Quincy was surveying the crowd, thinking again about how lucky she was to have so many wonderful friends when Gina put an arm around her waist. "I've been thinking."

Quincy drew her closer. “Always a dangerous thing.”

“Yeah, yeah. Anyway, you and Lindy talked about screening in the porch, and I just had a brilliant idea. Let’s make it larger and build it so the screens in the screened-in porch can be replaced by windows, converting it to a glass-enclosed sunroom in the winter. If we install under-the-floor heating, it will be nice and cozy. Lindy will love it.”

Gina was right. Lindy wanted a screened-in porch. And she’d love a sunroom in winter. “If she comes back?”

Gina hugged her. “No, you dodo. *When* she comes back.”

Quincy brushed the tears from her eyes. “You’re that sure?”

Gina grinned. “Yup. And I’m willing to contribute free labor to make it happen.”

“That would be a great gift.” Quincy pulled her into a hug. “I’m ready to start whenever you have time.”

CHAPTER TWENTY

Lindy

It's past ten o'clock and the community lights have gone off as usual. Except for the solar lights that line the path back to the dormitory, I am in the chapel in total darkness on my knees, sobbing. I can't stop. Emma and Michaela are asleep in the pew next to me. My poor babies.

The good news: the medication has taken hold. The bad news: the better I feel, the saner I am, the more I am my old self, the lonelier I feel. I long for Quincy. I long to be held, to be touched, to be loved. I curse myself for bringing us to this harsh, loveless environment. I think about Babs, about our friendship, about the love we feel for each other. I remember all our friends, my chosen family. I mourn Sarah, my chosen mother. And I sob.

I curse Letitia, Lauren, and Joanna for taking advantage of my weakness and planting the idea that my love for Quincy is vile and a sin, convincing me that we and the girls would suffer eternal damnation because of our love and encouraging me to leave all that I know, all that I love. What kind of religion destroys a loving marriage? Are those three polygamists? Are they paid for sending women here?

Finally, the tears are replaced by an overwhelming sadness. How will I survive this? How will I protect my babies? Thinking I was saving them from eternal damnation, I brought them to hell.

I lift Emma to my shoulder. She's grown so tall and heavy it's getting difficult for me to carry her. I lift Michaela next. She'll never be as tall as Emma but she's also grown from a baby into a little girl. And I can't help feeling guilty for depriving Quincy of seeing her change. I stagger along the dimly lit path to the dormitory and breathe a sigh of relief when I find the door unlocked. On the way to our room, I bump into Abby. She takes Michaela from me and deposits her on the bed without comment. We whisper goodnight. I arrange the girls on the bed and undress them.

I stare at the sky through the small window and wonder whether Quincy sees the same stars I see here in the desert. It's later in New Jersey. Is she at work or home in our apartment sleeping alone in our bed? Or maybe by now she's not alone. I push that thought aside. Quincy is nothing if not loyal. But I've done a horrible thing. I've stolen everything she loves. Dare I hope that still includes me? Does she think about us? Or has she moved on? And the tears, hot and painful, flow again.

Since women with children are excused from breakfast duty, we walk to breakfast with Abby and her daughter in the morning. I clear my throat. "Was it you who left the door open last night?"

"Yes. I was worried about you. I was afraid you'd run away."

"Really." I turn to look at her. "Where would I go in the dark?"

She shrugs. "Everyone knows you spend a lot of time in the chapel. I thought maybe you were meeting someone there."

I laugh at that. I certainly wouldn't choose to meet any of those men. And I haven't noticed any women of the lesbian persuasion around here. "You have a wonderful imagination, Abby. Are you sure you're not a journalist trying to write an exposé of the community?"

Abby stops short. "What? Of course not. I—"

She notices the smile on my face and cuts herself off.

I grin. "Sorry, just kidding. But that's just as likely as me having a rendezvous in the chapel." Has she been asked to spy on me or is she a friend? She hasn't shown any disillusionment with the community. In fact, she seems to accept that waiting for another man to choose her is the way things should be. As much as I need a friend, I can't trust her.

On the way into the dining hall, Hannah stops me. "I noticed you came in after lights out last night. Where were you?" The tone of her voice leaves no question that she's accusing me of some wrongdoing. Abby and Hannah erase any doubt that eyes are on me all the time. I will have to be very careful not to arouse suspicion when I actually do something wrong.

It probably isn't smart but I make no attempt to hide my annoyance. "Where would I be, Hannah? My daughters were with me. Did you think I took them to an orgy or maybe a rendezvous with a secret lover? Everyone in the community seems to know that I go to the chapel every night after dinner. I was praying and lost track of the time. I can't believe you didn't know I was there."

She huffs and brushes past me. I take a deep breath and go to where Abby is sitting with a smirk on her face. "Ooh, someone's in a bad mood today."

I hesitate but then I don't care. "Oh, right, bad moods are not tolerated around here. I know it's unchristian to be so snarky, but I feel Hannah's eyes are always on me, just waiting for me to screw up."

Abby pats my hand, then reaches for a slice of toast. "Don't let it bother you. She's like that with everybody. She's been here forever and no man will have her. What else does she have to do?"

Now I feel bad. These women measure their worth by whether a man finds them desirable. It must be hard. Continued rejection can make a person bitter. I watch Abby tending to her daughter and wonder how many years before she becomes like Hannah.

I turn to Emma and Michaela and make sure they have enough to eat. And what about me? How long before I become bitter about the pickle I've got myself into? I rejected murder and suicide when I thought we would all end up burning in hell for eternity. How long before it seems like the only possible escape?

CHAPTER TWENTY-ONE

Quincy

A week after the barbeque, Quincy invited Dorothy and Megan over for dinner. She gave them a tour since neither of them had seen the house beyond the kitchen and the nearby bathroom. Spotting the pictures of Michaela and Emma, Megan had a thousand questions: Where were they? When were they coming back? Did Quincy miss them? Would they like to play with her? Quincy knew the questions related as much to Kaitlyn's absence as anything and answered honestly.

She'd made spaghetti and meatballs, Megan's favorite, and when the girl went to wash up after dinner, Quincy broached the subject that had been on her mind. "Dorothy, please be honest. Would you rather we continue including you in everything or are you comfortable with Megan spending time alone with me in my house?"

Dorothy didn't hesitate. "I'm totally comfortable with you being alone with Megan. I see how good you are with children and how much you care about Megan. And your friends couldn't say enough good things about you at the barbecue."

So Quincy relaxed. When she worked days, she made a point of spending time with Megan after work and usually had dinner with Dorothy and Megan several times during the week. When she was on nights, she and Megan usually spent part of each day together, playing, cooking, reading, or doing jigsaw puzzles. Sometimes they went to the movies or the pool, and other times they visited Amelia and the girls. She lent Megan Emma's mitt so they could play catch. She taught her to ride Emma's bicycle and they often went for bike rides in the neighborhood. It wasn't the same as having her daughters, but they both benefited from the time they spent together—and so did Dorothy. And that felt good.

One afternoon they were playing Megan's favorite game, Monopoly, at a table in Quincy's backyard. "You're getting to be a real capitalist."

Megan giggled. "What's a capitalist?"

"People who make money from investing in businesses or from the labor of others, like the owner of a factory. People like you who own utilities, for example. Do you know what utilities are?"

"Railroads, electric companies, telephone companies, water companies."

"Right. Also people who build hotels on Boardwalk and other properties they own then charge people to stop there." She grabbed Megan and tickled her. "You are definitely a capitalist."

Seeing a movement at the side of the house, Quincy looked up. A soldier in sand-colored fatigues was standing there, glaring. Quincy recognized Kaitlyn from the pictures in Dorothy's house. She put the still-giggling Megan down and turned her toward the soldier. "You have a visitor, Megan."

The soldier and Megan locked eyes but neither moved for a few seconds. Then Megan screamed, "Mommy!" and dashed into her mother's arms.

"Megan, baby." Kaitlyn pulled the girl to her, kissing her, touching Megan's head and her back and her face as if trying to confirm Megan was real. "I've missed you so much."

She turned to Quincy. "My mom said Megan was playing with Quincy. Where is he?"

Quincy stared at her, then laughed. "I'm Quincy."

"You. But—"

"Your mom didn't explain? We play together all the time, right, Megan?"

"Yes, Mommy, and we go to the beach and the library and the museum. Quincy taught me to swim and throw and catch and ride a two-wheeler and—"

"Hey, slow down, kiddo. Give your mom a chance to catch up." She smiled. "Kaitlyn, I moved in here a couple of months ago and I've become friends with Dorothy and Megan." She stuck out her hand. "J. Quincy Adams at your disposal."

Kaitlyn shifted Megan in her arms and shook Quincy's hand. "You're kidding, right? That's not your real name."

"Johna Quincy Adams, it is. What can I say? There's some distant relationship and my parents thought it was cute, though they, and everyone else, have always called me Quincy, not Johna."

"I see. Well thanks for spending time with Megan. We'll go home now."

"I have to put our game away, Mommy."

"I'll make an exception this time, Megan, I'll clean up. Do you know what an exception is?"

"Not something you usually do?"

"Good, kiddo." She smiled. "How long are you home for, Kaitlyn?"

"Ten days."

"I'm sure I'll see you again. See you later, Ms. Megan."

Megan wiggled out of Kaitlyn's arms and kissed Quincy's cheek. "See you Ms. Quincy." She put her hand in her mother's. As they walked away, Kaitlyn turned to stare at Quincy. Quincy sank into a chair and slowly packed up their game. Her thoughts went to her girls. She wished she could show up and claim them as easily as Kaitlyn had just claimed Megan. She didn't know how long she sat there, but she could feel the dark cloud enveloping her, so she pulled out her phone and speed-dialed Amelia. "Can I come for dinner?"

CHAPTER TWENTY-TWO

Quincy

Quincy hadn't seen Megan or Kaitlyn for two days and on the third day when Dorothy showed up to invite her to dinner, she readily accepted.

Oblivious to the tension in the room, Megan was her usual bubbly self, going on and on about going to the zoo and the movies with her mom. Kaitlyn looked exhausted and was stiff and awkward when Quincy tried to engage her. Quincy could see the strain in her face and realized that as much as she loved her daughter, what she probably needed was quiet time to recuperate from whatever horrible things she was involved with in Afghanistan. Her inclination was to take Megan for a day but she sensed that Kaitlyn would be offended so she did the best she could, chatting with Dorothy, engaging Megan, and listening when Kaitlyn joined the conversation. When Kaitlyn went up to put Megan to bed, Quincy helped Dorothy clean up then went home.

Luckily, the next day, Quincy switched to days and kept her contacts with them to a few minutes so that Kaitlyn did not feel she was competing for Megan's attention. But she missed her daily contact with Megan and two nights before Kaitlyn's leave was up invited the three of them to dinner.

Kaitlyn made no bones about examining Quincy's house. She looked at the photographs of Quincy's children, then she picked up and studied several pictures of Megan—with Amelia's twins at the beach, with Dorothy at the pool, and one with her and Quincy standing by their bicycles. She glared at Dorothy. "You bought Megan a bicycle?"

Not getting the angry subtext, Megan responded. "It's Emma's, not mine, Mommy."

"Who is Emma?"

Quincy could tell Kaitlyn was frustrated, not knowing what was going on in her daughter's life. "She's my older daughter. They're with their mother." She really didn't want to discuss the situation in front of Megan. "And Megan uses things like her baseball mitt and her bicycle from time to time."

"Can I have a bicycle for my birthday, Mommy?"

"We'll see."

Quincy smiled at the stock parent answer Kaitlyn offered.

Megan dragged her mom over to a large board with a half-done jigsaw puzzle. "See, Mommy, we're halfway done with this."

"Isn't it too hard for you, honey?"

"Quincy is teaching me how to do it. Look. This whole side is mine. Quincy helps me find the pieces that might go there but then I have to put them together."

The buzzer went off and Quincy went into the kitchen to check on the roast. When she came back to say that dinner was ready and would they come to the dining room, Kaitlyn met her eyes. She looked away quickly but not before Quincy saw the pain in them. She noticed the pictures in Kaitlyn's hand. She knew Kaitlyn was afraid she would lose Megan but she wasn't sure how to reassure her. She pointed to the pictures. "That's Lara and Mia, my friend Amelia's twins. Megan likes to play with them, don't you, Megan?"

Over dinner, Quincy was aware of Kaitlyn sitting stiffly at the table while Megan talked about the things she and

Kaitlyn had done that day. She tried to draw Kaitlyn into the conversation, asking about Afghanistan, her job there, when her tour was over. Kaitlyn clammed up about Afghanistan but said her tour would be over in another six months. Trying to connect, Quincy offered to drive her to the airport when her leave was up in two days but she refused, saying she'd take a bus.

When Kaitlyn left to put Megan to bed, Dorothy stayed to help Quincy clean up. "You'll have to forgive Kaitlyn," Dorothy said. "She doesn't want Megan to be unhappy but I sense she's afraid you're going to replace her."

"Oh, God, Dorothy, not my intention at all."

Dorothy patted her hand. "I know, Quincy, but I think it's natural for Kaitlyn to feel insecure. Megan is a very different little girl than the one she left with me. You've not only made her happy but you're teaching her so many things and you've given her self-confidence. Being a single parent with the kind of responsibility Kaitlyn has in the army is not easy, though she's struggled to do both to the best of her ability."

"Is there anything I can do to help?"

"Just keep being there for Megan. She's the important one. She needs the love and attention that you give her every day. Kaitlyn will have to live with it. But I worry about you too. If Kaitlyn is transferred to another base or meets someone and gets married, she'll take Megan away and you'll have to deal with another loss."

"I've thought about that but if I know where she is, I can visit and keep in contact with her. I think I'll be okay. I was thinking we should do something special after Kaitlyn leaves to help Megan deal with her going away again."

"What?"

"I'm not sure yet."

Dorothy kissed Quincy's cheek and went home.

* * *

Quincy and Gina were enjoying the warm evening outside in the newly screened-in room that she and Gina had added to her backyard when Kaitlyn appeared. "Oh, sorry to interrupt, Quincy. Mom asked me to return your bowl."

Quincy stood and opened the screen door. "No problem. Come in and meet my friend, Gina." She put the bowl on the table. "Gina this is Megan's mom, Kaitlyn. Can I get you something to drink? Beer, wine, water?"

Kaitlyn shook hands with Gina, then shuffled uneasily.

"C'mon, join us. It's your last night of leave. You deserve a little quiet time with adults to relax and unwind."

Gina snorted. "I'm not really sure Quincy is an adult, but please join us, Kaitlyn. I've heard a lot about you from Megan. She's really proud of you."

Kaitlyn smiled, an unusual occurrence, and sat next to Gina. "It's nice to hear that. She's so young and I'm away and out of touch so much I'm afraid she's going to forget me."

Quincy was touched by Kaitlyn's honesty. She hesitated to respond because she knew she was the cause of her worries.

Gina patted her hand. "Not a chance of that happening. I've spent a lot of time hanging out with her and Quincy and we talk about you all the time."

"A beer would be great, Quincy," Kaitlyn said, avoiding looking at her.

Quincy pulled one out of the cooler and handed it her.

"What kind of work do you do, Gina?"

"I'm a cop, like Quincy, but she's a detective and I'm in uniform."

"I used to be an MP before I got into…what I do now. Sorry, I can't discuss it."

They exchanged cop stories. Gina and Kaitlyn connected, the conversation was lively and they seemed to enjoy each other. Quincy interjected now and then but mostly she sat back and listened. As usual with Gina, there was lots of laughter. Tonight was the first time Quincy had heard Kaitlyn laugh. It was a lovely sound.

Kaitlyn glanced at her watch and stood. "This has been great but I need to get to bed so I can be up early tomorrow to spend time with Megan before I get the bus to the airport. Nice to meet you, Gina. Thanks, Quincy."

Gina walked Kaitlyn to the door. "Um, I'm off tomorrow, if you'd like a ride to the airport. Megan can come with us so you'd have more time with her."

Kaitlyn glanced at Quincy.

Quincy could see Kaitlyn wanted to accept but felt uneasy since she'd rejected Quincy's offer to drive her to the airport. "You should accept Gina's offer. I hate the idea of you taking the bus and I'm sure Megan would love the extra time with you." She smiled. "Walk Kaitlyn next door and make arrangements, Gina. I'll move Emma's car seat to your car."

Twenty minutes later, Gina was back.

"All set?"

"Yes. She was embarrassed because she'd refused your offer, but I convinced her you wouldn't mind. You don't, do you?"

"No. I know I'm not her favorite person but I meant what I said. She shouldn't have to take the bus. You two seemed to connect."

Gina flushed. "She's nice. I like her."

When Gina didn't continue, Quincy changed the subject, knowing Gina would come back to it when she was comfortable. It had been a long time since Gina showed an interest in someone. It would be nice for her to get to know Kaitlyn.

CHAPTER TWENTY-THREE

Quincy

A few weeks later, Quincy had dinner at Dorothy's and after she put Megan to bed, Dorothy asked her to stay and talk. "I'm sure Megan told you her birthday is in ten days."

Quincy laughed. "She has mentioned it a time or two." And Lindy's birthday was two days later.

"Kaitlyn wants to give her a bicycle and a helmet and any other accessories she needs with it. She asked me to ask if you would purchase everything for her. She'll send you a check to cover the cost."

"Of course. Actually, I was planning to get her a bicycle but it'll be more special coming from her mom. I'll come up with something else. Also, Dorothy, I was thinking of having a party for her. I thought I'd invite Amelia's two and Babs' two. And now that she's back in school, I'm sure there are some friends she'd like to invite. Is that all right with you?"

"It would be wonderful. I'm planning to make cupcakes for her class but I get tired so quickly these days a party would be too much for me. Which reminds me, I want to show you something." She led Quincy into the living room, opened the bottom right drawer in her desk and pulled out a folder. "In case something happens to me, this folder has all my insurance information and medical history. I'm sorry to put this on you, Quincy, but with Kaitlyn not always available, there's really no one else I trust."

"I'm honored, Dorothy." Quincy hugged her. "Hopefully, I'll never need it but it's good to know."

The party was a huge success. Megan invited eight girls and three boys from her class so with the five children of Quincy's friends, she had sixteen kids six and under. Amelia, Babs, and Gina helped organize the food, decorations, and games. Quincy had gone all out. Besides birthday cake and ice cream and goody bags with candy, everyone received presents. Megan was thrilled with the party, thrilled with the bicycle, and thrilled with the iPad Quincy gave her, especially after they FaceTimed with Kaitlyn in Afghanistan and she could show her mom the gifts she'd received and demonstrate how good she could ride her new bicycle with her own helmet.

After all the children had gone home and Gina and Dorothy helped her clean up, Megan, Dorothy and Quincy were alone, having a quiet dinner. "I had a nice birthday, Quincy, thank you."

Quincy glanced at Dorothy who shrugged and raised her eyebrows. Clearly Dorothy hadn't instructed Megan to say that.

"It was fun seeing my mom when I talked to her. I felt like she was here. Will I be able to see her sometimes when I talk to her?"

"No, Megan, you'll be able to see her *every* time you talk to her now that you have the iPad. I'll show you and grandma how to do it."

Megan threw herself into Quincy's arms. "Thank you, thank you."

Later that night she received an email from Kaitlyn. *Thank you for buying my gift for Megan. The bicycle looks awesome. And thank you for having a party for her. I'd like to pay for it, if that's okay. Just let me know what I owe you for the bike and the party and*

I'll send a check. You know, when Megan told me you'd bought her the iPad, my first reaction was anger that you'd spent so much money on her. But I realize now it was anger at myself for not thinking of it. So thank you for buying Megan the iPad. It's a wonderful gift for both of us. I felt like I was at the party and part of my daughter's life, not an easy thing being so far away. I'm grateful for all you do for Megan and my mom. And for me. Gina says you're a really good person. I think I might be starting to agree.

CHAPTER TWENTY-FOUR

Lindy

Emma shows me the drawing she'd done in school today and I'm shocked by the date written on the paper. September 25th. Today is my thirty-fifth birthday and I had absolutely no idea. I've lost track of time. Does Quincy remember?

Some birthday. Instead of celebrating, I'm mourning. Hannah announced at lunch that Dr. Baumann is no longer the doctor for the community and anyone who needs a doctor will be taken to Chino Valley to see someone else. Rumors are rampant but I surmise that the doctor was going to help someone leave the community and the woman got cold feet and told Joel. I'm devastated by this news. Dr. Baumann is the only one I truly trust here and I had decided to ask her to help me and the girls leave. But not only did I not get to tell her of my fears and ask for her help, I didn't even get to say goodbye. Now I am absolutely alone. And I have never been so frightened. Not even when I stole my mother's secret rainy-day savings and ran away from home at fourteen.

I brush the tears from my eyes. Emma is already upset and the last thing I need right now is to add my tears to hers. Emma has become more compliant and accepting of the school rules. Today for the first time in a while she's been punished. Apparently she was running, pretending she was riding her bicycle. She hasn't mentioned her bicycle for months so I'm not sure what triggered it. I try to comfort her as we walk toward our play spot near the wall, but she throws herself on the ground sobbing. My own despair makes it difficult to console her. What am I going to do?

I've been checking the few cars parked near the dining room for keys and unlocked doors. So far, I haven't found any. My preoccupation with escaping spilled over into my dreams. Last night I dreamed I called Quincy and begged her to come and get us, but she kept saying "We have a bad connection, I can't hear you." I cried when I woke this morning. I'm angry at myself for following Letitia's orders about leaving the phone and throwing the battery away. When I left Hackensack, I was already breaking down and so afraid of Quincy all I could think about was making sure she didn't find us. How ironic. If I had the phone now I'd call Quincy.

I gather from my gentle inquisition of Abby that the closest town is twenty minutes to a half hour away by car. And while I came here voluntarily, Abby's comments and the experience of the woman who got cold feet about escaping, lead me to believe that once you're here you don't leave unless they want you gone.

More men have been coming in for dinner lately. And many of them pretend they're not checking me out when they slowly scan the room but their eyes come back to me time and time again. It makes me anxious. I pretend that I don't notice them but they scrutinize me as if I'm the dinner special. I'm finding it more and more difficult to eat and if it wasn't for needing to feed Emma and Michaela, I would skip going to the dining room. I'm hoping that being married will protect me but I'm afraid Abby is right, that my marriage doesn't matter to them.

Even as I play Simon Says with Emma and Michaela after dinner one night, a car slows, then stops. A man watches us for a while then blows his horn, waves and drives on. This is not good. This is not good at all.

Hannah stops me as I'm entering the dormitory with both Michaela and Emma asleep in my arms. I can barely stand with the weight of them, yet she makes no move to help me. Some Christian. But then I've noticed that there wasn't much of the kindness or gentleness that I'd hoped to find when I decided to flee to a Christian community.

I'm exhausted and not feeling very Christian myself, though I've been on my knees in the chapel for hours. My version of praying these days involves thinking of Quincy, our love, our life together, and searching for a way out of here. Hannah tells me that tomorrow night the community is having a special adults-only dinner. The children will eat earlier and Jemma will take care of Michaela and Emma while I have dinner with the other women and some of the men in the community. I smile and pretend I'm excited. I still can't believe they will try to force me to marry a man, but as I bathe the girls, I think of ways to make myself unattractive. I'm sweaty from playing tag so I decide not to wash and tomorrow morning I won't brush my teeth. I'll also eat garlic if I can get some. Maybe if I stink they'll leave me alone. I consider whether acting crazy will help. I wouldn't have to fake it either. The idea of being forced to marry a man or stay in this screwed-up place is fostering crazy thoughts, like stopping my medication. But I remember what Dr. Baumann said about Joel institutionalizing crazy women when I came here. The last thing I want is to abandon my girls to this place. I regret not asking Dr. Baumann to call Quincy to let her know where to find us. But there's no one to ride in and save us now. It's up to me.

Abby is flushed and vibrant, chattering like a chipmunk as we walk to the dining room. Unfortunately, her excitement isn't contagious. I think she doesn't notice my silence or my escalating anxiety. But then she takes my arm and pulls me to a stop. "You're worried, aren't you?"

I'm surprised by her sensitivity so I'm honest. "Yes, I am."

She pats my arm. "You don't have to worry. You're so pretty. I know of one man interested in you already so who knows how many will want you by the end of tonight?"

All right, not so tuned-in to me. When I look in the mirror, I see the face of a miserable scarecrow. My arms are so thin I look anorexic, yet under this much-too-large, faded cotton dress, I could weigh ninety or five hundred pounds. What does she see? And what do the men see? I offer her a weak smile and remind myself that as much as I need a friend, I can't trust her.

The night isn't as bad as I expected. Some of the men have brought wives with them, usually their first wife, and it's mostly the women I talk to. They are more open about scrutinizing me than their husbands but Abby whispers they are looking for different things like temperament, willingness to cooperate, and compatibility. The men are careful not to stare but I often feel eyes on me as I eat and socialize but I don't feel threatened with the wives there.

These women are different than I expected. None of them seem particularly religious. Most are down-to-earth and all of them are curious about me, though it's obvious they all know I found God and left a lesbian marriage. Their questions don't feel intrusive, rather I sense a desire to understand what a woman could see in a woman. As the evening comes to a close, some of the women make sure I meet their husbands and chat with them for a few minutes. I take this to mean they approve of me. Shit.

On the walk back to our dormitory, I'm relaxed. I enjoyed talking to some of the women, but there's still no way in hell I want to marry any of their husbands. Or any man for that matter. And, unfortunately, even though I talked about how much I loved Quincy and how happy we were, I don't think they got the message. Abby seems a lot less excited than earlier. "How did it go for you, Abby?"

She bites her lip and even in the dim light on the path I see her tears. "Not good. I think the old bitch spread the word about me and most of the women ignored me." She shudders. "I hope I'm not stuck here for the rest of my life."

"Aren't there any younger men looking for a first wife?"

She shrugs. "It's very hard for young men to get established. They're viewed as competition by the older men."

"Aren't there other communities? Maybe you could talk to Joel?"

"That's a wonderful idea, Lindy. There must be other places where I don't already have a bad reputation." She wipes her tears. "What about you? You seemed to have a good time."

"I liked some of the women and enjoyed talking to them but…I'm not ready to get married again."

She touches my arm. "The three women who brought their husbands over to meet you were signaling their approval. I expect all three will propose and you'll have to accept one."

"I can't refuse?" My anxiety skyrockets.

"I doubt it. But you can ask Joel."

The bile rises in my throat and I'm doubled over on the side of the path, throwing up the best dinner I've had since I arrived here. I wonder what Abby makes of it.

CHAPTER TWENTY-FIVE

Quincy

It was a windy late September morning and just home from work, Quincy was in the kitchen making coffee when she heard banging at the back door. At first she thought she hadn't hooked it properly but then she realized Megan was screaming her name. She tore the door open and pulled the girl into her arms. She was in her pajamas, sobbing. "What is it, Megan?"

"Grandma fell down and won't wake up."

Quincy spoke to 911 as she ran next door with the girl in her arms. Dorothy was breathing, but barely. "Go get dressed, Megan. We're going to the hospital with Grandma." The girl ran upstairs and Quincy knelt next to Dorothy. "Help is on the way. Stay with us, please." She heard the ambulance pull up and rushed to the front door to let the EMTs into the house. They acknowledged her and quickly went to work.

She dashed to the desk to retrieve the folder Dorothy had shown her. She was surprised to see an envelope with her name scrawled on it lying underneath the folder. Dorothy hadn't mentioned it but she stuffed it into her pocket and went back to watch them work on Dorothy.

Megan came down and stood next to her. Quincy pulled her close as she scanned Dorothy's notes on her medical condition. "According to this, she has high blood pressure and some heart problems and has had a couple of minor strokes." The EMTs nodded and continued checking vitals, administering oxygen, and inserting an IV. They moved her onto a stretcher and one of the EMTs asked, "Are you coming with us, Adams?"

"We'll follow in my car."

As they drove, Megan asked in a whisper, "Is Grandma going to die like my daddy?"

Quincy hesitated, then went for honesty rather than false promises. "I don't know, Megan, but it's a good hospital and she'll get the best medical care." She took the girl's hand. "Don't worry, I won't leave you."

At the emergency room, Quincy provided Dorothy's Medicare information to the admissions clerk and upon request passed her the advanced medical directive and a healthcare proxy. The clerk scanned the documents into her system, handed the originals to Quincy then directed her and Megan to the waiting room. Once they were seated, she opened the envelope Dorothy had left for her.

Dear Quincy,

I'm so sorry for dumping all of this on you but as I said, with Kaitlyn in Afghanistan there is no one else—no one else I feel who cares and whom I trust to take care of me and Megan. I hope you don't mind. The forms attached here should help you do what needs to be done. The healthcare proxy names you and Kaitlyn so you should have no problem making decisions for me if I'm not able and I've tried to make my wishes clear in the Medical Directive so you'll know what treatment I would want. If in doubt, try to get in touch with Kaitlyn or as a last resort talk to the doctors and make your best call. I trust you implicitly.

Dorothy

Quincy turned the page and found another note.

Dear Quincy,

It's me again. I asked Kaitlyn to have a legal document drawn up to give you responsibility for Megan if something happened to me. If you are reading this, she never did it. I know you understand her insecurity about you replacing her in Megan's life and I suspect that's what prevented her from following through.

In any case, as soon as you can get in touch with her in Afghanistan, get her to send you something giving you temporary responsibility for Megan. In the meantime, I've written the attached letter, which I hope will do. I pray you have no problems since the last thing Megan needs is another disruption in her life.

Love and apologies,
Dorothy

An hour later, a doctor entered the waiting area. "Anyone here for Dorothy Wilson?"

Quincy stood and positioned Megan in front of her. She put both her hands on the girl's shoulders and pulled her close. Megan was petrified and had held on to her one way or another since they'd arrived at the hospital, sitting on her lap, clinging to her leg, hanging onto her jacket, or reaching up to hold her hand in a death grip.

The doctor walked over. "I'm Dr. Monroe. What's your relationship to Mrs. Wilson?"

"I'm Quincy Adams and this is her granddaughter, Megan. I'm Dorothy's friend plus I'm her healthcare proxy and I have power of attorney. How is she?"

The doctor glanced at Megan. "We've done a CAT scan and confirmed she had a stroke. You got her here fast enough for us to administer a drug that should help reduce long-term damage. Right now she's very weak and very tired. She's sleeping. We won't know the extent of the deficits until she wakes up."

Quincy tipped her head toward Megan. "Can we see her for a minute?"

The doctor hesitated, then spoke to Megan. "I'll take you in for just a second but she really needs to rest so don't talk to her or touch her. Okay?"

They followed the doctor to a cubicle in the emergency room. Before she pulled the curtain, the doctor knelt in front of Megan. "Don't be frightened. She's hooked up to some machines and has tubes coming out of her to give her food, water, and medicine while she sleeps."

Her eyes huge, Megan nodded and they followed the doctor into the cubicle. Quincy kept her hands on Megan's shoulders. Dorothy was pale but she looked comfortable, and Quincy knew Megan would feel better for having seen her. The doctor moved the curtain aside and led them back to the waiting area. "Why don't you take a break? Have breakfast, take a walk, then come back in a couple of hours."

"Good idea. Thanks, Doctor." She smiled at Megan. "I'll bet you're as hungry as I am."

Quincy drove to the diner and while they waited for their food, she called Amelia. "Hey, it's me. Dorothy had a stroke this morning. She's semiconscious so they don't know the extent of the damage. Megan and I just left the hospital to grab some breakfast at the Chit Chat Diner, then we're going back to wait for her to wake up."

"Damn. Poor Dorothy. Poor Megan. The kid shouldn't have to sit at the hospital all day. Why don't I meet you at the diner and take her home with me? I can distract her until I pick up the twins after school."

"Good idea."

"Give her the phone, honey."

"Amelia wants to talk to you, Megan." She handed her the phone. She could hear Amelia inviting her, using the promise of the girls coming home in a couple of hours to lure her away from the hospital.

Megan's face brightened as she listened. When Amelia stopped talking, Megan's eyes settled on Quincy. "If Quincy thinks I should."

Quincy nodded. "Your grandma won't wake up for hours and there's nothing we can do at the hospital except wait. I think you should go with Amelia. I'll come and get you as soon as she can have visitors."

Megan hesitated. "Okay, Miss Amelia, I'll come." She listened, then handed the phone to Quincy. As the waitress deposited their breakfast, Quincy and Amelia made a plan.

Quincy watched Amelia drive away with Megan and then headed home to shower and change. Afterward she went next door and packed Megan's clothes, a few favorite books, her iPad, and the triple frame with pictures of her with Kaitlyn. She carried everything down to the kitchen, then remembered to check the calendar. Damn. Just as she feared. Yesterday was the start of one of Kaitlyn's blackout periods. She'd be leading a mission and would be unreachable for at least a week, maybe more. She copied the number for Megan's school from the bulletin board next to the calendar, then called from Dorothy's phone to say Megan would be out today but back in tomorrow.

She moved Megan's things into the guest room closest to her bedroom and unpacked everything. Before she returned to the hospital, she checked in with Amelia. They were baking cookies and Megan was fine.

Back at the hospital, she settled in to wait. And dozed off. She jerked awake when Gina touched her shoulder. "Quince, a hospital volunteer is waiting by the door to escort you in to see Dorothy."

She stretched and yawned. "How long have you been here?"

"About twenty minutes. I'm on lunch break and I thought you might appreciate some company." She lifted a bag. "And food."

"Thanks, I'll eat when I get back. Could you get me a coffee?"

"Yessir."

Quincy smiled as she went over to the volunteer. Dorothy was still in the emergency room cubicle, but she looked more alert. She attempted to smile and said something that sounded like "Quincy." Quincy pulled a chair over and took her hand. "You gave us quite a scare this morning but you're looking a lot better." Dorothy tried to speak but could only make sounds. "Don't worry, Dorothy, everything is under control. I've moved Megan into my house and she'll stay with me until you come home. Amelia and Gina will be there when I'm at work. In fact, Megan is with Amelia and her girls now."

"Than ooh."

"You're welcome. We'll take care of Megan. You concentrate on getting better. Okay?"

A nurse came in. "We're moving Ms. Wilson to a semi-private room on the fifth floor. The nurses there need some time to get her settled and she needs time to rest so the best thing all around is to wait a few hours before visiting again."

Quincy took that as a dismissal and went back to the waiting room. She and Gina took the food down to the cafeteria to eat before leaving.

Gina handed Quincy a sandwich. "Have you contacted Kaitlyn?"

"She's on one of her secret missions so she's out of touch but I'll email her tonight and ask her to FaceTime with me when she gets back. I don't know if she'll be able to get leave but if she can't, I need her to send me a legal document giving me temporary responsibility for Megan. Right now all I have is a letter Dorothy wrote but nothing official."

Gina sipped her coffee. "I'm available to help in any way I can."

"Thanks. I moved Megan into my house earlier. I'm working eleven to seven for this week and next so I'll be able to take her to school, pick her up, give her dinner and put her to bed, but I'll need someone there overnight. You on days or nights?"

Gina pulled their garbage together. "Days. I'll get some things together after work and come over this evening. Should I bring dinner?"

"Amelia will feed us tonight, but thanks. And thanks for stepping up to help."

CHAPTER TWENTY-SIX

Quincy

It was almost three weeks later when Quincy and Kaitlyn connected through FaceTime late one night. Megan was asleep and Quincy was updating her database with the latest sighting of Lindy and the girls in Oklahoma. Another dead end. The police there had followed up but it wasn't them.

"Quincy, I just got back and saw your email asking me to contact you as soon as I could. Is Megan all right?"

Kaitlyn looked and sounded so exhausted that Quincy felt bad telling her about Dorothy. "Megan is fine. But Dorothy had a serious stroke about three weeks ago. She's—"

Kaitlyn paled under her deep tan. "Shit. Is she okay? Where is she? What about Megan?"

"Everything is under control. Dorothy is alert and chipper. Thanks to Megan, we got her to the hospital in time for them to administer a drug that limits long-term damage. She was in the hospital about a week, then with my friend Amelia's help, I was able to get her into a very good rehabilitation center where they're working on her speech and helping her learn to walk again. She'll probably be there another three or four weeks."

"I don't have much money—"

"Don't worry about the money. Medicare will pay for everything."

She watched Kaitlyn relax, then tense again. "Where's Megan? Oh God, I've been dreading something like this. Did Social Services put her in foster care?"

"No. She's living with me. I hope that's all right?"

Captain Kaitlyn Dimarco put her head down, her shoulders shook and Quincy heard a sob. She waited. A minute passed before Kaitlyn raised her head and drew her arm across her eyes. "Sorry, I'm not usually so emotional."

"I'm sorry to lay all of this on you when you've just come back from...wherever you were. But you needed to know. Dorothy is weak but she's in good spirits and doing well. Megan seems happy and comfortable living with me, though I think she's worried about you. Do you think you could call again tomorrow morning before she goes to school? I know it would make her feel better."

"Of course. I need to see her and speak to her."

"And it might help Dorothy if we could do a FaceTime session with her tomorrow night. It would help both of them if you could come home for a while."

Kaitlyn looked away. When she turned back, tears were streaming down her face. "I can't get leave." Quincy could feel her anguish. "I have a critical mission in two days." Her eyes darted around the room. "You've no right to be making decisions for my mom and Megan. I'll figure out how to get them taken care of, maybe the military will help or maybe a foster family for a while." She raised anger-filled eyes to Quincy. "I won't let you take my daughter from me."

Quincy knew that Kaitlyn was stressed but she was stressed too. "Why are you being such an asshole, Kaitlyn? I'm not trying to replace you. Dorothy foresaw this situation, and before she got sick she gave me power of attorney over her affairs and named me her healthcare proxy along with you. She has a pretty specific advanced medical directive but instructed me to check with you if you were available, and if not, to make any decisions that needed to be made."

"I didn't know."

"She also included a letter giving me temporary responsibility for Megan because you never sent the official document she asked you to have drawn up. They both need someone to take care of them and I'm here, you're not. I'm just trying to help all of you. Why can't you accept that?"

"I—"

"You'd really rather send Megan to live with strangers than leave her in a familiar environment with people who care about her? People like Gina and Amelia and other friends of ours you haven't met? Megan is very dear to me but I am not trying to steal her from you. You do know I have two daughters of my own?"

"I…yes. I remember the pictures. Where are they?"

"My wife got involved with some religious nuts and kidnapped them. Didn't your mom tell you?"

Kaitlyn's eyes filled. "Sorry, I didn't know." She shook her head. "I can't even imagine." She took a deep breath. "My mom mentioned you were helping them despite your problems but we got distracted before she could explain. Self-involved ass that I am, I didn't ask her later. Your wife? So you're a lesbian?"

"That's not a problem for Dorothy. Is that what this is about?"

"No it's just…"

"Listen, Kaitlyn, I know how out of control I feel with regard to my girls, not knowing where they are and how they're doing. I would guess you're feeling out of control and wanting things to be the same as if you were here. But you're not and I am. You are going to have to accept that I'm just trying to help."

They were silent for a few minutes, then Kaitlyn spoke. "I'm sorry, Quincy. It's hard enough being separated from Megan when everything is okay. You're right, I do feel totally out of control and torn between family and duty."

"I appreciate the sacrifice you're making by serving and I want to support you and your family. Please believe me, Kaitlyn, I'm not against you. I'm for you and Dorothy and Megan."

"I'll try." Kaitlyn took a deep breath. "I haven't had more than two hours sleep for three days and I'm not thinking clearly but can you give me some details about my mom before we get off."

"Sure. She's awake and talking and starting to walk but she needs extensive physical and speech therapy. You should be prepared when we Face Time tomorrow that she doesn't look great and her speech is impaired."

"Has Megan seen her?"

"I take her to visit a couple of times a week but mostly I drop her off with Amelia or Babs, another friend with kids around her age."

Kaitlyn nodded. "I'll call in the morning to talk to Megan. Goodnight."

"Before we say goodbye, I really need to have papers from you giving me temporary responsibility for Megan. You know it could be something as simple as her falling off her bike and breaking a wrist. It's iffy whether Dorothy's note will be sufficient for me to make decisions for her and it could mean Social Services getting involved. Please don't let that happen."

Kaitlyn nodded. "Sorry, I let my jealousy get in the way of Megan's well-being. I'll take care of it immediately."

The next morning after speaking with Megan, Kaitlyn arranged a FaceTime session with Quincy for that night, after Megan was asleep.

"Quincy, I talked to the lawyer about drawing up the paper giving you responsibility while my mom is sick and I'm overseas." Kaitlyn's voice was tentative, almost frightened, a far cry from the command voice she often used.

"Is there some problem?" Quincy was annoyed. It seemed as if Kaitlyn didn't want to give her temporary custody. "I mean with me as her guardian, or whatever you want to call it."

"No. Well, um, maybe. The attorney pointed out that with me doing dangerous work in a dangerous environment and my mom's health so precarious, that I should really think about what happens to Megan if neither of us is able to care for her, whatever the reason, death or illness."

Quincy sucked in air. Kaitlyn was going to take Megan away. "You think I'm not fit?"

Kaitlyn paled. "Oh, God, Quincy, that's not it at all. You're wonderful with her, so wonderful that I've been jealous of you and I've let it get in the way of Megan's best interest."

Quincy breathed a little easier. "And now?"

"My attorney forced me to see how lucky I, we all are, that you're there and willing to step in and take care of Megan and my mom." She sniffed. "I don't know what I'd do if you weren't there." She cleared her throat. "I called to ask whether you would be willing to assume permanent responsibility for Megan if both my mom and I were dead or incapacitated?"

"Wow, Kaitlyn, I'm honored. I hope it's never necessary but of course I would. She's a wonderful kid."

"And if your own children come back?"

"Megan would be another daughter to me."

"There's no way I could ever repay you for everything you're doing for my mother and daughter, Quincy, but from the bottom of my heart, thank you. I'm so sorry I let my insecurities get in the way when I was home. I'm so sorry I doubted you. I hope we can start over."

Quincy relaxed. "I'd love to. But I should thank you for putting your life on hold to fight for our country and our freedom, so given what I owe you, maybe I'll catch up in a couple of years." They laughed and looked at each other, really looked, for the first time. Kaitlyn flashed one of her rare smiles. "There is one more thing I need to ask of you."

Quincy tensed. "Okay." She drew the word out.

"Would you call me Kate? It's what my friends call me."

Quincy let out the breath she'd been holding. "I won't just consider it, I will. Kate."

"I'll sign the papers when we end this call and they'll go out before I leave for my mission tomorrow. You should have them in a few days. Can we talk again when I get back in a week?"

"Anytime, Kate. I'll be on days that week and the following one, so I'll be home every night."

"Oh, I didn't even think about how you manage to take care of her. You're a detective so you can't always predict your hours."

"As I mentioned earlier, my friends help. Gina is here with her when I'm working nights and if for some reason neither of us can be here, Megan loves sleeping at Amelia's house because she has twin daughters the same age. Two other friends, Ellie and Kelly, are available to stay here with her if necessary. Believe me, other than having you and Dorothy with her, this is the best possible situation for Megan. You spoke to her this morning. How did she seem to you?"

"Thanks to you she's happy, Quincy. I know I sound like a broken record, but I really don't know what I would have done without you. And being able to see and talk to Megan so often makes me feel like I'm involved in her life again. Thank you for making me happy too."

Quincy blushed. "Well, if you must know, making you all happy makes me happy too." They laughed. "Stay safe, Kate, and call us when you get back."

* * *

It was near the end of October when Quincy brought Dorothy home from rehab. She was still weak and needed a walker, but she was on the mend. Quincy helped her out of the car, then guided her slowly to the rear of the house. The ramp into the sunroom would be easier for Dorothy to navigate than the front steps and they could enter the house through the connecting door. Who knew when Gina suggested the ramp instead of steps it would come in handy for Dorothy on a walker?

Inside the house, Quincy led Dorothy to the room she and Lindy had earmarked as the children's playroom. Since it was on the first floor and had a bathroom attached it was perfect for Dorothy, so Quincy had converted it to a bedroom. She helped Dorothy out of her coat and onto the bed. Dorothy's eyes filled with tears. "I don't know how to thank you."

"Just work on getting better. That will be thanks enough for me. Would you like to take a nap? I didn't tell Megan you were coming home today so she's going to be all over you when you see her."

"I will nap but first tell me how you're going to manage all this, caring for me as well as Megan?"

Quincy wasn't exactly sure how she was going to do it either but with the help of her friends she would work it out. Any effort to care for Dorothy paled next to the sacrifices she and Kate were making. She sat next to Dorothy and put an arm over her frail shoulders. "The beauty of having a former social worker as your best friend is that she knows her way around these things. First of all, we have an aide coming in for several hours three or four mornings a week to help you shower and dress. The other mornings I'll help you. You'll have physical and speech therapy here three times a week for two weeks and after that one of our team will drive you to the rehab center. Amelia is working up a schedule of our friends for days when I can't do it. We'll manage, Dorothy. We have a lot of support." She stood. "Let me help you lie down."

"What about the cost, Quincy? This hospital bed and that wheelchair must be expensive and I noticed a shower chair and a commode in the bathroom. Maybe I should give you my social security check."

"Medicare will cover all the equipment and the aides, so don't worry." *And I'll figure something out to pay for the extra hours Medicare won't cover.*

Quincy took advantage of the time Dorothy was napping to get a head start on lunch, soup with a side of rice and steamed veggies for Dorothy, who needed only soft foods, and soup and sandwiches for her and Megan. She was listening to a soft rock playlist at a very low volume so she would hear the bell she'd set up for Dorothy when a sound caught her attention. She paused her chopping and listened. Someone was knocking on the front door. All her friends used the side door so it was likely a salesperson. She dried her hands and went to see who was there.

She peeked through the curtains. A very tall Black woman faced the door. She looked familiar. She opened the door and was eye-to-eye with her.

The woman smiled and extended her hand. "Ms. Adams, I presume. I'm Nina Mayfair, Dorothy's pastor."

Quincy took her hand. “Pleased to meet you, Pastor. Please call me Quincy. Dorothy is napping but she should be up in a little while. Come in.”

After settling her in the kitchen with a cup of tea, Quincy continued making her soup. Pastor Mayfair watched her work. “It’s wonderful that you’ve taken it upon yourself to take care of Megan and Dorothy but it’s a lot for one person. When I visited Dorothy in rehab recently, she said your friends had stepped up to help. But I understand she still needs a lot of care and a lot of chauffeuring so I’m here to offer my services and the services of my parishioners to help ease the burden for you. Our people are available to support you and Dorothy. Whether it’s doctor or therapy appointments or someone to stay with Dorothy day, evening or even overnight, or someone to take Megan to school or pick her up, you tell us what you need and we’ll make it happen.”

Quincy stopped chopping and stared at her. “Wow, I swear just a few minutes before you got here, I was struggling to figure out how I could get all the help we need. My friends have jumped in but they’re all working, and some have children, so it’s been a juggling act just to make sure someone is always with Megan. Now with Dorothy home our needs have increased exponentially.” She sat. “Pastor, I can’t tell you…” Her voice broke. She reached for a tissue, then dabbed her eyes.

Pastor Mayfair took both Quincy’s hands in hers. “It’s Nina. And you don’t have to tell me. Anyone who’s ever cared for a sick person understands the demands. Dorothy and Megan and Kaitlyn are lucky to have you and your friends in their lives. We want to help, if you’ll let us.”

“I accept. But how would it work? Would I have a list of people to call when I need someone?”

“We could do that but then it means you have to spend your time calling around to see who’s available. I’d suggest we make a weekly plan. You anticipate the help you’ll need the following week and give me a schedule. I’ll be responsible for getting the volunteers and making sure they show up when needed. If something you hadn't planned comes up, you make one call to me and I'll get someone. How does that sound?"

Quincy relaxed her shoulders. "It sounds terrific. I don't know why I didn't think to ask the church for help."

Nina smiled. "I know your last interaction with a church wasn't a happy one but you should know some of us really do believe in the love of Christ and in loving one another."

CHAPTER TWENTY-SEVEN

Lindy

I sit on the edge of the chair. In the eleven months I've been in the community I've seen Joel, the spiritual leader, but I've never once spoken to him, so I'm concerned about being summoned to his office now. I wonder if my anguish and doubts are obvious to the members of the community. Despite the relentless daily religious lectures inflicted on the women to ensure we understand our subordinate role to men as wives and bearers of children, I still love Quincy and more than anything in the world, I long to be home with her. I vacillate between thinking Quincy would never love anyone else and thinking she's already replaced me.

I often think of my childhood, growing up in that harsh, loveless, religion-focused family and my heart breaks that I brought our girls to this rigid, loveless environment. This is hell for them. Although they aren't physically beaten or mistreated the way I was, the brainwashing we all received every day is sucking the life out of Emma and me.

The door opens. I look up as Joel walks in and sits behind the desk. He tents his hands and gazes at me for a minute before speaking. Pompous ass. "So, Lindy, you've been with us a little over eleven months and how hard you work and how much time you spend in the chapel praying, hasn't gone unnoticed."

I don't know what to say, so I nod.

"You're a very lucky woman because you've come to the attention of three men in the community looking for wives. I believe you met Jeff Melingham, Efraim Fieldstone and Jeremy Porter at the dinner last week."

So it's about getting married. My eyes go to the large glass ashtray on his desk and I imagine using it to knock him out, steal his keys, get the girls from school and escape. I blink and force myself to look at him. I need to play this game.

Abby had identified those three as definitely interested after the big matchup dinner. And since then, I've been waiting for the ax to fall, not knowing what, if anything, is happening behind the scenes, or whether I get a voice in this marriage. I still can't wrap my mind around the fact that they will force me into a sham marriage—with a man—knowing I am already legally married to a woman.

"I met several of them and their wives at the…dinner. Are you, and they aware that I'm already legally married?"

He looks condescending. "Oh, I'm aware. But that's Satan's marriage, not God's. And my dear, I thought getting away from that is what brought you here."

"I…yes, I just thought you should know."

"Now I can choose a husband for you or if you prefer you could meet them and decide for yourself."

"They would take my daughters?"

"It would be up to them. If they didn't want the girls, we'd keep them here in the school."

They would take my girls away. I fight the panic and nod as if it's every day I talk about being forced into bigamy and abandoning my daughters to become uneducated, subservient harem members. "What if I choose not to marry?"

"We can't support you forever. You're free to leave, if you'd rather."

"I didn't know. Would someone drive us someplace where we could get a bus or train."

"Oh. The children would have to stay. You kidnapped them and are a fugitive, after all. Besides, on the street with no money, how would you a take care of them?" He offers a gotcha smile.

"I…I didn't realize I was a fugitive. Uh, could I have some time to think about it, to meet these men and maybe get to know them before deciding?"

He stands. "Of course. We wouldn't force you to marry someone you didn't want. We'll start with the formal introductions next week and you can take some time to decide."

I stand. And turn toward the door. "Thank you." With my back to him he can't see my panic. My instinct is to run as fast as I can, but I exercise great control and slowly walk away. As I close the door, I turn and manage to smile but I'm having difficulty taking in enough air. Outside, I stumble. I force myself to breathe and walk back to my room at a normal pace.

I want to drag the girls out of their classes and run but I know better. In the beginning I was too confused, and though I hate to admit it, too crazy to think about where we'd ended up. But after several months of trial and error, Dr. Baumann found the right dose of a medication that worked for me and when it kicked in I felt like my old self. With my eyes open, I saw the truth of this community and I seriously considered taking the girls and walking out of here. However, once I took the time to look around, I realized we were in the middle of the desert and I'd never seen a car drive past. We must be off the main roads. I have no choice but to go along with this charade while I search for a way out for all of us. That big glass ash tray pops into my mind and I push it away.

* * *

One evening a few days later, Hannah and Abby show up with a dress that is almost my size and relatively stylish. They tell me they will fit the dress to me so I look attractive when I have dinner with my suitors. Not wanting to alert the enemy to my aversion to the whole idea, I bite my tongue and make no comment. But the way I look in my raggedy tent dress hasn't kept the animals at bay so why worry about it now? In three days I will have a private dinner with Efraim Fieldstone, one of the suitors whose wife I'd liked.

I'm running out of time.

My asthma is rearing its ugly head. I've been struggling with it since I arrived in Arizona but I think the stress is making it worse. Even the inhalers prescribed by Dr. Baumann are not helping as much and there are times I struggle to breathe. So now I'm stressed worrying that I'll die and leave Emma and Michaela here alone.

Thankfully, the private room where Efraim and I are having dinner is air-conditioned and I breathe easy for the first time in weeks. I try to strategize as I wait for him to show but I'm so scared I have to force myself to sit still and act composed. I wonder what will happen if the three suitors all reject me.

I'm standing at the window when the overweight fifty-something, his breathing almost more labored than mine in the middle of an asthma attack, walks in wiping his brow with a white handkerchief, which is probably washed and ironed by one of his many wives. As he lumbers across the room, I enjoy a seconds-long fantasy of him dropping dead immediately after we're pronounced man and wife, leaving me free to leave with my daughters. And then I focus. I really liked Nora, his first wife. I found her open, warm, and kind. I gathered from Abby that most decisions with regard to the household fall to the first wife and Nora seemed sympathetic to my worry about leaving my daughters, and though she hadn't committed, she'd hinted she would let me take them with me. I take a deep breath. I need to play this right so if I am trapped into marrying, I make the best choice for me and the girls.

Joel is right behind my suitor. "Lindy, I believe you've met Efraim Fieldstone?"

"Yes, of course, Mr. Fieldstone." I extend my hand. Fieldstone hesitates, then touches it briefly. Oops, was I not supposed to touch him?

"Lindsay, so nice to see you again. Nora sends her regards. Shall we sit?" He nods at Joel.

We wait for him to leave and once the door is closed, Fieldstone leans toward me. "Please call me Efraim." He smiles. "Would you like some wine?"

"No thank you, I don't drink alcohol." And that's the truth.

He beams as if I'd just given the correct answer to the sixty-four-thousand-dollar question.

We both turn at the knock on the door. A woman I don't recognize enters wheeling a cart with two covered dishes and utensils, glasses, bread, salad, water, and two desserts. She serves us and leaves.

We eat in silence for a minute, he slicing and chewing his steak and me enjoying the vegetarian meal I'd requested, the second meal since I arrived that had any taste. A good sign? Hopefully, I won't throw it up later. "So, Lindsay, tell me about yourself."

Damn, Efraim if you're trying to seduce a girl at least get her name right. "It's Lindy, not Lindsay. A lot of people make that mistake." I hasten to add that last so as not to alienate him. I'm sure Nora filled him in on my story but I guess he wants to hear it from the horse's mouth so I tell all, including my crazy arrival here and the treatment by Dr. Baumann. He smiles and nods as I talk, seeming unfazed by the tale. Suddenly thirsty, I pick up my glass. We both notice my hand shaking.

Surprising me, he reaches out and covers my hand to still the shaking. "There's nothing to be nervous about, Lindy." A few seconds later, I bring the glass to my lips and take a long drink. It's a sweet gesture, intended to comfort me but it makes me angry instead. He shouldn't have the right to touch me. He shouldn't be colluding to force me to marry him. I close my eyes, shutting him out, and breathe deeply. In a few seconds I'm in control of my anger but not the churning in my stomach. Hopefully he'll think I'm overwhelmed by his compassion.

When I open my eyes, he nods and smiles, probably proud of himself. "So are you a virgin?"

I'm glad I've finished drinking before that direct question because if I had water in my mouth I'm sure I wouldn't have been able to keep from spraying him. I don't hesitate to answer. "Well, no, I've been married for six years. In fact, I'm still married." I'm ambivalent about my goal here. On the one hand, based on what I've learned from the other women, Efraim and his wives are highly regarded and are my best bet for having my girls with me, so I want him to want me. On the other hand, I don't want any of this. I want out of this place. I want Quincy. And I want him to reject me.

"Well, if you haven't ever been with a man, then you're a virgin in my book." He stares into my eyes, triumphant.

"I haven't ever wanted to be with a man so I guess it's true, by your definition, I'm a virgin." I temper my snarky answer with a smile that I hope is shy, even virginal.

Suddenly he looks sly and wolfish, as if he's sorry he's had dinner because he has no room to devour me right now. But later. Maybe it's my imagination.

Images of him naked on top of me, invade my mind. I feel an urge to vomit. I swallow a few times to keep the bile down and force another smile. Since both our minds are already there, I ask a question. "How does it work? The sex, the multiple wives?"

"I try to be fair and pay equal attention to each one of my wives, but it's not always possible because sometimes I desire a particular one and so she's the one I visit at night. And then someone is always pregnant, so it depends on my mood and the situation."

Christ, like he's God's gift to women, allocating his scarce resources to fuck everyone fairly. I swallow again. "I've heard stories of problems between wives. Do your wives get along?"

"You've met Nora. She likes you a lot and that's very important to me since she's the one who organizes the household and keeps the peace. My other three wives are all compatible with her and I assume they will be with you. I'll arrange for you to meet them if you'd like?"

I swallow, trying to push the fear back. "That would be nice." Once I agree to marry him I'll lose any power I have so I decide now is the time to negotiate the most important point. "Would you take my daughters? Michaela is almost seventeen months and Emma is six."

"I hear that Emma is quite a handful but yes, I would take them. Can't have too many girls." He smiles again.

I've lost my appetite so I push the food around on my plate. "Can I ask how you support your…" I catch myself before I say harem. "…large family?"

He leans forward, clearly happy to tell me about his three businesses—a lumberyard, a construction company, and a fledgling trucking firm. He is excited to learn I was a scheduler in a long-distance trucking firm before I got married and had children. I wonder if I can convince him to give me a job instead of marrying me but I hold off on that for now.

He walks me back to the dormitory but makes no move to kiss or touch me. "I'll meet with you again after you've talked to your other two suitors. If you're interested, I'll take you round to meet the rest of my family."

I thank him and go inside. Abby is sitting on the steps waiting for all the details. Having no doubt that everything I say will be reported back to Joel, I spin a positive tale and speak of how much I like Efraim. If I ever get out of this hellhole, I might have a career on the stage.

The girls are asleep when I finally close the bedroom door and collapse at the foot of the bed. This is moving too fast for me. Suddenly, I have a brilliant idea. I'll reject all three suitors and ask to leave, even though they'd keep the girls here. Once they drive me into town I'll call Quincy to come and rescue the girls.

No. I don't trust them one bit. I have no guarantee they won't send me to a mental hospital. Or worse, let me go and send the girls to another community where they'll be lost to us forever.

I'm desperate. I have to find a way to leave with the girls. First thing, though, is to determine how much money I have. I pull out my jeans and search for loose change and bills and find thirteen dollars. I search every drawer and crawl on the floor of the closet, but I don't find anything else. I collapse on the floor and sob in frustration. When I open my eyes, I blink to clear them. Am I hallucinating or is that my suitcase under the bed?

Careful not to wake the girls, I pull the suitcase toward me. The snapping of the buckles echoes like gunshots in my ears. I pause, but the girls don't stir. I listen for footsteps in the hallway but I only hear the usual night sounds, a cough, a snore. I lift the top of the suitcase and stare at the jumble of clothing. I'm a neat person, a neat packer. The state of my suitcase probably mirrors the state of mind when I left New Jersey.

The girls' clothing is a jumble on the top. I don't even bother going through it. They've grown so much nothing I brought with us will fit so I stuff their things into my garbage bag. I take a breath and methodically go through the three pairs of my jeans looking for more money but I come up empty. I pull out a pair of sweats but the pockets are empty. I hesitate. No tees or underwear or socks for me? I was crazy so why am I surprised? I'm starting to panic when I see another pair of my jeans. I pick them up but as I put my hand in a pocket I spot a credit card in the bottom of the suitcase. I dump the single sneaker, box of tissues and woolen sweater on the floor and find another two credit cards. And then, nestled in the corner, I see my wallet, my cell phone, the battery and the charger. I sob with relief.

I have a vague memory of tossing the cell battery out the car window, but I guess my stubborn streak prevailed or maybe I imagined it. I have absolutely no memory of packing my wallet or phone. I'm thrilled to find another thirty dollars in my wallet.

Praying there's cell phone coverage out here and that Quincy hasn't canceled my contract, I replace the battery and plug it in. My heart racing, I watch it. But just as it starts to charge, the power goes off as it does every night at ten. I stare at the phone, surprised to find myself actually praying for a signal, praying that we will be saved from the hell I've brought us to, praying for Quincy to rescue us. I'm confident she'll come for us, or at least for the girls. But what if she's canceled my cell contract? I sink to my knees. After a few minutes, I remember Quincy telling the judge she hadn't changed anything after I left so I still had access to all our joint accounts, my phone, and my car. And now that I think about it, I'd wager my life that she still hasn't canceled my cell contract. When the power comes back on at five a.m., I'll call. Quincy will know what to do.

At five the next morning, I watch the phone charge, see that I do have a signal, then suddenly afraid Quincy won't want me, I turn it off and put it back in the suitcase.

I think about the phone all day. I'm so distracted that several women in the kitchen ask what's wrong. "Nothing," I reassure them. I lean in and confide that three men are interested in marrying me. "I just can't stop thinking about my dinner with Efraim last night. I wonder what the other two will be like. I'm getting married soon." I hope sending positive messages to Joel will take the pressure off while I work up my courage to call Quincy. I haven't given up the idea of stealing a car from Joel or one of my suitors, but I don't know what to do once I make it out of this place. I don't have much cash and I'm not one hundred percent sure my credit cards are still valid but mostly I fear they will catch me and bring us back here, cutting off all possible avenues of escape. Quincy will come if I call, I'm sure, but will she take the girls and me?

In the quiet of the chapel I go over and over every idea, every objection until I'm near tears again, and once the girls are asleep on the bed in our room, I go over all of it again. The next morning Hannah tells me I'll be meeting another suitor tomorrow night and I resolve to chance it. How can I sentence Michaela and Emma to grow up in the midst of the misogynistic hypocrisy of this so-called religious community? They deserve a normal life. I trust that even if Quincy doesn't want me back, she'll come for the girls. And I know in my heart she won't leave me here. I'll call when the power comes back on in the morning. I am so excited that I show the girls their lockets and the pictures inside, then talk to them about Quincy, about what a sweet and good and loving Mama she is. It helps me to talk about her, but I worry when Emma turns away.

Once Emma and Michaela fall asleep, I try on the jeans I was wearing when I arrived. I'm shocked at how much weight I've lost. I knew I was much thinner and I did notice I resemble a concentration camp victim but still I'm jolted by the reality. I reassure myself Quincy will come for me no matter how I look. I close my eyes and remember Quincy taking my hands and gazing into my eyes as she spoke our marriage vow. "*I love you and I promise to take care of you in sickness and in health and I commit my life to making you happy as long as we both may live.*"

Quincy would never forsake me. Our commitment was forever. I'm the one who broke our vow.

CHAPTER TWENTY-EIGHT

Quincy

Quincy bolted from a deep sleep as the alarm rang. Not the alarm, the phone. She squinted at the clock. Eight a.m. on a Sunday. Had to be an emergency call out. As she opened the drawer to get her underwear she checked her phone display. Her heart skipped a beat. Lindy's number. She dropped onto the bed. "Quincy."

Heavy breathing. A sob. A sniff. Then the familiar husky voice whispered, "Quincy?"

Lindy. Her breath caught. "Lindy. Are you and the girls all right?"

"Yes. Please can I come home?"

Quincy's heart broke, hearing the fear in Lindy's voice. "Oh God, yes. Where are you?"

She hesitated. "I'm so sorry for running away, Quincy." She sobbed. "I've been sick. I don't know how I feel, I mean about us, but I miss you terribly. The girls and I need to come home."

"Don't worry about that, Lindy. We'll figure things out after we get you all home. Tell me where you are and I'll come for you."

"We're in the desert about twenty minutes to a half hour away from Chino Valley, Arizona. In a walled religious community. There's nothing around that I can see. I've been told it's about an hour and a half outside Phoenix." A sob escaped. "They've told me I can leave but the girls will have to stay because I'm a fugitive. I want to come home but if you have to choose, take the girls and leave me."

"Lindy." Quincy waited a second. "I won't leave you there unless it's what you want." She was anxious but she hoped her voice was strong, reassuring. "Is it?"

"No." Lindy's firm answer, left no doubt. "I want to come home with you and the girls." Quincy heard her quick intake of air. "If you'll have me."

Tears pricked Quincy's eyes. Lindy sounded so vulnerable. "Lindy, honey, I love you and I want you home with me. Now tell me again what you know about where you are." Quincy picked up the pen and pad she kept next to the bed and wrote down the information. "I'll call you when I arrive at the airport and let you know when I'll be there."

"No, you can't call. We're not allowed to have phones and if anybody hears it, they'll confiscate it. I didn't even know I had it with me or I would have called sooner. I was kind of crazy when I left and they wanted me to leave it behind so I must have blocked out putting it in the suitcase. I was surprised to find it and the battery yesterday with the stuff I brought with me. Thank God, you've left the service on." Lindy hesitated. "Um, Quincy, that reference to God was a figure of speech. I'm past that craziness."

"That's good to know." Quincy smiled. Did that mean she wasn't Satan anymore? "I'll be on the first flight I can book and hopefully I'll pick you up tonight. Can you leave the phone on for a couple of hours? I won't call but maybe we can use the signal to figure out exactly where you are. Make sure it's charged then leave it off until about six your time tonight. Turn off the sound and put it in a drawer or someplace no one will hear it beep when I text you instructions. I'll be there tomorrow morning at the latest. Only take what's essential. We'll buy anything you need when we get home. Be ready to go." Quincy took a breath. "You're sure this is what you want?"

"Yes."

"I love you. Hold tight. I can't wait to see you."

"Thank you." Lindy was silent for a few seconds, then she said something so softly Quincy wasn't sure whether she'd imagined Lindy had whispered, "I love you" before she disconnected.

Quincy stilled her breathing, afraid to let herself feel happy. She'd flown all over the country following up sightings of Lindy and the girls. But this was different, wasn't it? Lindy wanted to come home. She'd been careful to let Quincy know she wasn't making promises about things going back to the way they were. Well, they'd cross that bridge when they came to it. It sure sounded like Lindy had said she loved her. She shook her head. It didn't matter. Right now, she needed to figure out what had to be done to bring her family home. She looked at the pen and paper in her hands and started a list.

She booked her flight on American Airlines, a 1:55 p.m. flight out of Newark arriving in Phoenix at 4:01 p.m. Phoenix time. Then she booked four seats on an American flight leaving Phoenix at 8:45 a.m. the next day, arriving in Newark at 4:30 p.m. She arranged for a rental car and a hotel room at the airport in Phoenix.

After she showered and dressed, she made coffee and sat at the table and made her calls. "Amelia, Lindy called this morning. I'm flying to Arizona later to get her and the girls and I can't get back until tomorrow early evening. Gina will stay with Dorothy and Megan tonight. Can you spend the day here today and tomorrow?"

"Whoa. Slow down, Quince. She called? How did she sound?"

"Strung out, but she says they're okay. She wants to come home but she's not making any promises about us. We'll see."

"Oh, honey, I'm thrilled for you. Of course I'll stay with Dorothy. It's a little easier now that she's well enough to be left alone while I pick Megan up for lunch, then go for Megan and

Lara and Mia later, after school. My two will be ecstatic about playing with Megan. I can be there by ten."

Her next call was to Chief of Police Connie Trubeck. She brought her up to date. "Connie, I need at least the next two days off and maybe the week."

Chief Trubeck laughed. "Christ, Quincy, go get Lindy and the girls. You have tons of vacation and comp time coming so take what you need."

"Thanks. Could you call the Chino Valley police chief to request a patrol car follow me when I go to pick up Lindy and the girls? I don't expect trouble, but you never know. I don't want to give them too much notice in case they're in cahoots with whoever she's with so I'll let you know when I'm getting near Chino Valley."

"Okay. Call me if you need anything while you're there. And, let me know when you're back."

"Thanks."

She called her partner, Tony, to brief him, then made one final call. "Babs, Lindy called this morning. She wants to come home."

"Holy shit, Quincy. Where is she?"

"In Arizona. I'm getting a flight out later today to pick them up. If all goes well, we'll fly back tomorrow. I'm going to need your help."

"Whatever you need."

Quincy explained the plan and hung up. Since she'd told Lindy to leave everything behind, she packed a bag with toothbrushes, pj's and a change of clothes for all four of them. She couldn't find Lindy's coat and the girls must have outgrown theirs in the last year. She'd have to buy them coats in Arizona. Then she went into the room where she stored the girls' toys and picked a favorite stuffed animal for each, the book of fairy tales, and coloring books and crayons.

By then Dorothy was up. Quincy filled her in as she helped her wash and dress. Megan came down and Quincy made breakfast for the three of them.

"Megan, I'm going to get Michaela and Emma this afternoon, so I won't be home until tomorrow night."

"Will I be able to play with them when they come?"

"Absolutely. I'll bet they love you. But they might be kind of tired for the first few days."

"Will Emma be able to ride her bicycle?"

Quincy studied Megan. "Well, I think it will be just about the right size for her now but we'll have to see how she feels. Go get ready. Amelia is going to stay with you and grandma today and tomorrow, so you'll get to play with Lara and Mia."

"Yay." Megan jumped off the chair and hugged and kissed Quincy and dashed out.

Dorothy squinted at her. "Are you going to be able to deal with all of this?"

"All of what?"

"Me, Megan, Michaela, Emma, Lindy? It's a lot for one person. Maybe we should move back to my house."

"Hey, Dorothy, haven't you ever noticed I have broad shoulders? And besides that, it may be easier for Lindy if there's someone else in the house, someone neutral."

"I'm not exactly neutral when it comes to you."

"I meant not a lesbian but not a religious fanatic either."

"Ah, yes, I see. In that case, I'm neutral."

Quincy cleaned up breakfast, walked Megan to school and chatted with Amelia when she arrived. Later, she went upstairs for the suitcase she'd packed. On an impulse, she packed Lindy's iPod, closed the suitcase and headed for the stairs. She stopped to gaze at the pictures Patsy had taken of them just hours after they'd met. On the way down the stairs she scanned the pictures of her and Lindy and their daughters. She'd missed a year in her daughters' lives but she would make it up to them.

Waiting for her flight at Newark Airport, the memory of the other time Lindy ran floated through her mind. They'd spent an intense nonsexual weekend talking and eating and walking, getting to know each other, making a strong connection. As they got ready to separate Monday morning, Quincy asked Lindy out on a date. And Lindy fled.

After almost a month Lindy called. Sounding as unsure as she'd sounded this morning she asked if Quincy still wanted to go on a date with her. Her heart had responded then, exactly as it did this morning. Yes. Yes. Yes.

CHAPTER TWENTY-NINE

Lindy

I can't believe it. Quincy is coming for us. Today. She said she loves me. I'm as excited as I was on our first real date. To avoid making anyone suspicious, I concentrate on going about today like any normal day. We have breakfast in the dining room, I take the girls to school and go to my job in the kitchen. I can't stop thinking about Quincy, can't stop smiling. I realize how badly I've hidden my unhappiness when person after person comments on how different I look, how I seem to be glowing today. Once again I use the three suitors as cover, saying not only am I excited about getting married but I'm also relieved because one of my suitors says I can take my daughters with me. And because it's what they all want, they believe me. Despite my best efforts to avoid looking at the clock, my eyes seem to go there of their own accord. The day drags.

I pick up the girls after school, go for our usual before-dinner walk around the grounds, stroll past the entry as usual, and then return to our room. While the girls nap, I decide what to take. Definitely the lockets. I consider my medications.

Although Dr. Baumann is no longer allowed on the grounds, refills arrive each month. I know she sends them to keep me sane. I shove the bottles in the pocket of my dress along with my driver's license, credit cards, and the little money I have. The cell phone and charger go in the other pocket. Luckily the damned dress is shapeless so no one will notice that my pockets are full. I join the girls on the bed and let myself think about Quincy and our friends, the people I've abandoned. It will be difficult facing everyone but not as difficult as staying here, being forced to marry a stranger—a man—and being separated from my children. It comes to me that I have complete faith in Quincy, trust her totally and know she will help me through this. Yet I don't trust these so-called religious people at all. I try to recall why I'd felt I had to leave Quincy, but the effort makes me anxious so I think about our apartment instead. And when Emma kicks me in her sleep, I remember the king-size bed.

At last Quincy's text arrives. Twenty minutes. I can barely breathe. I wake the girls and wash their faces with the always lukewarm tap water to wake them. I put their lockets on and we leave the room, on our way to freedom. As I start walking, Joel's assistant, Peggy, stops me. "Joel would like to see you in his office now, before you go to dinner."

Shit. "Um, please tell him I'm so excited I'm taking a walk to calm myself. I'll stop by right after I finish my walk."

Peggy's eyes widen, her jaw drops. "Oh, no, when Joel invites one they must go immediately." She clasps my arm. "Besides." She greets two women exiting the building, watches them until they are out of earshot, then whispers, "One of your suitors has come by unexpectedly and is waiting to have dinner with you. Go ahead. I'll take the girls."

No way. I need to get rid of this woman before I lose the opportunity to escape. "I need a few minutes to compose myself and while we walk I plan to explain what's happening to the girls. Why don't you meet me at Joel's office in ten minutes and then you can take them with you." I hoist Michaela, grab Emma's hand and start walking toward the exit to meet Quincy. Michaela is heavy so I can't run but I walk as fast as I can, dragging poor Emma. As I near the exit I hear people calling my name. Sure that it's Joel, Peggy, and probably my suitor, I don't look back. *Please be there, Quincy, please be there, Quincy.* Wheezing, and dragging Emma along, I repeat it over and over, like a prayer. *Oh no, please don't let my asthma kick in now.*

"Mommy, I can't go so fast. Can we stop?" Emma is slowing down, falling behind me.

"Just a little more, honey. Just to where the cars come in. See it's just ahead."

"Mommy, somebody's calling you, look they're running after us." I reposition Michaela in my arms, getting a firmer grip.

"Don't worry, Emma baby, it's just a game. Show them how fast you can run. Don't let them catch us." As we close in on the gate I spot the police car, then standing there in all her splendid glory is Quincy. *Quincy.* My hero from the first time we met. Always my hero. I fight back the sob rising in my throat and tighten my hold on my daughters. Our daughters. "Run, Emma, run."

We dash past the guards, around the wooden arms blocking the road, but I'm jerked to a stop as Emma is dragged away from me.

CHAPTER THIRTY

Quincy

The flight seemed like it would never end. She tried to doze, she tried to read, she tried a movie, but nothing distracted her. She walked up and down the aisle as often as she could without people thinking she was some crazy person. When they finally landed, she turned on her phone. Lindy had sent her a selfie, a picture of the three of them, and a text. *So you don't go into shock when you see us.* Well, she was shocked. And sick to her stomach. All three looked undernourished. Both Emma and Michaela had long, badly shaped hair. Michaela was a little girl, not the baby Quincy pictured. Emma was taller, but she looked miserable, sullen, and her spark was gone. Lindy's beautiful golden hair looked as if someone had chewed it off and half of it was almost orange; her eyes were sunken in black shadows and lifeless. Quincy felt her anger rise as she walked to pick up her rental car. She looked at the pictures frequently as she drove and each time she wept with rage. She fantasized about the damage she would do to those who caused this pain to her family, starting with the three fanatics in New Jersey. After about an hour she pulled off the road and texted Connie. *About a half hour out of Chino. Plse call police chief.*

She sat for a few minutes, breathed deeply and calmed herself enough to back off from her revenge fantasies. Her goal, her only goal, was to get her family out of that place and bring them home where she could care for them. Later she would see if there was something illegal about what these people were doing. Just before she turned off the highway, Connie texted to say she'd arranged an escort and she should head directly to the police station.

The call from Chief of Police Trubeck must have been the highlight of the guy's year because Chino Valley Chief of Police Norman Corbett greeted her like a long-lost friend.

"Detective Adams. Welcome. Chief Trubeck told me you've come to retrieve a woman and two children from the polygamist community just outside of my jurisdiction. She says you don't intend to enter their property. Is that right?"

Polygamist? "I didn't realize they were polygamists. Is that even legal?"

He leaned back in his chair. "No. But we have a live and let live philosophy out here. As long as they keep a low profile, let women leave if they want, don't force them to marry, and aren't dumping boys out on the streets to cause trouble for us, we don't bother them."

Quincy leaned forward. "I have no desire to go on their property. But I will if they try to detain the woman or the children. I hope you'll back me up."

He straightened the folders on his desk before answering. "They try to avoid drawing attention to themselves, so I don't think they'll give you any trouble, especially when they see a police car with you."

"Thank you, sir. I appreciate the escort. Lindy, the woman, asked to be picked up so I'm hoping there won't be a problem. Chief Trubeck thought you'd want to be involved in any case." Quincy stood. "What's the layout so I can tell her where to meet me?"

"There's a guardhouse with barriers blocking entry to, and exit from, the community. It would be best if she could meet us there so there's no question of trespassing."

"How long a drive is it?"

Chief Corbett thought for a second. "Twenty minutes should do it. I'll meet you out front in the patrol car."

She shook his hand. "Thank you, Chief."

Back in the car, she texted Lindy. *Be there in twenty minutes or less. A police car will be right behind me. Meet us at the guardhouse where cars enter. Text me if you don't know what I mean. I'll open the back door of the car. Come out and get in the car immediately. All of you. We'll talk later.*

She kept her eyes on the police car in front of her and took deep breaths trying to relieve the tension. She fluctuated between feeling happy that she would see them soon and anxious that they wouldn't be there. At last the police car stopped near the entrance of what appeared, as Lindy had indicated, to be a walled compound of some sort. This was it. Quincy took a deep breath. The chief of police and his deputy exited their car. They stood hands resting on holsters but didn't approach. She stepped out of her rental car, nodded at the chief, then walked around and opened the back door. Two men wearing guns came out of the guardhouse, heads swiveling between the police and her, trying to figure out what was happening.

Thirty seconds later she spotted her ragtag family running toward the guardhouse. Lindy was carrying Michaela and dragging Emma with her. Quincy's heart did a flip. It was happening. Lindy was coming. The shouting pulled her eyes from Lindy to two men and a woman chasing her and shouting something she couldn't make out. Instinctively, she moved up to the property line where Lindy would exit. She glanced at the police. They had moved closer as well. As Lindy dashed around the barrier arm blocking vehicle entry to the compound, one of the men following her grabbed Emma and pulled her away. Emma started screaming, "Mommy, Mommy."

Lindy turned to go after her but Quincy held her back. "Get in the car. I'll get Emma."

Gasping for breath and clearly exhausted, Lindy nodded, and limped toward the car, trying to soothe Michaela who was screaming for her sister.

Quincy faced the grinning goon holding Emma's shoulders. "Let her go." Her voice was low and threatening.

He glanced at the guards and straightened. "She's on our property so she's ours. And that woman is a fugitive."

Quincy stared and took a step closer. "Emma is my daughter and I've come to take her home. And, for your information, my wife Lindy isn't a fugitive. If you don't give me my daughter right now, not only will the FBI be crawling over this place in an hour, but I will slap you with a lawsuit so big you'll work the rest of your life to pay off the settlement." She turned toward the police chief who was now standing next to her. He nodded. "They're on standby, Joel. And you know there's nothing they'd like better than—"

"Take the little brat." He pushed Emma toward her so hard she stumbled.

Quincy caught the girl and lifted her into her arms before she fell. "Hi, Emma, I have you now, baby." She started toward the car, then turned. "Don't think this is over."

Quincy and the police chief walked toward her rental car. "Thanks, Chief. I appreciate the backup."

He grinned. "Nice bluff."

She grinned back. "Yeah, it was either bluff or get into a fight and a tug of war, so I decided to try peaceful first."

"I hope to get the FBI in there someday." He patted her shoulder. "We'll follow you to the town line. Good luck to you and your family, Quincy."

Lindy was waiting by the open car door. She took the sobbing Emma from Quincy. Their eyes held for a moment and Quincy touched Lindy's cheek. "Let's get out of here." Lindy ducked into the car. Quincy shut the door and Lindy and the girls were alone in the air-conditioned car, silent except for the sobs of the girls and the rasp of Lindy's breathing. Lindy hugged the girls, then dried their tears. "Yay, we won the race."

Quincy stood at the driver's door, removed her sunglasses and glared over the roof of the car, almost daring the group, the two men, a woman and the two guards, to try something but they didn't approach. She waved to the police, got behind the wheel and drove away. Her eyes kept darting to the rearview mirror but it didn't look as if anyone was following them except the police car, which escorted them all the way to the Chino Valley city line on the highway. The chief honked as the police car peeled away. Quincy honked back, lifted her hand to thank them again, and turned toward her future.

More relaxed now, she glanced at her family in the rearview mirror—all three pale and frightened, the two girls clinging to their mother. They'd been driving about a half hour before Quincy spoke. "We're okay now. Hi, Lindy, hi, Emma, hi, Michaela."

The girls buried their faces in Lindy's lap. Lindy seemed dazed but when she noticed Quincy watching her in the mirror she offered a shaky, lopsided smile. Quincy's heart somersaulted. She couldn't help herself. As awful as Lindy looked, even though she'd hurt her and the girls, Quincy still loved her dearly.

They drove in silence for another few minutes. "Thank you for coming for us, Quincy." Lindy's normally raspy voice cracked, as if she hadn't used it in a long time. She coughed, seemingly unable to stop or catch her breath. Quincy handed her a bottle of water.

Lindy drank, inhaled and her breathing calmed. She raised her eyes to meet Quincy's in the mirror. "Sorry, the desert dust has done wonders for my asthma." She ran her hands through Emma's hair. "Emma, do you remember Mama?"

Emma sat up. She didn't say anything, didn't meet Quincy's eyes in the mirror but she stared at the back of Quincy's head and her hand went to her throat. Quincy saw the gold chain and realized she was fingering the locket that contained the picture of them together. She smiled. Emma's features had changed and she looked even more like her than she had before they left. "Hey, Emma, you have our picture I see." Emma ducked her head again.

"You know, Lindy, I think the clothes I brought from home are way too big for you and way too small for Michaela and Emma. Are you okay with pulling into the first store we see along the highway so we can buy you guys a few things?"

"Do you think we'll be safe?"

"You don't have to worry, Lindy. I'll take care of you. If you let me."

Lindy wiped the tears that sprang into her eyes. "I know." A sob escaped.

Quincy pulled into the parking lot of Target and helped Lindy and the girls out of the car. She hesitated, not wanting to freak Lindy by touching her, and was thrilled when Lindy threw herself into Quincy's arms. "Thank you, Quincy. I knew you would come. I'm so sorry, so sorry." The girls clung to Lindy's legs.

Quincy held her close. "I've missed you so much. It's wonderful to have the three of you back." She looked down at her daughters; they'd grown so much in the year they'd been gone. Michaela was walking and talking and Emma had shot up and was on her way to being tall like Quincy. "Come on, let's get you guys some clothes that fit."

It turned out that Lindy had dropped two sizes since she left home and it took several trips to the dressing room to find clothing that fit. She bought jeans, several T-shirts, a couple of long-sleeve turtlenecks, a sweater, a package of panties, a bra, three pairs of socks, pajamas and leather ankle boots. Emma and Michaela had been brainwashed into believing it was a sin for girls to wear pants so they each got three dresses that fit, tights, sweaters, some underwear, pajamas, shoes and socks. Quincy threw a suitcase into the cart but she wasn't sure about finding coats out here in the desert. She asked and was directed to the ski shop. They selected down jackets for each of them, a pink one for Michaela, a purple one for Emma, and a fawn-colored one for Lindy. Quincy paid and then the four of them went to the ladies' room so they could change into their new clothes. Lindy packed their new clothing into the suitcase, added their sandals and tossed the dresses they were wearing into the garbage.

Lindy refused to leave Quincy's side so they all went to drop off the car before going to the hotel. In their room, Lindy marveled at the space. "Our room was less than a quarter of this one. I wanted to keep the girls close so the three of us slept in a single bed. And I have the black and blues to prove it."

Quincy relaxed. She'd anguished over the room when she made the reservation, but she was glad she'd reserved just one room with two king beds. Lindy liked the space but more important, it was clear she didn't want to be separated. Quincy would sleep on the floor if it made Lindy feel comfortable.

Emma sat on the edge of the bed. Michaela tried to sit next to her but she slid down to the floor. Emma giggled and patted her sister's head. Quincy and Lindy shared a smile but the silence that followed was awkward. Lindy prowled around the room, touching the tourist magazines on the desk, examining the TV remote, gazing out the window, running her hands over the pillows, staring into the bathroom. Quincy cleared her throat. "You all must be starving." She brought the room service menu to Lindy who was back at the window. "Let's figure out what everyone wants to eat, then we can relax." They stood close, fingers touching as they held the menu. Quincy experienced a pang of loss. She no longer knew what her daughters liked to eat. On the other hand, her fingers tingled and she felt a rush of love. She glanced at Lindy and hoped her pink cheeks meant she was feeling it too.

While on the phone giving room service their order, Quincy watched Lindy settle into the chair by the window. Even seated she seemed restless and anxious. Was she still afraid Quincy was the devil? Was she thinking she'd made a mistake? "You seem anxious, Lindy? Can I do anything for you? Do you need anything?"

Lindy shook her head. A tear trickled down her face. "I…I'm having a hard time believing I'm here with you and not in that place." She wiped her face with the back of her hand and offered a weak smile. "And I'm not sure how to be myself or how to be with you or what it all means."

"Oh, sweetheart, be kind to yourself. You don't have to do or decide anything right now. If you feel safe with me, try to relax. We'll work the rest out as we go along. Okay?"

Lindy nodded. "Thanks." She turned toward the window.

Quincy saw the tears flowing but decided to give Lindy space to feel what she was feeling instead of rushing in to comfort her. She unpacked the few toys she'd brought and got down on the floor with the girls. She gave them the stuffed animals they'd left behind. Was that a glimmer of recognition on Emma's face? She showed Emma her favorite fairy tale book. "Can I read you a story?"

Emma looked away, shaking her head.

Lindy sniffed and cleared her throat. "It's all right for Mama to read you a fairy tale. Nothing bad will happen, I promise."

Emma shook her head.

Lindy shrugged and mouthed, "I'm sorry."

"Maybe later," Quincy said. "Would you like to color? I brought you some coloring books and some construction paper so you could draw." She offered the crayons, colored pencils, paper and books.

Their faces brightened but they waited for Lindy's nod, before reaching for them. Quincy helped them choose a coloring book. "Can I draw while you color?"

Emma nodded but still wouldn't look at Quincy. Quincy selected a purple pencil, sketched a bicycle, then began to color it with a purple crayon. She didn't look directly at Emma, but with a quick sideways glance she could see Emma had stopped coloring and was staring intently as she filled in the sketch. When she'd finished, she held it up. "Do you know what this is?"

Emma's eyes flicked from the drawing to her coloring book to Lindy, then back to the paper in Quincy's hand. She stared at the drawing for what seemed like hours but was probably less than a minute, then with the beginnings of a smile tickling her mouth she raised her eyes and looked directly at Quincy for the first time. "A…my bicycle?" she whispered.

She remembered. Quincy felt a surge of happiness. "That's right. It's waiting for you at home. Would you like this picture?"

Emma had lowered her eyes to the coloring book but she nodded and reached for the drawing. Quincy shot a grin at Lindy who was watching them with the sweetest smile. Quincy's heart swelled. She was pleased that Emma clutched the drawing and from time to time looked at it with an almost smile on her face. She had no idea what the future held for the four of them but she knew for sure this was her family and she would never be separated from them again. She lay on the floor watching the girls color until room service arrived with dinner.

They sat at the table and when Quincy uncovered their spaghetti and meatballs, the girls' eyes got big but they made no move to eat. Quincy frowned, wondering whether she'd ordered the wrong thing.

Lindy took Quincy's hand. "We need to give thanks before we eat, Quincy." Emma reached for Quincy's other hand and for Michaela's. Lindy, Michaela, and Emma lowered their heads. "Dear Lord, we give thanks tonight to Mama Quincy for taking us back into her loving arms." Lindy looked up and met Quincy's eyes. "We pray she will forgive us our sins. Amen." They stayed connected for a few seconds, then Lindy turned to the girls. "You may eat."

"What is this, Mommy? Did we ever eat it before?" Emma almost looked afraid of the pasta.

Lindy put her hand on Emma's shoulder. "It's spaghetti and meatballs with tomato sauce, Em. You had it a long time ago and you used to love it. Taste it."

Emma warily brought a forkful to her mouth, chewed and swallowed. "Um, I like spaghetti." She tried the meatball. "I like meatballs, too."

Quincy poured apple juice for the girls, prepped her hamburger and fries, then poured her beer. Lindy stirred the vegetables into her pasta then poured her Dr. Pepper. "Mommy, please cut my paghetti." Lindy turned to help Michaela but Quincy put a hand on her arm. "Is it okay if I help you, Michaela, so Mommy can eat her pasta before it gets cold."

Michaela nodded. Quincy cut Michaela's food and turned to Lindy. "Can she feed herself?"

Lindy smiled. "She can but she's not the neatest eater. That's why I tied the towel around her neck."

"Do you need help, Emma?" She was doing a good job but Quincy asked anyway.

"No, thank you."

The girls ate like they were starving. Lindy groaned with pleasure as she sipped her Dr. Pepper, and then issued a low moan when she tasted her pasta. Quincy quirked an eyebrow.

"The food there was bland, actually mostly tasteless. Water, milk and watery iced tea were the only drinks allowed. I haven't had a Dr. Pepper in…" Her eyes filled. "Too long."

Quincy touched her hand. "Enjoy. We'll order more if you need to fill up."

Lindy blotted her eyes, then smiled. "Thanks."

Lindy was less tense after dinner and they bathed the girls together. The new Cinderella and Ninja pajamas were a huge hit.

Quincy turned on the TV and found *The Little Mermaid*. It was halfway over but Emma and Michaela stared open-mouthed at the riot of color, the characters and the music. While Lindy showered, Quincy invited the girls to sit with her on the bed and positioned herself between them. She watched them watch the movie.

Although they had occasionally allowed the girls to watch movies, Michaela was too young to remember and Emma seemed to have forgotten. Quincy's heart soared when Emma kept turning to her as if to confirm they were allowed this pleasure. When she lifted her arms, both girls crawled to her and she held them close. She sighed.

Lindy came out of the bathroom in her new pajamas, looking a lot more relaxed after the very long, very hot shower. She'd washed her hair, and though it was damp, cut badly, and multicolored, she looked beautiful.

Lindy smiled, seeing Quincy with her daughters in her arms. "Well done," she mouthed, then kissed her fingertips and threw Quincy a kiss. Quincy's heart lurched, but she reminded herself not to consider it sexual. Lindy picked her phone off the desk, took a picture of the three of them, then sat on the bed beside Emma.

The girls fell asleep watching the movie so they turned off the TV and moved to the sofa near the windows.

"We don't have to talk, Lindy. I'm just happy to have you all with me again."

"It looks like the girls are starting to reconnect with you. Love is always attractive."

Quincy thought for a minute and realized she meant that her love for the girls would bring them back to her. "I hope so. I notice they still have the lockets I gave them. I'd have thought jewelry—"

"I found them when I was rearranging things in my drawers. I was teetering on the edge of insanity when I left New Jersey and I fell over somewhere on the way to Arizona. I was stark raving mad by the time we arrived." Lindy checked Quincy's reaction to what she said, but she looked fine. "I remember saying goodbye to you in the park and shoving the lockets in my pocket but everything after that is a blur. I didn't even know I'd brought a suitcase with me until I spotted it under my bed the other night. If I'd known I had the phone, I would have called you much sooner." She yawned. "I'm exhausted. Is it all right if I go to bed?"

Quincy showered and when she came out, Lindy was asleep. In the bed with the girls. Disappointed that she'd chosen not to sleep with her, and feeling excluded from her family still, she contemplated getting into the same bed, keeping the girls between them so Lindy wouldn't freak out. But remembering her therapist's warning about letting Lindy lead, she watched her precious family sleep and allowed herself to feel the pain of the loss of a year and the happiness at having them back in her life. After a few minutes she turned out the light and got into the empty king bed, trying to hold on to the good feelings. It took her a long time to fall asleep.

"Quincy." Lindy's voice woke her. "Are you awake?"

She smiled. Lindy had always done this, woken her, then asked if she was awake. "I am now. Is something wrong?"

"No. I just… I don't have the right to ask any more of you than you've already done by saving me and I don't know what will happen with us because I'm far from feeling sexual, but I feel so alone and so scared. Would you consider letting me share your bed and holding me? Just holding me?"

She didn't answer. She couldn't. Lindy had done just that for her the first weekend they'd met when she was on the edge of slipping into the darkness. She moved over, shifted to her back and lifted the covers. She was so thin that Quincy barely felt the mattress move as Lindy slipped in and rolled over onto her. Lindy sighed and adjusted her position. Quincy wrapped her arms around the woman she stilled loved more than life.

Lindy's body felt so fragile, all bones. She was shaking. "I'm here, Lindy. I won't let anyone harm you." She gently stroked Lindy's hair, something she knew would comfort her.

Lindy fell asleep immediately and Quincy listened to her congested breathing, felt the warmth of her breath on her neck. She kissed the top of Lindy's head. She had so many questions, so much she wanted to know about why she left and why she came back and did she still love her? Would they have a life together again? But she thought again of the conversation with her therapist while she'd waited for her flight to board in Newark. Denise had advised her to avoid trying to rush Lindy to go back to where they had been before. Denise had reminded her that Lindy had serious problems she had to work out, problems that had caused her to leave. She'd encouraged Quincy to be patient and loving. She sighed. The loving would be easy. The patience not so much.

CHAPTER THIRTY-ONE

Quincy

She'd accumulated so many miles flying all over the country as well as Mexico and Canada following leads on Lindy and the girls, that she booked them first-class seats. It was tricky at first because both girls wanted to sit next to Lindy, and of course they couldn't, at least not on takeoff. And though Emma had finally agreed to sit in the aisle seat next to Quincy, she leaned toward Lindy on the other side of the aisle. Quincy spoke softly to Emma about the plane, explaining what would happen on takeoff and asking her to select the movie she'd like to watch. By the time they taxied on the runway, she was holding Quincy's hand, albeit with lots of glances at Lindy for confirmation that it was all right. After they were in the air, Emma was engrossed in the movie they'd selected and Michaela fell asleep. Lindy moved Michaela into Quincy's seat so they could sit together.

"Am I a fugitive, Quincy?"

Quincy squeezed her hand. "No. Judge Fleming didn't issue any kind of restraining order against your leaving and as the girls' parent, you have the right to take them out of state. But you did miss the psych eval and our court date. I'm sure Shayne Elliot can easily fix that."

Lindy leaned in and kissed Quincy's cheek. "I deserve to be punished for what I did to you, Quincy." She glanced at the girls, Michaela asleep and Emma engrossed in a movie. "And, especially for what I did to them."

"What's done is done, Lindy. Let's look forward not back. But I would like to know more about where you were and why you decided to leave." She waved the stewardess over. "Can we have a Dr. Pepper and a black coffee, please?"

Lindy recounted what she remembered about making the decision to leave, then being spirited away in the middle of the night. She had only flashes of what happened after that but she related what Dr. Baumann told her about the endless drive to Arizona, changing cars often, eating at fast-food restaurants or highway rest stops, sleeping in the car, and washing up in the restrooms of gas stations. She described the drab religious community with even drabber people, not violent people like her parents, but not kind or loving or welcoming either. "I was crazy, Quincy. I thought you were Satan, I heard voices and the TV talked to me. God talked to me and told me to leave you. When I arrived, I was totally out of control but I was lucky that the doctor who came to deal with me recognized my symptoms and knew how to treat me. It took a while, but I calmed down and began to enjoy the quiet and uneventful life they allowed me. When the medication kicked in and I started to feel better, I realized I'd made a mistake. You were always in my thoughts. I remembered how much I love you, how loving you are with me and the children and what a good person you are." She took a long drink of Dr. Pepper. "Besides, they didn't have Dr. Pepper there," she joked.

Quincy laughed, happy to see a spark of the old Lindy.

"I thought about just walking away but I noticed there was no traffic on the road and I thought it might be dangerous to take the girls into the desert not knowing where we were. So I was feeling trapped and then the head of, I don't know what to call it since nobody ever explained it, called me in to tell me I would have to marry one of three men and if my new husband didn't want the girls they would have to live in the community school. By then I knew it was a polygamist community, and of course, I wasn't interested in marrying a man. Or anyone other than you."

"And our marriage?"

"Didn't count for them. Anyway, I was desperate to get away but, as I told you last night, it wasn't until I started looking for money that I discovered the suitcase with the phone and the charger. Someone must have shoved the suitcase under the bed the day I arrived but I didn't know I had it." She smirked at Quincy. "I have a vague memory of Letitia insisting I throw the battery and the phone away but crazy or not, my stubborn streak must have kicked in and I did what I wanted." She looked down. "It took me a couple of days to get up the nerve to call you. But here we are, flying…home." She looked at Quincy and smiled shyly. "I am going home with you, aren't I?"

Quincy took her hand. "You are definitely coming home with me and if I have anything to say about it, you'll never leave again. But there are a few things you need to know about home before we get there."

Lindy's hand tensed.

"I have a woman and a child living with me." Lindy gasped and pulled her hand away. "Wait, not a lover." She took a deep breath. "Lindy, I love you. That hasn't changed for me. I know you're not sure of how you feel or what you want, but you are the love of my life and all the love in my heart is for you and our daughters. There is no one else for me. Okay?" Quincy reached over, took Lindy's hand again, then kissed her knuckles trying to reassure her. "It's my elderly neighbor and her six-year-old granddaughter. I've gotten very friendly with Dorothy, the woman, and Megan, her granddaughter, helped me deal with not having the girls. Dorothy had a massive stroke a month or so ago. She has no family around because her daughter is an officer fighting in Afghanistan so Megan has been living with me since the stroke and I brought Dorothy home with me when she came out of rehab."

Lindy looked at her. "Won't it be crowded with all of us in our…your apartment?"

She'd intended to surprise Lindy with the house when they got back to Hackensack but Denise had advised her to go slowly until she knew where Lindy stood. Was she still hallucinating? Was she still enthralled by religious fantasies? Don't overwhelm her, she'd advised. "Actually, I bought the house we wanted so there's plenty of room for all of us."

This time Lindy's gasp was a gasp of pleasure. "Really? And you're living there? Is that where we're going?"

"Yes, to all of the above. I hope you like it. I painted it the way we planned and moved our things in, so you'll get to decorate when you feel up to it."

Lindy stared straight ahead. Her shoulders shook. She had sounded happy to hear about the house, but something was wrong. "Did I upset you?"

Lindy lifted the arm between the seats, wrapped her arms around Quincy's waist, and put her head on Quincy's chest. Quincy held her as her fragile body vibrated with quiet sobs. Finally she stopped crying but she didn't move out of Quincy's arms until lunch was served. They helped the girls eat, ate their own lunches, then Lindy dozed, with her head on Quincy's shoulder. Quincy thought about how much this year had cost all of them. Especially Lindy. The captain's message announcing two more hours to Newark woke Lindy and the girls. After finding appropriate movies for Michaela and Emma, Lindy turned to Quincy. "Who will be at the house? How will I ever face everyone?"

"Our friends have been worried about you and they'll be overjoyed to see you again. Dorothy still can't be alone for long periods so Amelia and the kids are spending the day with her and Megan, but by the time we get home only Babs will be with them. Can you deal with seeing her?"

"Babs doesn't hate me?"

"Honey, nobody hates you. We all just want you to feel better." Quincy cleared her throat. "This year has been traumatic for you and the girls, and for me, and we have so much to process. Would you be willing to meet with me and my therapist?"

"When did you go into therapy?"

"A couple of months after you left. I was having trouble dealing with…everything."

"And you feel it helped?"

"Yes. Please say yes. We need someone to help us deal with everything that's happened."

Lindy flushed and looked down at her hands.

Quincy put a finger on Lindy's cheek and turned her so they were face-to-face. "That was not intended to make you feel guilty. It was a statement of fact. If we don't work through this together, we risk losing…each other. Do you still want to try to be with me?"

Lindy gazed into Quincy's eyes. "I do." She took a deep breath. "All right, I'll meet her. But the girls are so anxious. I probably shouldn't leave them alone."

"Denise has agreed to come to the house to meet with us tomorrow, if we want, and I think they can stay in the room if we give them something to do."

"With us? Together?" Lindy paled. "I'm not sure I can talk about this with you in the room."

Quincy sensed Lindy's anxiety rising. She started shaking. She covered Lindy's hand. "Would you prefer to see her alone at first?"

"Would you mind?"

Quincy smiled and rubbed Lindy's hand trying to reassure her. "Whatever you need, Lindy. I meant what I said. I love you and I'll wait until you figure out what you want." Quincy's voice shook. "I just need you and the girls to stay with me. I couldn't stand losing you again."

Tears filled Lindy's eyes. "I promise I won't run again but I'm afraid I might relapse and if I do, I don't know how good my word will be."

Quincy squeezed her shoulder. "We'll take it as it comes. As long as you commit to working with Denise, I'll be right there with you. And this time I'll be paying attention so whatever happens, you won't go through it alone."

Lindy brushed the tears away and laughed. "I cried so much in Arizona I was sure the desert would be fertile and I would never cry again. It looks like I was wrong. What did I do to deserve you?"

When they landed, Quincy texted Amelia to let her know what time to expect them so she could order pizza and ice cream. Then she texted Babs, so she could go to the house to meet them. She reminded Babs to let Lindy take the lead, let her come to her.

Luckily Quincy had carried on their one suitcase so when they deplaned, they were able to head right out to the car. Though they'd all napped on the plane, the girls were exhausted and once they were in their car seats and the car started moving, they drifted off to sleep again. Lindy was awake, staring out the window, with the occasional sniff and the twitching of her fingers.

Quincy sensed her anxiety escalating the closer they got to home. She was anxious herself. Almost of their own accord, her eyes flicked from the rearview mirror checking on the girls, to Lindy, to the road, then back, assuring herself her family was truly there with her. They were all stressed but hopefully they would relax once they were home. When they turned onto their street, Lindy leaned forward checking out the houses. She tensed as they turned into the driveway. Quincy touched her cheek. "Babs is your best friend and she loves you. It'll be okay. I promise."

Lindy nodded and got out of the car. They helped the girls out of their car seats and into the house. Other than the low monotone of the TV, it was quiet. Lindy stopped to admire the entry hall. "It's beautiful, Quincy. Are these the colors we picked?"

"Yes."

"How long have you had it?"

"Not that long. After you left I gave up the idea of buying it and it was sold. But about six months later the wife in the couple took a job in California and the house came back on the market. I bought it in hopes we would one day live here together. After the signing, I pulled out our dream house folder and it was a no-brainer to paint each room the color we'd chosen."

Lindy ran her hand over the wainscoting. "It's more beautiful than I imagined."

Quincy put her hand on Lindy's shoulder. "Ready?"

Lindy reached for her hand and Quincy led them into the living room. Babs wasn't there but Dorothy noticed them and used the remote to turn off the television. Just then Babs came in from the kitchen with a glass of water. She froze, smiled, and gave the glass to Dorothy before facing Lindy. They stared for a second. Lindy squeezed Quincy's hand. "Babs." She hesitated but went to Babs and took her hands. "I'm so sorry, Babs." Lindy burst into tears and fell into Babs' arms.

Quincy knelt and put her arms around the girls who were starting to get upset. "Mommy is crying because she's happy." Megan was so excited she was practically levitating in her seat but she stayed put. Quincy turned the girls toward Dorothy. "Dorothy this is Emma and Michaela. Girls, say hello to Miss Dorothy. She lives with us."

Dorothy didn't wait for them to speak. "I'm so happy to meet you Emma and Michaela. Welcome home."

Quincy smiled. "Megan, please come here. Michaela and Emma, this is my friend, Megan. She lives with us too and she's been waiting to play with you."

The girls eyed each other shyly. "Do you want to play with my dollhouse? It's over there." Megan pointed to the area behind the couch, near the bookcases, where Quincy had moved the play table for her. She extended her hands. Emma looked at Lindy. "Mommy?" But Lindy was still locked in Babs' arms. Emma fingered her locket, then turned to Quincy. She whispered something that might have been "Mama." "Go play. We'll be right here with you." Holding hands, the three girls went to the table where Megan began to talk about the dollhouse. Hands on hips, Quincy watched them.

Emma spoke softly to Megan. "Is she your mama?"

Quincy sucked in air.

Megan looked up. "No, she's *your* mama. My mama is in the army fighting bad men to keep us safe." She pulled the girls closer to the bookcase and pointed at a photo. "This is me with my mama." She pointed to another. "And this is you two with your mama before you went away." Emma's hand went to her locket again as she examined the photo, then she turned to look at Quincy.

Quincy smiled.

Megan pulled Emma to stand in front of other photos. "That's your bicycle." She handed Emma the picture of Quincy kneeling next to a grinning Emma in her new helmet, standing with her bicycle between her legs. "This is my bicycle. Your mama let me ride your bicycle when she moved to this house, but she was saving it for you so my mama bought me my own bicycle for my birthday."

"Where my 'cycle?" It was the first time Michaela had spoken.

"Look, that's you, Michaela." Megan pointed at a picture of the infant Michaela. "You were a little baby when you went away so you didn't have a bicycle." Megan turned to Quincy. "Will you buy Michaela a bicycle?"

Michaela ducked her head and moved closer to her sister but Quincy knew she was listening.

"Yes. She's a big girl now so we'll go shopping soon. Then I'll teach her to ride it like I taught Emma and you. What color would you like, Michaela?"

Michaela lifted her head and her eyes darted to Quincy. "Pink." She said it quickly, then buried her head in her sister's shoulder.

Emma studied the picture Amelia had taken of them at her birthday party, the last time they'd seen each other before yesterday. She was sure Emma was starting to remember. Quincy silently blessed Megan for moving her daughters closer to her.

"Let's play now." The girls followed Megan to the dollhouse but Emma held on to the photo and looked at it from time to time as they played.

Quincy met Dorothy's eyes and said, "And the child shall lead the children." She sat next to Dorothy.

"Ye reap what ye sow." Dorothy patted her hand. "You've given Megan so much and though I'm sure she has no idea she's doing it, she's paying you back a little."

Quincy looked at Lindy huddled on the loveseat with Babs, holding hands and talking softly. She sighed. It was going even better than she'd hoped.

After about forty-five minutes, Babs and Lindy stood. Hand in hand, they walked to Quincy. Babs leaned over to kiss Quincy's cheek. "I'm leaving but I'll be back tomorrow. If you're going to work, I can come early and spend the whole day. Otherwise, I'll come in the afternoon."

Quincy stood. "Thanks. I'm taking some time off so I'll be home." She looked at Lindy. "But if Lindy is up to seeing you in the afternoon, please come."

Lindy leaned into Quincy. "I'd like Babs to come for a while tomorrow but nobody else except, um, your therapist, Denise."

Right after Babs left, Lindy sat next to Dorothy. "I'm sorry I was rude, Dorothy, but—"

"No need to explain, Lindy. I could see it was important for you to reconnect with Babs. I'm assuming Quincy told you Megan and I are living here so we'll have plenty of time to talk." Dorothy stopped to catch her breath. "Sorry, it's still an effort to talk. Anyway, welcome home. I've heard so much about you."

Lindy flushed. "I'm sure you have." Her voice communicated unease.

"Don't be embarrassed." Dorothy placed a hand on Lindy's thigh. "Quincy never said a bad word about you. You must know how deeply she feels, how fiercely she loves you and the girls. She missed you something terrible."

"I hurt her and the girls."

"You did. But looking back won't help. You need to focus on the future."

"Uh, ladies, you do remember I'm here?" Everything Dorothy said was true but still she felt as if she was eavesdropping.

Saved by the doorbell, Quincy went to retrieve their food, then reappeared in the doorway. "Hey, anybody want pizza for dinner and ice cream for dessert?"

Megan jumped up and down. "Me, me." She looked at Michaela and Emma. "Don't you like pizza and ice cream?"

Emma looked puzzled. She shrugged.

Quincy positioned Dorothy's walker and helped her stand. She pulled Lindy up. "Come into the dining room everyone and let's find out who likes pizza and ice cream."

"I like pizza and ice cream," Michaela repeated periodically after eating. It turned out that everyone liked pizza and ice cream.

CHAPTER THIRTY-TWO

Quincy

Quincy put Megan to bed and settled Dorothy in for the night while Lindy got the girls to sleep. Though Emma and Michaela would each eventually have their own room, Lindy and Quincy decided it would be better if they stayed together until they adjusted to being home.

When Quincy left Megan's room Lindy was standing in the hallway holding the suitcase they'd bought in Arizona. Her face was flushed and she avoided looking at Quincy. "Um, what should I do with my things?"

"In here." She led her into her bedroom, the room she hoped they would share.

Lindy emptied the suitcase onto the bed, separating the clothing they'd bought for the girls from hers. Quincy went to store the suitcase in the basement and when she returned, Lindy was sitting on the bed holding her clothing, staring at the floor. "Need help?"

She didn't meet Quincy's eyes. "I'm not sure exactly what you meant."

Quincy knew Lindy was unsure of her position in her life, in this house. "Hang your jeans in the closet and put your T-shirts and underwear in your side of the dresser."

Lindy nodded. She opened the closet, then spun around to Quincy, her eyes wide. "You hung my clothes in your closet?" She burst into tears. "I thought you would throw them away or maybe store them in the basement."

Quincy moved closer. "Lindy, honey, I love you and your leaving didn't change that. I never lost hope that you'd come back to me."

Lindy stepped into Quincy's arms and sobbed.

Blinking back her own tears, Quincy held her and despite the angst-filled year of separation, her body responded to the feel of Lindy's slight body, to her pain and gentleness. Reminding herself this was the time for comforting and reconnecting, Quincy rubbed Lindy's back. "I understand you don't know what you want our relationship to be now. I love you and I'll live with whatever you decide as long as I can have you and the girls in my life." She kissed the top of Lindy's head. "There's a bedroom for you if you want to sleep separately but I would love for us to sleep together, no sex unless you decide that's what you want." She tilted Lindy's face up. "It's up to you. Okay?"

Lindy sniffed. "One of the most horrible things about that place was how cold it was. I don't mean temperature. There was no warmth, no caring, no kindness, and for the entire time I was there no one but the girls touched me. I've never felt so alone in my life." She tightened her arms around Quincy. "I need human contact. And not just any human. I know you care and you won't hurt me. I feel safe with you. If you really don't mind, I'd like to sleep with you."

"Come on, I'll help you hang the clothes and then we can get ready for bed." It didn't take long to hang Lindy's few new things and then they took turns in the bathroom. When Quincy came out, Lindy was brushing her hair. A simple thing but a reminder of their previous life together. She'd always enjoyed watching Lindy brush her hair at night.

Lindy smiled. "I didn't even know I missed this. I left in such a hurry I forgot my hairbrush. Is Cut and Set still in business? I'd love to go after we settle in. Maybe Sienna can shape my hair and do something with this horrible color." She put the brush down and got into bed. Quincy shut off the lights and slid in beside her. As she had the previous night, and all the nights they'd slept together except the first weekend when Quincy slept in her arms, Lindy rolled into Quincy's arms. And Quincy was happy to hold her. She thought of how safe and comforted Lindy had made her feel that first night, the first weekend they'd met when she slept with and held Quincy, a virtual stranger, in her time of need. Exhausted from the stress of the day, they both fell asleep immediately.

It was light outside when Quincy woke with Lindy still asleep in her arms, the cadence of her congested breathing as comforting as it had always been. She loved this woman with all her heart and would give her life to protect her from the pain and anxiety she was suffering. She hoped her love and that of their friends, combined with Denise's counseling and guidance, would bring Lindy back to her, back to their life together. She kissed Lindy's hair, breathed in the familiar smell of her shampoo, and floated in the warm cocoon of love until it was time to start her day. At her normal time, Quincy slipped out of bed, dressed, woke Megan and helped her select an outfit, then went downstairs to get Dorothy up and make breakfast. Dorothy's Medicare aide would come later to help her shower and dress, but she joined Quincy and Megan in the kitchen for breakfast.

Megan chatted happily about the girls as she ate. "Can I stay home from school and play with Emma and Michaela, Quincy?"

"They'll be here when you get home. Come on, kiddo, we'll be late for school if you don't get a move on."

* * *

I come to consciousness and lie with my eyes closed, enjoying the coolness of the room while snuggling under the comforter in the comfortable bed. Coolness? My eyes pop open. I jerk to a sitting position, then roll to my feet, wide-awake. Where am I? Where are the girls?

Then I remember. Quincy. October in New Jersey. And we always sleep with the window open a bit, even in winter. It isn't a dream. I'm really here in Quincy's house. But where is Quincy? I check the bathroom but she's not there. Nor is she in the hall. I peek into the girls' room and they are sleeping peacefully but Quincy isn't there. Megan's room is empty, her bed is neatly made. The next room is empty. I run down the steps calling for Quincy in a loud whisper so as not to wake the girls.

"In the kitchen, Lindy."

The voice is creaky and weak. Dorothy. I push through the swinging door and scan the kitchen. "Where is Quincy?" I hear the panic in my voice.

"Good morning." Dorothy smiles. "She walked Megan to school. She'll be back in a few minutes. She made coffee in case you woke up before she got back."

I start to panic. I have to find Quincy. But which way to go?

"Have a cup of coffee and sit with me." Dorothy extends her hand. "She'll be back soon, really."

Panting, I hesitate, then grab Dorothy's hand and sit next to her. I know I have a death grip but I'm petrified. Has Quincy left me?

Dorothy covers our hands with her free hand. "It's just a few blocks, she won't be long."

I hear the front door open. I bolt into the hall and throw myself into Quincy's arms. "I was afraid you'd left me." My voice and my body tremble.

"Hey, it's okay, sweetheart. I'm here now." Quincy holds me away from her so she can look into my eyes. "I'll never leave you, Lindy. I promise."

"Mommy, where are you?" Emma sounds panicky. She's awakened with me in the same room almost every day for a year. Finding herself alone with Michaela in a strange bed must be scary.

"I'm here, Emma. I'll be right there."

Quincy kisses my forehead. "Are you okay?"

I take a deep breath. "I just…yes, I'm fine now that you're here."

"Don't worry. I'm not going anywhere without you." Quincy hugs me and steps back. "Go get the girls and I'll get the pancakes going."

* * *

"Are you taking some time off?" Dorothy watched Quincy pull out the ingredients for the pancakes. "Lindy is really fragile and she needs you to be close."

"I've requested two weeks' vacation but I have a lot of accumulated compensatory time and unused vacation so I can extend it if she needs me. I'll do whatever is necessary to bring her back to herself. And hopefully, to me." She sliced a kiwi and started on the strawberries.

Dorothy popped a slice of strawberry into her mouth. "She's confused now, Quincy, but your love will restore her."

Quincy looked up. "I hope you're right." She mixed the batter and when the girls came down, she cooked the pancakes and decorated them with fruit so they looked like faces. The girls loved them. She made a few extra and put them aside for Megan in case she wanted a snack later. After they had all eaten, Lindy took Michaela and Emma upstairs to get dressed while Quincy cleaned the kitchen. Dorothy's aide arrived and she went to take a shower and dress for the day. Her physical therapist would arrive in a couple of hours.

Quincy whistled while she filled the dishwasher and washed the griddle. She felt the girls warming to her but she was worried about Lindy. She was so close to the edge. Patience, she cautioned herself. It hadn't even been a full day yet. And hopefully, with therapy and time, Lindy's confidence would return.

She heard the three of them on the stairs and when they didn't appear in the kitchen, she went to look for them. They were on the staircase looking at the pictures. Quincy and

Lindy locked eyes over Michaela's head and for a minute the old connection flared in Lindy's eyes, then she turned to the pictures. "Emma, do you remember I told you Mama is a police officer?"

Emma nodded but continued to clutch Lindy's leg and avoid eye contact with Quincy.

Lindy shifted Michaela to her hip. She pointed to the picture Patsy had taken that day in the hospital. "This is our first picture together. And here she is in her uniform getting a medal for saving twelve people from burning cars. She was very brave because she could have been hurt too." She glanced at Quincy as she carefully moved down a few steps. "All the people Mama saved in the accident wrote letters to this lady telling her how Mama saved their lives, and in this picture, the lady is giving Mama a prize because not many women are as brave as she is." Emma glanced at Quincy, then quickly looked away.

Quincy smiled. What Lindy wasn't saying was that the Silver Foundation gave women deemed exceptional in some way a lovely engraved glass award and fifty thousand dollars. And she and Lindy had used most of that money to pay for the two invitro fertilizations it took for one of Quincy's eggs, the one that was Emma, to adhere to Lindy's uterus and go to full term. With Michaela they'd just had to inject their donor's sperm into Lindy so it could link up with one of her eggs.

"This is Mommy and Mama on our wedding day." Lindy traced their faces, a gentle smile on her lips, then moved to the next. Skipping the picture where she was hugely pregnant with Emma, she went to Emma's first picture. "Here you are, Emma. Mama Quincy is holding you when you were just born. And here you are when you started to walk." She skipped a few more of Emma. "And look Michaela, here you are with Mama Quincy holding you in the hospital right after you were born."

Michaela reached out and touched Quincy's face. "Mama."

Lindy smiled. "Yes, sweetie, she's your mama." She shot a grin at Quincy before turning to the next few pictures taken at Emma's birthday party in the park right before she'd run to Arizona. Lindy paused in front of the one of her sitting on the bench with Babs, then moved on. "And here is Emma the day Mama taught her to ride her two-wheeler." She pointed to the picture of Emma on her new bicycle with Quincy steadying her as she learned to balance. Emma glanced from it to the one she held in her hand, the one she'd refused to give up last night.

Emma looked up at Quincy. "Is my bicycle here?"

The doorbell rang. Quincy knelt in front of the girls. "It is, Emma. But Mommy's friend is here. Let me talk to her a few minutes then we'll go to the basement to look at your bicycle and all the other toys. Maybe later we'll all go buy a bicycle for Michaela. Okay?" She stood. "Why don't you go into the living room with the girls, Lindy?"

CHAPTER THIRTY-THREE

Lindy

Quincy escorted Denise into the living room. "Denise, this is Lindy and Emma and Michaela."

Lindy was ready to vomit. Unfortunately, the girls seemed to sense her anxiety and were clutching her legs.

Denise took Lindy's hand and made eye contact. "Don't worry, I don't torture my clients until the second session."

Lindy almost smiled.

Denise rubbed Lindy's hand. "I'm so happy to meet you, Lindy." Denise knelt. "And you too, Michaela and Emma."

Quincy touched Lindy's cheek. "I'll take the girls to see their toys, if you're okay."

Lindy grabbed Quincy's hand. She swallowed then nodded and knelt in front of Michaela and Emma. "Go with Mama. I'll be right here in this room if you need me."

Quincy smiled at Lindy and left the room with the girls.

Denise closed the door. "Is someone with Dorothy?"

"Quincy arranged for her aide to stay until someone from her church arrives."

"Why don't we sit?"

Lindy sat on the sofa, gazing at her hands clasped tightly in her lap. Denise sat in the chair facing her. Neither spoke for a minute, then Denise broke the silence, her voice gentle. "It's been almost a year. How do you feel being home, Lindy?"

Lindy kept her eyes down and didn't respond.

"I'm on your side, Lindy. I want to help."

Lindy nodded.

"Can you tell me what you're feeling now?"

Her shoulders lifted.

"All right, I'll wait until you feel able to speak."

Lindy's mind raced. How could she talk to this total stranger? This was all too much. Had she made a mistake coming back into Quincy's life? Images of Hannah, Joel, Efraim, the women flashed through her mind and she remembered the uncaring coldness, her fear for her daughters, the panic, despair, and helplessness she'd felt. And then Quincy came for her, even though she done a horrible thing and took her daughters away from her for an entire year. She straightened. Coming home to Quincy was what she wanted, being with Quincy made her feel loved and safe. Happy. Yes, Quincy made her happy. If she wanted to be deserving of Quincy's love she needed to face her fears. "I…I'm scared." She spoke softly and Denise leaned forward to hear what she said.

"What are you afraid of?"

Should I tell her I'm afraid I'm crazy? Dr. Baumann knew I was crazy and she helped me. Quincy thinks Denise can help me. She took a deep breath. *I need to do this so I can get better for my daughters, and for Quincy.* "I'm afraid I'm not really well. I'm afraid God will start talking to me again now that I'm here. I'm afraid Quincy is the devil, like God told me. I'm afraid I'll hurt Quincy and the girls again." Lindy raised her tear-filled eyes. "I'm afraid I'm crazy."

Denise nodded. "Yet you left the safe place, the religious place, you were taken to."

Another long silence. "They talked about God but that place felt mean and hard and…loveless. And even though I'm married to Quincy, they were going to force me to marry a man and leave my daughters. I didn't feel safe there and I didn't want my daughters to grow up in that kind of environment."

"Why did you come back to Quincy?"

"When it came down to it, other than Sarah, Quincy was the only person I..." Lindy made a helpless gesture with her hands. "Because I trust her and feel safe with her. And I knew she would come for us, even though I hurt her, even if she hated me."

"And does she hate you?"

"No." Lindy broke down. "But what if she is the devil and she's tricking me into trusting her again." She wiped her eyes with the back of her hand. "Now do you think I'm crazy?"

"Is God still talking to you? Are you hearing any voices?"

She shook her head.

"Have you had any thoughts of hurting yourself or the girls or Quincy?"

"I thought about it briefly before I went away but I wanted to save Emma, Michaela, and myself from eternal damnation and suicide and murder wasn't the way to do it."

"What about Quincy?"

"Never. I thought she was going to leave me all alone because she was cheating on me with Babs and other women. I was sure she and our friends were plotting against me. Then I realized, um, then God told me she was the devil and I should get away from her."

Denise touched Lindy's arm. "None of this is your fault, Lindy. Be gentle with yourself."

A sob escaped Lindy and tears streamed down her face. Denise waited until she regained control. "Tell me about Arizona."

Lindy took a tissue from the box on a table next to her and blew her nose.

"I presume Quincy told you about the community I was involved with. The three women who helped me go there repeatedly told me Quincy was Satan and she was going to take the girls to hell with her. I'm not entirely sure but I think I was already hallucinating and hearing voices, but it was sometime after I met them that God started talking to me."

"Did you tell them?"

"No. At the same time I knew I was so special that God was talking to me, a part of me knew it was crazy and I shouldn't tell anyone. They convinced me I had to get the girls away from Quincy to save them from burning in hell. They kept pushing me to run away but I don't like to be bossed around so I ignored them until the day of Emma's birthday party in the park when I realized that Quincy would use the psychiatric evaluation to take the girls away from me. That afternoon I agreed to leave and late that night a car came for us. I had no idea where I was going, just that I and the girls, would be safe."

She opened one of the bottles of water Quincy had left for them, and drank. She took a deep breath and described how crazy she'd been when she arrived, how Dr. Baumann had given her a shot to make her sleep, how later Dr. Baumann had diagnosed her with postpartum psychosis, then convinced her to wean Michaela and take the medicine she recommended.

"And the medications helped?"

Lindy shrugged. "It took a while to get the right medication and the right dose. Maybe it was the drugs or the quiet or the lack of stress or not having to pretend I wasn't crazy. Or all of the above, but I started eating and sleeping. And though God still talked to me and I still had auditory hallucinations, I didn't have to hide them and I became less agitated."

Lindy took another swig of water. "Until the drugs started to kick in and I calmed down, women watched me twenty-four hours a day to ensure I didn't hurt myself or the girls. Once I was feeling better, we were pretty much left alone. I spent a lot of time praying in the chapel while the girls colored or napped with their sitter in a nearby pew. Eventually, the girls had to go to school and I had to work in the kitchen but I went to the chapel every night and some afternoons. And somewhere along the way, I stopped praying and instead, thought about my life and my friends but mostly about Quincy, about how we met, about the kind of person she is, and remembered our love."

Denise jotted a note on the pad at her side. "Is that when God stopped speaking to you?"

"No. He stopped talking about Quincy being Satan but he occasionally commented on what was going on around me. In fact, it was God who pointed out that I was living in a polygamist community. I was shocked. I'd been so involved with my internal struggle that I'd barely noticed the community."

"So God had become an inner voice describing what you saw rather than a threatening voice?"

"Yes, but I didn't get it until about two months ago, when I realized that God hadn't spoken to me since telling me I was in a polygamist community. At first I attributed it to my prayers but then I realized I'd stopped praying months ago. It was around that time that I started thinking about leaving.

"But now that I'm back here where it started with no warning, I'm worried that I'll hear voices and hallucinate again. And even though I know those were crazy thoughts, I've found myself wondering whether Quincy could be the devil. How can I know?"

"I hear that you feel crazy, Lindy, but you've been through a major psychological trauma and it's normal to fear you'll relapse. Based on what Quincy told me of your behavior and what I'm hearing from you, I'm tending toward Dr. Baumann's diagnosis of untreated postpartum psychosis. You're lucky that it was Dr. Baumann who treated you. Many doctors either don't recognize postpartum psychosis or have decided it doesn't exist."

Lindy frowned. "Like my gynecologist. Michaela was almost four months old when this started and my doctor said postpartum depression comes right after the baby is born, not months later."

"Your doctor was wrong and Dr. Baumann was right. You have some of the classic symptoms, like operating in two realities at the same time, floating back and forth between being completely rational one moment and in a psychotic state the next. You knew the hallucinations and voices and delusions weren't normal so you hid them.

"The good news is that while postpartum psychosis is much more serious than postpartum depression, it's considered an acute episode, not chronic, and it's treatable with therapy and medications, which it sounds like Dr. Baumann provided, and a good support system, which you have here."

"Will it happen again? I mean can I go crazy again?"

"If you haven't had a history of mental conditions, it's unlikely you'll ever have another episode unless you have another baby. If you take your medications, continue with therapy, make sure you get enough sleep and eat a balanced diet, and exercise, you should live a long and healthy life."

"We only wanted two children, so that's not an issue."

Denise nodded. "If you continue to see me, we'll address fixing what caused the PPP and then work through the effects it had on your confidence, relationships, and self-esteem."

Lindy was quiet, staring down at her hands. "I don't have any money."

"Do you love Quincy? I know you're frightened she might be the devil, but you said deep down you love her. Can you stay with that feeling?"

Lindy continued to stare at her hands. Finally, she nodded. "I do love her." She looked up and smiled.

"Well, Quincy loves you too and she wants to help you get better. Let her worry about the money. If you'd rather see someone else, I can make a recommendation."

"No. I'd like to see you. When?"

"Tomorrow and Friday at eleven. Then on Monday we'll shift to twice a week. I don't usually make home visits so if you feel up it, I'm sure Quincy will drive you to my office and wait for you. There are toys and books there for Emma and Michaela to play with while we talk. Are you okay with that?"

"Yes."

"I'd like to see the medications Dr. Baumann prescribed, if that's okay with you."

Lindy handed her the three bottles she'd placed in her pocket earlier.

Denise read the labels and looked at the pills in each bottle. "We'll stick with these until I get to know you better." She smiled. "Is Dr. Baumann a gynecologist?"

"Yes. She says she sees, um, PPP occasionally in her practice and more often in the women in...that place. They get shipped off to the state hospital then she treats them when they're released."

"Interesting. Did she say why she thinks there's a high incidence?"

"The lifestyle and a high occurrence of mental issues."

"Would you mind if I contact her?"

"Not at all. I'm sure you can get her number in Chino Valley. Please tell her I'm home safe and thank her for everything she did for me."

"How do you feel, Lindy?"

Lindy closed her eyes and gave it some thought. "Hopeful?"

"That's a good start but I want you to call me any time of the day or night if the voices come back or you feel frightened or out of control. Here's my card with my cell phone number. Also, I think you'll feel safer if you confide in Quincy when you're frightened or anxious. And I know it will be hard but start to see your friends. Let yourself feel how much you're loved." She stood and took Lindy's hand. "Welcome back."

After she walked Denise to the door, Lindy went up the stairs, touching the glowing wooden banister, admiring the color of the wall, remembering their excitement choosing the colors they would paint each room. Quincy made their dream come true. At the top, she turned and slowly walked down examining the pictures of their life together, letting the memories roll over her.

Just as Lindy reached the bottom, Quincy came up from the basement with Emma and Michaela. The girls ran to her. She knelt to embrace them as they both talked happily about the toys and the bicycles in the basement. Over their heads, she gazed at Quincy and basked in the love shining on her face. Lindy's heart flipped and her lips curled into a smile almost of their own accord. This is where she belonged. Her family was only complete with Quincy.

"Lindy, I'd like to show you something." Quincy led the three of them through the kitchen and along a hall. She opened a door and threw her arm out, signaling them to enter ahead of her.

Lindy gasped at the brightness. She twirled slowly, taking it in. A sunroom. A place to sit and feel as if you were outdoors. She leaned into Quincy. "I don't remember this being here."

Quincy put an arm over her shoulders. "It wasn't. Gina and I built it for you. It converts to a screened-in porch in the summer. I hope it's okay that I put your stereo and your records and CDs out here?"

Lindy turned into Quincy, tucking her face into her armpit, trying not to cry, but unable to keep some tears from sneaking out. "Thank you, thank you. I love it now and I'm sure I'll love it in the summer. Did you believe, or did you just hope I'd be back?"

"I guess it was mainly hope, but a part of me refused to accept that I'd lost you and the girls forever."

Michaela pulled on Quincy's pants. "I want my 'cycle, Mama."

Quincy laughed. "I promised I'd buy Michaela a pink bicycle today. There's a bicycle shop near here. And we should be able to get it done before I have to pick up Megan for lunch. Want to come, Lindy?"

CHAPTER THIRTY-FOUR

Lindy

Lindy sat in the easy chair Denise indicated, then took a deep breath, trying to ease her anxiety about being separated from Quincy and their daughters.

"Good morning."

Lindy peeled her eyes from the door to the waiting room where she'd left her family and looked at Denise sitting in a chair opposite her. Their eyes met and Lindy quickly turned her attention to the large sunny room that smelled vaguely of cinnamon and spices. The muted earth-colored walls and furnishings were restful and the watercolors on the walls, the large bowl filled with seashells and a small bouquet of white flowers on a low table added to the warmth. Lindy felt embraced by the serenity. She turned back to Denise and found her watching her. "I like your office."

Denise's smile was warm. "Well, that's a good start." She put her feet up on the hassock in front of her then sipped from a steaming cup, tea judging by the tag hanging out of the cup. "How did you feel after our session yesterday?"

Lindy looked toward the window and thought about how at first she'd been relaxed, then she'd reminded herself she needed to be careful. Could she trust Denise? She had to trust somebody or she'd...no, she didn't want to think about that. She'd chosen to come back to these people and she needed to trust her instincts. Dr. Baumann had helped her. And now Denise said she could help her. "At first I felt good, then wary, then I decided to trust my instincts that this is where I belong. I feel better. A little lighter." Her eyes went to her hands tightly clasped in her lap. "I decided to take a risk and tell Quincy a little about when I arrived in Arizona."

"How did she react?"

"She listened, then she squeezed my hand and said she was sorry I had to go through that alone. She confessed that she felt guilty for not noticing the pain I was feeling before I left because if she'd been more attentive maybe we could have avoided a painful year for all of us." Lindy looked up. "She was very loving and caring and I felt close to her. But then I wondered if she was Satan trying to seduce me. I know you said I should tell her when I feel these things but I was afraid to tell her about God and Satan."

"There are no shoulds, Lindy. Only do or say what feels authentic to you. Therapy takes time, so just go with what you feel, unless what you feel is that you want to hurt yourself or anyone else. Has God spoken to you again?"

Lindy shook her head.

"Was this the first time feeling close to Quincy made you think she was Satan seducing you?"

"Yes." Lindy chewed the cuticle on her thumb, thinking. She nodded slowly. "No, not the first time. I think it happens a lot." Tears streamed down her face. *How can I be sure you're not Satan trying to trick me?*

Denise's voice was gentle. "I know you're frightened, Lindy, but underneath the thoughts of Satan, I believe you know you're with people who love you and care about you. Remember yesterday you said part of you knew your thoughts were crazy and you shouldn't share them? Well the part of you that knows what's real hasn't gone away. You know what's real. You just have to trust yourself and those who love you."

She felt safe with Quincy even as she was afraid she was Satan. And she felt safe with Denise even as she feared *she* was Satan? Should she let Denise help her? "But can I trust you?" The question came out as a sob.

Denise waited until Lindy stopped crying, then leaned forward. "From what you've told me, even at your most paranoid, out-of-control moment you allowed yourself to trust Dr. Baumann, a stranger, in order to protect your daughters. And look how far you've come since then. Quincy loves you with all her heart and she trusted me enough to bring you to me. Only you can answer whether you can trust me, trust that I want to help you deal with your illness. But be sure you let the part of you that knows what's real make the decision."

Denise sat back, sipped her tea and waited.

Lindy took a tissue from the box on the table next to her, dried her tears, then stared out the window again. Denise's warmth, her compassion, and her openness reminded Lindy of Sarah and she'd felt an immediate connection with her yesterday. She hadn't thought about Sarah since her death because she couldn't bear to acknowledge she was gone. Maybe the part of her that knew what was real was letting her know she could trust Denise. She sat up straighter, then offered Denise a wobbly smile. "I'd like to continue."

Denise nodded as she put her cup down. "You said Michaela was about four months old when this started. Do you remember any events or situations around that time that might have set it off?"

Lindy shrugged. "I told you God started talking to me after I started hanging out with Joanna, Letitia, and Lauren but I…" Suddenly it hit her. "Sarah died."

"And who was Sarah?"

Lindy smiled, thinking about the woman who'd saved her the first time she was lost. "Sarah was the warm, kind, loving mother I didn't have growing up. Sarah was so much more my mother than the woman who gave birth to me, the woman I lived with for the first fourteen years of my life, the woman who was going to trade me for money and prestige." Lindy proceeded to tell Denise how Sarah had spotted her cowering at the bus depot the day she ran away from home and how, for all intents and purposes, she had adopted her. "She showed me what love and kindness and goodness are and encouraged me to open myself up to them. She taught me to trust, introduced me to books and music, showed me how to experience life, convinced me to let people and art touch me. She molded a person from a hardened lump of clay."

When Lindy didn't go on, Denise intervened. "How did Sarah die?"

Lost in memories, Lindy was confused for a second. "A drunken driver plowed into her car, killing her instantly. I never had a chance to say goodbye."

"What a tremendous loss. Was Quincy there for you?"

"Oh, yes. We left Emma with our friends Babs and Danni, and Quincy and I went to Florida with Michaela. Quincy was with me every minute, taking care of me, doing everything but breastfeeding Michaela. And then, two weeks after we got back from Florida, Quincy's partner, John, was killed on the job."

"That must have been a great shock for you both."

"Yes. Quincy and John stopped for lunch. It was his turn to go into the deli to order their sandwiches but his back was bothering him and she volunteered to go so he could rest in the car. While she was in the deli, a guy they'd arrested several times for ignoring his wife's restraining order knocked on the window of the car. John rolled the window down and the guy shot him in the head. Quincy went after him and killed him. As best they could determine, he happened to see John sitting in the car shortly after he'd killed his wife and two children. John's death devastated Quincy. All of us really. He was a good guy. It was a shock, yet the family and friends of police worry every day about this happening. I spent as much time as I could with John's wife. Quincy was a basket case. I did my best to console and support her but for the first time in our relationship, I felt the very real possibility that I could lose her in an instant like John. I was petrified."

"Did you talk to her about it?"

Lindy looked offended. "No, she was devastated. How could I burden her with my fears?"

Denise nodded. "So first you lost the parent you loved, then you feared you'd lose Quincy?"

"Yes." Lindy pulled on a lock of her hair. "It wasn't so clear then but that's what happened."

Denise sipped her tea. "Anything else unusual or stressful you can think of?"

Lindy sorted through things in her mind, trying to remember anything that had upset her. She nodded. "About a month before Sarah's death, we stopped in at an open house just to look around, and fell in love with a house. Actually, the house Quincy lives in now. We'd earmarked a $50,000 award Quincy had received for bravery as the down payment when we were ready to buy a house, but then we decided to have children. Quincy didn't have any desire to carry a child, so we spent most of the award on doctors and tests and whatever, to harvest Quincy's eggs, fertilize them and implant the fertilized egg that was Emma, in me." She took a second to breathe. "We didn't have enough for the down payment. I thought I should go back to work but we figured out childcare for two small children would eat up anything I could earn. Quincy had been offered work as the head of the security detail for stars performing at venues in the area. The money was good and the hours dovetailed with her regular job and we agreed she'd work the two jobs for a few months. She left the house at six thirty every morning and didn't come home again until twelve the next morning at the earliest."

"So basically, Quincy left you too."

Lindy hadn't thought of it that way, but that's the way it felt. "After John was murdered, I started to feel down in the dumps. I'd had postpartum depression for a few weeks after Emma was born, but this was worse. At first, I couldn't sleep, I'd cry off and on all day, and then I couldn't eat. I was afraid to drive with the girls in the car, afraid I'd fall asleep at the wheel. That made it hard to shop, hard to go anywhere. Between her two jobs I barely saw Quincy. I couldn't seem to pull out of it, so I went to see my doctor. And that's when he ridiculed my suggestion that I had postpartum depression. He said if I really thought I needed something, I'd have to stop nursing and he'd prescribe sleeping pills and Valium but he made it sound like I was a junkie looking for a fix. I left there feeling inadequate and guilty, ashamed that I was failing as a mother."

"Oh, Lindy, I'm so sorry you recognized the symptoms and reached out for help but were slapped down due to ignorance. Before you leave, I'd like his name so I can educate him." She studied Lindy for a minute. "Are you okay?"

Was she okay? Not yet. She wanted this to be over, to be herself again, not this frightened shell of herself. But she needed to get this out so she could move ahead. She shook her head. "Quincy was working such long hours that she basically came home to sleep a few hours then went back to one of her jobs. I hardly saw her. We barely talked. It was around then I became convinced Quincy and my best friend, Babs, were having an affair. I also thought she was having affairs with Connie, the chief of police, her friends Amelia and Gina, and an old woman who lived next door to us. I began to obsess about her leaving me for someone else. Eventually, I thought they were all plotting against me.

"And I couldn't read a book or a magazine. The words made no sense. TV shows seemed garbled and I couldn't follow them. Even the girls' books were unintelligible so I couldn't read to them at night. Except some nights I could.

"One night I was nursing Michaela when a voice in the upstairs bedroom said, 'What do you think you're doing, sinner?' I jumped. Our apartment was all on one floor, so we didn't have an upstairs bedroom. I knew it but I didn't; it's hard to explain. After that I started having other auditory hallucinations, people talking and plotting against me and commenting on my inadequacies from the refrigerator, the TV, the toaster, the showerhead. Sarah spoke to me from the newspaper once or twice telling me to relax. It was around then I met the three religious women and they started on me. Soon after, God started talking to me."

"Did you recognize his voice? Did he remind you of anyone?"

"No it was just loud and scary and commanding." Lindy thought about it. "Well, maybe a little like my minister growing up."

"That's an important association, Lindy. We'll talk more about it tomorrow, but we do have to wind down now." Denise wrote something on the pad on the table next to her chair and tore it off. "I'd like you to see Dr. Mary Miller, an internist and a friend of mine who I really trust. She's had lots of experience dealing with postpartum psychosis and depression. She'll do a physical and take some blood tests to rule out any physical problems that might have caused the psychosis." Denise stood. "I know you're still anxious and it's your decision, but if you can see her, it will help us move ahead." She handed the paper to Lindy. "See you Friday at eleven."

CHAPTER THIRTY-FIVE

Lindy

Relishing her quiet time in the sunroom while Dorothy enjoyed her daily tea and newspaper ritual and Quincy watched the three girls playing in the basement, Lindy relaxed and let her mind wander over bits and pieces of her discussion with Denise earlier today. She didn't understand why talking to Denise made her feel better, but it did. Just two sessions and already she felt easier than she'd felt in a while. Could all of her…craziness—that was the only word for it—could it all have been just a biochemical imbalance? She closed her eyes.

Something woke her. Dorothy's bell signaling she needed help? She glanced at her phone. Probably not at this hour. Besides Quincy was home. Must be the front door. She slowly opened the sunroom door and crept down the hall. She wasn't ready to see any of their friends, but she was curious. When she reached the intersection of the hallway and the foyer, she peeked around the bend, then staggered back against the wall. Oh, no, Quincy was hugging a soldier. A female soldier. Lindy was stunned. Her heart racing, she stumbled to the sunroom, closed the door, and leaned against it. Hadn't Quincy said Lindy was the only one for her? Had she lied? Her legs felt rubbery, her body icy. Had she lost Quincy?

No. She breathed deeply a few times to calm herself and straightened. Quincy would never lie to her. Never. There had to be another explanation.

She opened the door just as Quincy raised her hand to knock. "I almost knocked on your nose, Lindy." They laughed. Lindy stepped back. "Come in."

Quincy entered with Michaela and Emma, followed by the soldier, who had Megan in her arms. Right. Megan's mom, the soldier, what was her name?

"Lindy, this is Kate, Megan's mom and Dorothy's daughter. Kate, my wife, Lindy."

Lindy moved close to Quincy then extended her hand to Kate. "Nice to meet you. How long are you home for?"

Kate put Megan down then shook hands with Lindy. "Just three days. I had to come in for some business at the Pentagon yesterday and I was able to wrangle a couple of days to see mom and Megan." She pulled Megan against her. "I'm happy to meet you, Lindy. I've heard so much about you from Quincy."

"Really?" Lindy looked up at Quincy. Not being sure what information Quincy had shared about her always made her feel exposed when someone said that.

Kate didn't seem to notice Lindy's surprise. "You're a lucky woman, Lindy. Quincy has done so much for Megan and Mom and me. I hope we aren't imposing too much now that you're back."

Lindy tensed. She was out of practice with this social stuff. She didn't know if Kate was zinging her for abandoning Quincy, signaling that she was interested in Quincy, or just being nice? She leaned into Quincy, and some of the tension eased when Quincy tucked her under her arm like she used to and pulled her close. Was she being territorial? Maybe. But she didn't want Quincy to want someone else. Oops, they were waiting for her answer to…what question? Oh, imposing. "Actually, having Dorothy and Megan here has made things easier for the girls. And for me."

They were silent for a few seconds, then Quincy pointed to the gold leaf insignia on Kate's shoulder. "When did you make major?"

Kate's hand went to her shoulder. She grinned. "They promoted me while they had me in Washington." She straightened her already-straight posture. "And I can't tell you why, so please don't ask."

"Congratulations. I'm sure you earned it." Quincy turned to Lindy. "Kate does top secret work in Afghanistan."

"Congratulations on the promotion."

Kate flushed. "Thanks. I'll go sit with Mom, if that's okay, and let Megan get back to playing."

Megan struggled out of her mom's arms. "Quincy, can Emma and Michaela play with me in the living room?"

Quincy knelt to the girls' level. "Do you want to? I'll be right there."

Emma nodded. Megan took their hands. "Let's go." Kate followed.

When the door closed behind them, Quincy looked down at Lindy. "I hope you don't mind, but I invited Kate to stay in the guest room. She'll be spending most of her time here anyway and it hardly pays to open Dorothy's house for just three days."

Lindy was quiet. "Kate's impressive and sexy in her uniform. Are you involved with her?"

"What? No, of course not." She took Lindy's hands in hers and looked into her eyes. "Believe me, Lindy, you're the only one for me." She smiled. "Besides, I think there's something happening between Kate and Gina. How would you feel about Gina coming for dinner tomorrow?"

"I'm not sure I'm ready to see Gina yet. Can I think about it?"

"Of course. Kate will understand."

"She knows about me? About the crazy things I—"

"Yes. No. I mean she knows about you, that you took the girls and left, but she doesn't know anything more than that, though she did hear a lot about how much I love you and how much I missed you."

"Do you write letters or talk on the phone?"

"As I said, Kate does some kind of secret work in Afghanistan and she's often off-base for weeks at a time. I bought Megan an iPad for her birthday and they FaceTime when Kate is available. She worries a lot about Megan and Dorothy so often after everyone is in bed, we'll FaceTime so I can bring her up to date on things and sometimes we talk about me. She knows how devastated I was when you were gone and how much I missed you and the girls. In the beginning she thought I was trying to take her place with Megan."

"You would never."

Quincy smiled. "No, I wouldn't. And neither would I expose you by discussing anything so personal with someone you wouldn't choose to share your feelings with. I did my best to protect your privacy while discussing my feelings with friends. In fact, only Gina, Amelia, and Babs know the whole story. After they saw you in court, most of our friends surmised you had a breakdown but they don't know much more than that."

Snug in the protection of Quincy's arm, Lindy processed what Quincy had told her, then kissed Quincy's cheek. "Thank you." The surge of love she felt for Quincy surprised and frightened her. She ducked out of Quincy's arm. "We should start dinner."

"Are you…?"

Lindy didn't stop to hear Quincy's question. She walked quickly down the hall to the kitchen, listening intently. Had Quincy tricked her into loving her and now would she hear the voices again?

All was quiet in the kitchen. Quincy hadn't followed her so she relaxed into washing and chopping vegetables, putting up the quinoa, toasting nuts, prepping the acorn squash and baking it so she could stuff it later. She washed and cut up the cauliflower, chopped some garlic and grated the parmesan cheese that would be added after roasting. As she started on the salad, Quincy poked her head in the door. "Is it all right if I come in and help?"

Lindy felt bad. She had Quincy walking on eggshells for no reason. Contrary to her expectations, she'd not heard voices and the clutch of fear she'd felt about loving Quincy had not turned into anxiety about her being the devil. She smiled. They'd always been good together in the kitchen. Actually, they'd always been good together period. "Sure, would you make the salad while I stuff the squash?"

She watched Quincy pull the ingredients from the refrigerator and reach for the salad bowl. If Gina came for dinner, Kate, not she, would be the focus and that would make it easier because she wouldn't have to relate so much. Quincy said her friends weren't angry so this would be a good test. While Quincy was drying the lettuce in the salad spinner, she decided to risk it. "Uh, it would be fine with me if Gina joins us for dinner tomorrow."

Quincy turned to her. "Are you sure? They can get together on their own."

"I'm sure, sugah." Where did that come from? *Come on, admit you're feeling close to her.* She blushed, seeing Quincy's smile, the same twitch of the lips as Emma when she was pleased with something but not sure it was all right to show it.

CHAPTER THIRTY-SIX

Lindy

Lindy followed Denise into the office and settled into what she now considered her chair. Though they'd covered a lot of ground in the previous month and she felt comfortable with Denise, she wasn't sure where to start this morning. They sat in silence for a few moments.

"Tell me about your childhood." Denise listened intently and made an occasional note as Lindy spoke, but she let Lindy tell her story without interruption. There was a brief silence when Lindy finished. "Did your mother ever show affection?"

Lindy thought about her mother. She was worn out, resigned, and mostly silent at… Wow, she couldn't have been more than thirty-four or -five when Lindy ran away. Had she shown any affection? Lindy chewed her cuticle as she searched her memory. "Mostly I remember resentment and anger, not warmth or affection."

"Did she use the strap on you?"

"The strap but not the buckle. My father and my brother used the strap and the buckle as I got older."

"You felt your father and brother had sexual feelings for you. Did she try to protect you from them?"

"No." She rubbed her temples, then sat up straight. "Um, maybe. Now that I think of it, I don't think she ever willingly left me alone with them. And, oh, I'd forgotten. She put a lock on my bedroom door when I was twelve or thirteen. On the inside and insisted I lock myself in at night. I thought I was being punished. What do you think?"

"It's what you think that matters, Lindy."

"Probably she was protecting her investment. Making sure no one deflowered me before she could trade me to the highest bidder."

Denise raised her eyebrows. "You're still really angry."

"Darn tootin' I'm still angry. She was hard and bitter, and I often caught her looking at me with hatred. I don't understand it. I never did anything to deserve that treatment. What kind of mother hates her child?" She reached for a tissue and dabbed her eyes. "Yeah, it still hurts."

"Did you have any contact with them after you left?"

"Absolutely none. I never even considered it. Sarah taught me to look to the future and not dwell on the past and it worked just fine for me until...until I went crazy."

"Go easy on yourself, Lindy. You know your so-called craziness was the result of an illness, biochemical changes in the brain, not a personal failing. Even though your terrible childhood might have left you fractured, hard and bitter like your mother, you are whole, a warm, loving, strong woman."

"I didn't feel whole, or anything, until Sarah. It was almost as if she sat on me, broke through my shell, and brought me into the world. She taught me to dance and sing and laugh. We talked about everything. She gave me books, she took me to the theater and to movies and concerts. She showed me around Atlanta and helped me make friends. She taught me about love and goodness and kindness. At first I was confused and pained and saddened by the flood of feelings I'd never experienced, and I cried a lot. But eventually I found my footing and began to understand where I'd come from and how wounded I was.

Sarah helped me heal and showed me that I had value. She told me I could let my parents define me or I could be the person she saw and loved—a generous, giving, loving and happy person. I miss her so much." Lindy doubled over with pain as the tears flowed.

"She sounds like the mother we all dream about." Denise waited until Lindy lifted her eyes and looked at her. "I think her death got all mixed up in your psychosis. I'll bet you've never mourned her."

Lindy sniffled and dried her eyes with the sleeve of her shirt. "If I did, I don't remember."

"I'd like you to think about Sarah over the weekend, maybe share your thoughts with Quincy and Babs or even Dorothy but let yourself remember her and mourn. It's okay to cry." Denise stood. "I'll see you Monday."

CHAPTER THIRTY-SEVEN

Lindy

Letting herself experience the sadness of losing Sarah, Lindy was even more quiet and withdrawn than usual after her therapy session. Quincy gave her space and kept the girls busy. Dorothy seemed to sense her sadness but refrained from commenting. *Poor thing probably thinks I'm going to start talking to the toaster again.* Lindy smiled, then realized it was the first time she'd joked about her psychosis. Surely that was good. She'd have to tell Denise.

Once the three girls were asleep and the three adults were having tea in the kitchen, Lindy decided to do what Denise had suggested. "Quincy, I've been thinking about Sarah today and missing her. Did I mourn her death?" She turned to Dorothy. "Sarah was my adoptive mother, sort of, not legally, but she found me at fourteen and raised me. I'm not exactly sure when, but she was killed by a drunken driver around the time I started to lose it. Denise asked me think about her death today and I don't really remember much." She looked at Quincy.

Quincy sipped her tea and took a minute to remember. "I think you were in shock. It was so unexpected that I don't think you accepted it until we flew to Florida and you saw her in her coffin. Do you remember you passed out?"

"Uh-uh. I remember you doing everything for me except nursing Michaela, but I don't remember passing out."

"Each time we walked into the room during the two-day wake, you fainted when you saw her. It was like your body refused to acknowledge she was dead. I tried to keep you in the lounge area but you insisted on going into the room and boom you would be out. Her other daughters were also devastated, of course, but you were the only one who reacted physically by fainting and crying nonstop. Do you remember giving a eulogy?"

"What?" Her voice rose. "Me?"

Quincy patted her hand. "Yes, you, at the church and since the coffin was closed by then, you were able to stay on your feet and deliver it. You spoke from the heart about how much Sarah meant to you. You were…it was beautiful. You had everyone in tears. I recorded it, so whenever you're ready, you can listen to it. I expected that the burial would be particularly difficult but giving the eulogy seemed to calm you, and you got through the burial and the repast after it, with dignity. Do you remember Angela asked you to stay a couple of extra days to help her go through Sarah's things?"

"No. Was I…okay?"

"Yes. The two of you, not quite sisters, but closer than friends, cried together a lot while you sorted her clothing and other belongings. The jewelry of hers you took—your favorite bracelet and pin and necklace—are in your jewelry box. And the photo album that she kept for you is in the study. Should I get it?"

"Yes."

Quincy left the room.

"I can do this another time if it's boring, Dorothy."

Dorothy smiled and reached out to touch her. "It's not boring at all. I just worry that I'm intruding now…and in general."

Lindy got up and hugged Dorothy from behind. "I'm so grateful you and Megan are here. She's been wonderful helping the girls adjust." She glanced in the direction Quincy had gone. "And I still have a way to go before I feel totally at ease with Quincy so I'm comforted by having you as a sort of buffer. Please don't worry about intruding."

As Quincy walked in with the album, Lindy returned to her chair and scooted close to Dorothy. "Pull your chair over, Quincy, so we can all look at the photographs."

Quincy arranged her chair on the other side of Lindy and before she sat, moved the box of tissues from the sideboard to the table.

Lindy stared at Quincy for a few seconds, pulled a tissue from the box, then opened the album.

Once Sarah had realized Lindy had never seen a picture of herself, she'd started photographing her constantly to give Lindy a sense of who she was, physically at least, and to start to build a history for her. In the very first picture Lindy, a gangly fourteen-year-old, with blond hair down below her rear, self-consciously avoided looking at the camera, but as they progressed through the album, she flowered into the confident, mature, younger version of the woman Quincy had met that snowy night years ago.

Lindy had memories attached to many of the pictures and she laughed and cried as she explained them and talked about Sarah—her warmth, her love, her generosity, and how much she missed her. By the time they were through the album, Lindy was exhausted, but she felt less sad, more centered. While Quincy helped Dorothy get ready for bed, Lindy straightened the kitchen, then clutching the album, went up to their bedroom.

By the time Quincy came into the room, Lindy was sitting in bed thumbing through the album again, stopping every now and then to smile at a memory prompted by a picture. She waved Quincy over to her. "Thank you, Quincy, I think this was exactly what Denise was hoping would happen tonight, that you would help me mourn and remember." She kissed Quincy's cheek. "Thank you for everything." She put the album on her night table and got under the covers, remembering Sarah, thinking about Quincy.

She nestled into Quincy's side as soon as she turned off the light. She could see Quincy's smile in the dim light filtering in through the blinds. Lindy felt it too. Tonight they'd made the first connection since Quincy rescued her from the religious compound, that wasn't based on her fear. She felt good. And hopeful.

"Quincy?"

"I'm here."

"I never noticed before how like Sarah you are."

"Really?" She could hear the smile in Quincy's voice and felt pleased that she'd put it there.

"Really." Lindy yawned. "Good night."

Quincy shifted and Lindy smiled at the sound of her sniffing her hair. Maybe they'd be all right.

CHAPTER THIRTY-EIGHT

Lindy

Quincy was in the basement playing with the girls.

Lindy and Babs were sitting in the sunroom. Lindy loved the airiness and brightness of this room and spent most of her time here. Sarah would have loved it too. Sarah had seen something in Quincy the first time they'd met and had quickly come to love her. Maybe Sarah had seen what Lindy had realized the other night, that Quincy with her quiet consideration, her thoughtfulness, her consistent love and her inner strength was very much like Sarah and would take good care of Lindy. Recognizing the similarity between the two most important women in her life made her love Quincy even more.

Lindy sighed, contented. Babs took her hand. "I'm so happy to have you back. How are you doing?"

"I'm still a little shaky but I feel like I've come home." She smiled. "Leave it to me to utter the obvious." She shifted to face Babs. "Denise is helping me understand what happened to me. I still have work to do, fences to mend, and I feel hopeful that one day I'll be able to explain it to you, to everyone."

"Ah, honey, the important thing is you're back and feeling better." Babs chewed her thumb. Lindy remembered she did that when she was nervous. "Have you and Quincy discussed Thanksgiving?"

"Thanksgiving?" Lindy looked puzzled. "What about it?"

"It's next week and I was hoping you'd come to Grace and Mike's. We missed you last year."

"Oh." Lindy stared out the window for a few minutes before she spoke. "I didn't realize. I lost touch with the calendar in that…in Arizona. All of our friends will be there?"

Babs squeezed her hand. "Sorry, I don't mean to pressure you. But yes, everyone will be there as usual."

"Are they angry at me for what I did to Quincy? To all of you? Especially, saying lesbians are sinners doomed to suffer in hell for eternity."

"Some of our friends were angry at first, but once they understood, I mean we knew before you left that you weren't yourself. Mostly we were worried sick, not angry. Think about Thanksgiving, talk to Quincy." Babs lightly punched Lindy's shoulder. "Hey, didn't you want to show me the album Sarah made for you?"

Lindy smiled and pulled the album off the table beside her. "Quincy said we brought it back after her funeral but I didn't remember much about Sarah's death or the time between then and when I left, so I was surprised when Quincy mentioned it Friday night. You knew Sarah and you're in some of the pictures, so I thought you might enjoy looking at it with me." She opened the book and went through the photographs with Babs, telling her the story behind each.

Later that night, lying in bed waiting for Quincy to come in, she realized that Denise had been right. The more she talked about Sarah, remembering, laughing over memories, the less she felt the sadness and sense of loss. Though Sarah was gone, she would always be in her heart, in her memories. And she had the pictures to prove it.

She sat up when Quincy came out of the bathroom drying her hair with a towel. She hesitated, then smiled, and noticed

Quincy's body relax. Poor Quincy, always sensitive to her moods, and other than Dorothy and Babs, dealing with her totally on her own. "Quincy?"

"Yes?"

"Um, Babs reminded me this afternoon that Thanksgiving is next week. Are you?" She cleared her throat. "Are we invited? Do you want to go? I mean all of us?"

"Yes, we're all invited." Quincy sat on the bed and took her hand. "I didn't know if you'd be up to seeing everyone so I was thinking we could do our own dinner here. But I would love for all of us to go and I know Grace and Mike would be thrilled to have us there again." She hesitated. "But it's totally up to you and whether you think you can handle seeing all our friends at once."

Lindy played with Quincy's fingers as she thought through what she wanted. Yes she was afraid, but Babs had reassured her that no one was angry with her. And after she and Gina had cried and reconnected, it had been wonderful spending time with her and Kate. Denise had encouraged her to branch out, see more friends. Was she strong enough? Was she ready to deal with the emotions she would be sure to feel? Denise seemed to think she was, that she was stable, that she didn't have to worry about…going crazy again. Over this weekend she'd confronted Sarah's death head-on and now she was feeling good. She would do this, for her and for Quincy. She looked Quincy in the eye. "Okay, let's do it." She kissed Quincy's cheek. "I appreciate how considerate you are. Reminds me of why I let you seduce me."

Quincy's shocked expression at her teasing made Lindy laugh.

Quincy stood and flicked her with the wet towel. "I seem to remember you seducing me, Ms. James." Quincy reached over and tickled her. "Behave yourself or I'll…" They stared at each other.

Surprised by the surge of desire she felt, Lindy took a deep breath, then looked away. "We should go to sleep." She turned off the lamp on her side of the bed and slid under the covers, struggling to get control of her feelings.

As Quincy walked into the bathroom to hang up her towel, Lindy noted the joyful look on her face. Lindy smiled. No denying the sexual connection was still there.

CHAPTER THIRTY-NINE

Lindy

Though Lindy was now driving herself to therapy, one of them needed to be at home with Michaela and Emma and sometimes Dorothy, so Quincy was working a few hours a day as a way of easing them back to a regular schedule. And, she guessed, Quincy was also easing her back into taking responsibility in the house but she didn't mind. While the girls and Dorothy were napping, Lindy would prep dinner, chopping, mixing, seasoning, doing everything except the things that had to be done at the last minute and the actual cooking. In reality, Lindy was still nervous without Quincy nearby, so cooking kept her mind and hands occupied and she didn't feel Quincy's absence so acutely.

She spent most of her quiet time in the sunroom indulging in her secret pleasure, listening to music. She thought Dorothy knew but she hadn't said anything about it. She wasn't quite sure why she was reluctant to let Quincy or Babs know she'd begun to play her records and CDs, but Denise assured her the need for privacy was part of the process of reclaiming her life, reclaiming her independence, reclaiming the Lindy she had been.

It was almost time for Quincy to come home with Megan, and Dorothy and the girls would be awake soon, so Lindy turned off the CD player and replaced the disc in the rack. She cocked an ear and listened. It was Dorothy's bell indicating she was awake and needed help getting out of bed. Lindy hurried down the hall. She knocked then entered Dorothy's room. "Hi, ready to get up?"

"Yes. I'm in dire need of the facilities." She nodded toward the bathroom.

Lindy threw back the covers, then opened Dorothy's walker and placed it in front of her. She watched Dorothy swing her legs over the side of the bed, lean forward and pull herself up. Dorothy was getting stronger every day but she was shakiest when she woke up and starting to move so they were being careful to avoid a fall. Lindy followed her into the bathroom. Dorothy turned her walker in front of the toilet to face Lindy, took hold of the grab bar Quincy had installed, and nodded. "I'll be okay now."

"Call if you need me." Lindy left to give her some privacy. She stopped when the front doorbell rang. She tensed. This was unusual. "Dorothy, are you expecting any of your therapists or church helpers?"

"Not today."

"Hmm, Babs and Amelia always call before they come. Do you think I should answer?"

"Not if it makes you anxious, Lindy. If it's important they'll come back when Quincy's home." The toilet flushed. "You could peek out the side window and only open the door if it's someone you know."

Good idea. Lindy went to the foyer and moved the curtain to get a look at who was ringing the bell so insistently. She gasped and stepped back, shaking. It was them. Then she heard Denise's voice in her head. "You're not the person you were when you were in the middle of your psychosis. You're strong and centered and very much in touch with reality. Those people can't hurt you now." She realized she wasn't afraid; she was angry, very angry at what these three had done to her, at how they'd manipulated her.

She threw the front door open, stepped out onto the porch, and stood face-to-face with Letitia, Lauren, and Joanna. It was obvious they didn't recognize her. Well, of course, she was intact now, not fragile and crazy. She'd gained some of the weight she'd lost and had her hair dyed and styled to repair the damage they'd done with their stupid pixie cut. Plus, she was filled with rage. Letitia held out some religious pamphlets as she started the saving the sinner pitch.

"How did you find me?" The words flew out of Lindy's mouth with the force of quills from a cornered porcupine.

Three heads jerked up and stared. Three bewildered faces. One face reddened. "Lindy?" Three jaws dropped. Lauren was the first to recognize her. "What happened? We heard you were kidnapped from the sanctuary. How did you—?"

"Sanctuary? Is that what you call a so-called religious place that forces a woman to commit bigamy? You call yourself Christians? Instead of helping me when I was sick, you preached archaic religious drivel and filled my mind with unhealthy, insane religious thoughts that caused me to fear my wife and flee from her."

Letitia stuck her chin out and moved closer to Lindy. "We didn't make you crazy. You were already there when we met you. We tried to help by bringing the Lord our savior to you."

Lindy stepped into Letitia's personal space and stood eye to eye with her. Letitia paled. "Help my ass. You cost me a year of my life by sending me to a place where neither my friends nor my wife could help me."

Letitia held her ground. "We heard you got better. But it appears you have reunited with Satan." She knelt. "Let's pray." Lauren and Joanna remained standing, looking from Lindy to Letitia. "Dear Father, please forgive this sinner, our sister Lindy, for—"

"You three are Satan. You're doing the devil's work. Sending helpless women to a place where they're deprived of their children and married to the highest bidder in the name of God. I don't know what Joel and his minions pay you, but Quincy is looking into what kind of crimes you all can be charged with." She looked up at the sound of the car pulling into the driveway. "And speaking of Quincy."

Letitia got to her feet, the three of them scrambled down the stairs, then ran down the street without looking back to see if the devil was on their heels.

"You'd better run," she called after them. "If I ever see you in this neighborhood again, I'll call the police and have you arrested." She was still watching them when a very pale, shocked Quincy walked cautiously up the stairs holding Megan's hand. Oh, no, she had to explain. "Quincy—"

"What were they doing here? Are you? Have you been seeing them again?" Her voice was low and even but filled with tension.

"Absolutely not. They just showed up here a few minutes ago and I sent them away. I told them you were looking into what crimes you could charge them with. You don't have to worry. I've had enough of their God."

Quincy let out a breath.

"She's right, Quincy." Dorothy spoke from inside the house through the open door. "I got here a minute after Lindy opened the door and I heard everything. She let them have it good."

"Who are those ladies?" Megan looked from Lindy to Quincy to her grandmother.

"No one you know, Megan." Dorothy waved her inside. "Go to your room and change, Emma and Michaela will be up soon."

Lindy glanced behind her. "Thanks, Dorothy. I didn't realize you were there." She took Quincy's hand. "Are you all right? Please trust that I would never have anything to do with those women or anyone like them."

Quincy squeezed Lindy's hand. "It was such a shock seeing them talking to you on the porch that everything flashed in front of my eyes in a matter of seconds."

"I'm so sorry you had to experience that, but I was as shocked as you to see them here, all pious with their brochures, holier-than-thou attitudes, and save-your-soul faces." She giggled. "But you should have seen their faces when they realized it was me." She pulled Quincy into a hug. "I'd have to be crazy to go with them again." She giggled again. And snuggled in Quincy's arms.

Quincy smiled. "I can't tell you how happy I am to hear you laugh and joke again. And how happy I am that you told them off." She held the door for Lindy. "I'm going to ask the patrols in the neighborhood to keep an eye out for those bitches and harass them about soliciting."

CHAPTER FORTY

Quincy

Quincy helped Dorothy into the front seat of the van while Lindy herded the three girls into the back with her. "Everyone buckled in?" Hearing a chorus of yeses, she started the motor and turned up the heater. She glanced in the rearview mirror and met Lindy's anxious eyes. "You'll be fine, sweetheart, try to relax." She'd been reassuring Lindy from the minute they'd opened their eyes this morning and Dorothy had pitched in since breakfast.

Quincy had her own anxieties about Lindy seeing everyone at once. She hoped being supportive and positive would reduce her anxiety a little. She and Lindy had discussed the best way to handle it and Lindy suggested they ask Grace and Gina and Amelia and Jackson to casually let the other guests know that Lindy would come to talk to them, so they didn't rush her. Then this morning Quincy had realized her focus had to be on getting Dorothy out of the car and into the house, so she'd texted Babs to ask her to come out and walk in with them.

As Quincy parked, Babs appeared. She helped Lindy get the three girls out of their car seats while Quincy set up Dorothy's walker and eased her out of the van. Quincy put a hand on Dorothy to steady her. Lindy grasped Quincy's other hand. Babs picked up Michaela and grabbed Lindy's other hand. Megan and Emma held hands and followed the adults into the house. They stripped off their coats and handed them to Mira, the maid.

Lindy smiled. "Hi, Mira. Nice to see you again."

Mira's eyes flicked to Quincy. Seeing Quincy's grin, she relaxed. "Hello, Lindy. Nice to see you too. Happy Thanksgiving." She walked away with the coats.

Lindy took a deep breath. "That wasn't so bad." She looked at her entourage. "Onward to battle. Ready troops?"

Quincy, Babs, and Dorothy responded with a chorus of yeses, which the three girls echoed.

Lindy straightened her shoulders, grabbed Quincy's hand and marched them into the great room where Grace and Mike had hosted the Thanksgiving dinner for sixty or more guests every year since Quincy rescued their family. More than half were Lindy and Quincy's friends and people Quincy had rescued. The fireplace was blazing, waitresses circulated with trays of hors d'oeuvres and drinks, and the room was filled with the low roar of many conversations and laughter. Lindy hesitated in the doorway.

Dorothy whispered, "Go with her, Quincy, Amelia or Gina will help me find a place to sit." Quincy nodded.

"Okay, here we go." As Lindy led them into the room toward Grace, conversation ground to a halt and the only sounds were the soft jazz playing in the background and the tinkle of ice cubes in glasses.

Lindy was pale and she was squeezing Quincy's hand so hard it was getting numb but she didn't falter, except for a second or two when she was face-to-face with Grace. Then she stepped closer, raising her arms as if to hug Grace but then, unsure of her welcome, dropped them. Grace smiled. "Lindy. I've missed you." She burst into tears. Now Lindy didn't hesitate, she wrapped her arms around Grace. "I'm so happy to see you,

Grace. Thank you for having me." They cried together for a minute before separating.

Grace took Lindy's hands in hers. "I'm so glad you're here, Lindy. Now we're whole again. I want to catch up with you, but I think there are a few people here who want to say hello." She turned Lindy to face the crowd.

Lindy flushed. Quincy leaned close. "Are you up to this?"

"Yes. Yes, I am, but I need you with me. Babs, could you take the girls while we circulate?"

"Sure. We'll go to the children's area. They know Daniel and Ben and Amelia's twins will be there as well as other children."

Lindy knelt in front of the three girls. "Go with Auntie Babs. You can play with Lara and Mia and Daniel and Ben. Mama and I will be here if you need us."

Megan jumped up and down. "Oh boy, Lara and Mia and Daniel and Ben."

As they walked away, Quincy turned to Lindy again. "Ready?"

They moved around the room, taking a few minutes with each of their friends and a little longer with Quincy's grandmother. Lindy was expecting anger and judgment but she got lots of hugs and tears along with love and acceptance. By the time they'd covered the room, stopping even to talk to friends and family of Grace and Mike, guests they knew from previous Thanksgivings, Quincy could feel Lindy's exhaustion and steered her in the direction of some empty chairs. Lindy resisted. She insisted she needed to speak to Grace for just a minute, so Quincy stood back while the two women whispered.

When they sat, a waitress brought them a beer and a seltzer with lime. Quincy saw Mike watching and tipped her bottle in thanks. Lindy sipped her seltzer and watched the crowd over the rim of her glass. She glanced at Quincy. "That was intense, so many people at once. It was overwhelming, but I feel good." She laughed. "Tired but good." She reached for Quincy's hand. "Thanks."

"Any time." Quincy kissed Lindy's knuckles. "Do you think I should check on the girls?"

Lindy shook her head. "Amelia said Grace had hired the usual gaggle of teenagers to watch the kids. I think as long as we don't hear them screaming and nobody comes for us, we should let them be. It's a good start on them being more independent for when Michaela goes to nursery school and Emma starts kindergarten in January."

Just then, Grace banged a gong to get their attention. "Welcome, everyone. Mike and I are pleased to have you all here to celebrate Thanksgiving with us. As most of you know, it was in October eight years ago that we and our four children almost burned to death in our vehicle after a multivehicle pileup on the highway. We've gathered every year since then with our friends and family and the friends and family of the woman who, against all odds, saved me from a fiery death and saved Mike and our children and six others who are here, to thank her and to give our thanks for all that we have in our lives. We're also thankful to have Lindy back with us tonight." She took a sip of water.

"With so many of us, we don't have the room for a sit-down meal at a table, so, as usual, four separate tables have been set up with the entire meal, so you can go to any table to fill your plate, then find a place to sit and eat, then refill at any table. Ask the staff if you don't find what you need on the table. Waiters will continue to circulate to fill your drink orders. If you have children here, the sitters will serve them and help them eat. Now. Before we start, Lindy James Adams has asked to speak to the group for a few minutes."

Quincy was shocked. "What are you doing, Lindy?"

Lindy kissed Quincy's knuckles. "I've got this." The room erupted with conversations as Lindy walked to stand beside Grace. She took the microphone and held it without speaking until the room quieted. "Thank you so much for welcoming me back with open arms and hearts, and I hope, forgiveness. I'm so thankful to be spending this Thanksgiving with so many dear friends. I look forward to many more Thanksgivings together." She handed the microphone to Grace and walked into Quincy's arms while the crowd applauded. They stood together, Lindy's face nestled on Quincy's shoulder. "You were wonderful. Had you prepared that?"

"No, I was struck by the contrast between the coldness of the religious people and our welcoming and loving friends, and I wanted to acknowledge how grateful I am to be accepted back."

Grace waited for the crowd to settle. "I think I speak for everyone, Lindy, when I say you were missed last year and we are thankful to have you with us again," Grace grinned. "And now, let's eat." The crowd surged toward the tables.

Later that evening, as people were leaving, they stopped to say goodbye to Quincy and Lindy. Oren and Neil, a gay couple that Quincy had been friendly with for years, kissed the two of them. "Glad you're back, Lindy. I hope it's for good, because you almost killed Quincy the last time."

Lindy paled.

Neil kicked Oren. "Don't pay any attention to this loudmouth, Lindy. We'll see you." He dragged Oren away.

She turned to Quincy. "You almost died? What is he talking about?"

Quincy's face darkened. It's a good thing Neil had pulled Oren away because she would have beaten the passive-aggressive bastard to a pulp. "I'll explain when we get home."

They were quiet as they loaded Dorothy and the three sleeping girls in the van, then at home they separated to get everyone into bed. Finally, they came together again in their bedroom. Both were exhausted but a red-eyed Lindy sitting up in bed with her arms wrapped around herself, shot questions at Quincy, rat-a-tat. "Tell me, Quincy. Why don't I know you almost died because I left? What happened? Did you try to commit suicide?" Tears streamed down her face.

Quincy wanted to hold her, to reassure her, but instead, she sat on her side of the bed. She cleared her throat. "No, I didn't try to commit suicide. But yes, I put myself in danger and I could have died if I hadn't gotten help." She shifted. "To say I was distraught when you left is an understatement. You and Emma and Michaela are my world…" She walked to the windows and stared out into the darkness while she fought to regain control.

"And you were all gone in an instant, without a word." She turned and slid down the wall to the floor, clasped her hands around her knees, and lowered her head. She breathed deeply for a minute before looking up. "I was devastated. I had to find you because without you I'm a lost soul drifting in the darkness without purpose."

"That's not—"

"Let me finish." Quincy hadn't meant to be so harsh. "Sorry. As uncomfortable as this makes you, it's how I felt and now that I've started, I need to get it out so you understand."

Lindy nodded and dried her tears with the end of the sheet.

"I was determined to find you. I'm a detective, after all, and I had the support of the department. And I threw myself into the search. At first, Tony and I were assigned to the case full-time, and we worked relentlessly to develop leads and follow up sightings. But eventually we had to go back on regular cases. And though Connie assured me the department would continue the search, I couldn't stop. I was driven. So after work I'd come home and spend most of the night following up on any mention of a blonde with two children, dead or alive, anywhere in the country. On weekends or days off, I flew all over the country checking out possible sightings of you and the girls. I forgot about eating and drinking and sleeping. I lost twenty-pounds-plus. I refused to take time out to see friends, turned down all invitations and was isolated." She grinned. "A recipe for disaster. And sure enough after three months I collapsed. Luckily, I was at work so I was rushed to the hospital." She got up and went to sit on the bed. "My whole body was out-of-whack. I was dehydrated to the point my kidneys were about to shut down, my potassium, salt and other levels were dangerously low. I almost died."

Lindy leaned forward and took Quincy's hand. "Oh, Quincy, I—"

Quincy grasped Lindy's hand between both of hers. "It's all right. I didn't die. After three days, Amelia took me home with her to make sure I ate and drank and slept. And when I was feeling better, she invited all our friends and Denise to her house and staged an intervention. Amelia convinced me that while no one thought I was trying to commit suicide, it was clear that if I kept up what I was doing, I would kill myself. The intervention was very emotional and the result was a plan for living—eating well, exercising, spending time with friends, and seeing Denise three times a week. I continued to track leads but Grace and Mike paid for a private detective to follow up sightings so I wouldn't have to travel. Then I bought this house, the house we wanted. Dorothy and Megan were a lifeline. Dorothy treated me like a daughter. Spending time with Megan, teaching her things, playing with her, seeing her blossom and be happy in spite of missing her mom, gave me pleasure and helped me understand that I too could be happy even though I was missing you and the girls. In addition, I stuck with the program, though I now only see Denise once a month, and I've been happier and centered and healthy since." She looked into Lindy's eyes. "So you see it was dramatic but not as dramatic as Oren made it sound."

"Why didn't you tell me?"

"Oh, honey, I knew you would feel guilty, and you were so fragile when you came home. The last thing you needed was to deal with something you couldn't change. I promise I would have told you at some point."

"You can see by how I handled today that I'm not so fragile anymore. And I know I've said I'm sorry before, but I am truly sorry I put you through that. The thought that I caused such pain for you and our daughters crushes my heart, but I can bear it and I want you to tell me everything."

Quincy nodded. "If you mean it, I do have something else to share with you."

"Yes, I mean it. I need to know all the damage I did."

"This isn't about damaging me. It's more about you…your past. Um, when Tony and I couldn't find any trace of you, we went to Newtown Springs."

The look of shock on Lindy's face confirmed that as her sister said—Lindy knew better than to ever go back there. "Oh, my, you of all people should know I'd never go back to those people."

Quincy shrugged. "I was desperate. And you weren't exactly the Lindy I knew and loved when you left. Based on your notebook, I thought there was a chance you might have gone home."

Lindy frowned. "Notebook?"

Quincy's stomach did a flip-flop. Damn, she'd really put her foot in her mouth this time. She swallowed. "You don't remember you were keeping a notebook while…during…uh, before you left?"

"No. I don't remember." She swung her legs over the side of the bed, sat next to Quincy and put an arm over her shoulders. "Christ, Quincy, you're white as a ghost. You opened Pandora's box and it's too late to slam it shut. What the hell was in the notebook?"

"There were drawings and scribbles and written entries detailing what was happening for you, what you were feeling, your fears and things like that."

"And? What are you scared to tell me?"

Quincy sighed. "It was horrible to read, partly because your pain came through and partly because of what you were saying, about Satan, about me being Satan, about me cheating on you, about the girls burning in hell because we're lesbians, about God talking to you, stuff like that. It was scary. And it was painful to realize you were having a breakdown right in front of me and I hadn't noticed. But what hurt the most was when I did figure out something was wrong, I let you convince me you were fine and allowed you to leave with the girls. I should have persisted. I'm sorry."

"Oh, sweetie, you were working so hard to buy us this house and we barely saw each other. It was bad timing that you weren't around much after Sarah and John died, and of course, neither of us could control whatever it was biochemically that set off the psychosis. It wasn't your fault. Did you keep the notebook?"

"Yes. But maybe you should look at it with Denise tomorrow."

"Did you show it to Denise?"

"No. I did show it to Amelia when I found it because I was so freaked out. Later, when I was in therapy, I discussed my feelings about it with Denise, but Amelia and I are the only ones who read it. I wanted to protect your privacy but I confess if I had found you and the girls, I would have handed it to the judge to support my claim for custody."

"Fair enough." Lindy nodded. "Are you afraid I'll go back there if I read it now? Get psychotic again?"

"I, uh, I think it might upset you. And, uh, I guess I'm afraid you'll react badly."

Lindy patted Quincy's thigh and pulled back. "Denise has been after me to share more with you and now I see why. From what she's said and what's in the books and articles she's given me to read, it's highly unlikely I'll ever have another episode unless I have another baby and then the chances are fifty-fifty. So I doubt I'll relapse. However, I'll honor your request and take the notebook to therapy with me tomorrow. Okay?"

Quincy smiled. "Thanks."

Lindy took a deep breath and eyed Quincy. "Somehow we got off the track of your visit to my pa...my family." Her grin was mischievous. "So how did that go for you?"

"Not so good. Your parents were even nastier than you described. I didn't even mention your name to your dad and he was all over me because I was wearing a pantsuit. Aaron seemed kind of beaten down by your father. We talked to him outside the store and I intimated I'd seen you in Atlanta. He asked if you were okay, then said you were the smart one getting away and sent his regards."

Lindy wrapped her arms around herself and began to rock back and forth.

"Later we went to your parents' house hoping you were there. When I mentioned your name to your mother, she said she assumed you were in hell with the devil, which was ironic given our situation, and slammed the door in my face. Hope was more related. Someone in town told us she was married to the preacher's son. She spoke to us on the porch but kept looking over her shoulder so I assumed he was in the house. She was pretty clear that you'd know to never go back there."

"Even in my craziness, I never considered it." Lindy rubbed her upper arms. "I've always regretted not taking her with me, but I was just a kid myself and I was so scared. All I could think of was to run. Did she seem angry? Did she ask for me?"

"She wanted to know what you'd done that we were looking for you. I said we just needed to ask you some questions. She asked whether you were married. I said you were but I didn't say you were married to me. She asked about children and I told her you had two daughters. She apparently can't have children. She asked me to tell you she loves you and misses you every day."

Lindy looked as if she might cry.

Quincy hesitated but put a hand on Lindy's neck and gently massaged. "Hey, you had no idea where you were going or whether you'd get away. You were lucky Sarah found you, but you could have ended up being prostituted and becoming a drug addict." Quincy removed her hand. "She looked hopeless but when I asked if she wanted help getting away she refused, said it was too late." Lindy's hand went to her neck as if feeling the loss of Quincy's touch.

"Good thing this house is so big. Would you have brought her here or put her in a shelter somewhere?"

"Actually, I didn't have the house then. It didn't matter since the only thing I cared about was finding you. I would have brought her back to the apartment. I knew you would have wanted me to help her."

"I would. I wish she'd left with you, though I don't know how she'd feel about…us, about our family. Maybe someday, we can—" She shrugged. "It's academic at this point. So when did you buy the house?"

"About six months after you left it came on the market again because the owner got transferred to California. The broker called to see if I was still interested."

Lindy yawned. "I'm feeling a little overwhelmed. Can we go to sleep?"

CHAPTER FORTY-ONE

Lindy

Before Quincy left for work the next morning she handed Lindy a bag with the notebook. Lindy hesitated, placed it on the table near the front door so she wouldn't forget it, and surprised them both by kissing Quincy goodbye, not a sexy kiss but a real kiss. Now, driving to Denise's office, Lindy's eyes kept flicking to the bag. Though she had assured Quincy it wouldn't trigger the psychosis again, she was feeling anxious about what the notebook contained. But she had promised Quincy she would look at it with Denise and a promise was a promise.

Clutching the notebook, Lindy settled into her chair facing Denise. She knew she should start but for the first time in months she felt frightened.

Denise leaned forward, peering at her. "You're very pale, Lindy. Is something wrong?"

Lindy nodded, then shook her head. "I...Quincy told me about the notebook I kept before I ran away. I have it here." She held out the bag. "I promised her I'd only look at it with you but now I'm afraid to see how crazy I was."

"Put it on the table next to you. Let's talk for a few minutes." Denise watched Lindy place the bag with care. "Do you remember writing in the notebook?"

"No. I was surprised to hear about it. Quincy said it was hidden, so obviously I knew it was something I had to keep secret."

"Yes, we've talked about knowing what's real even in the midst of the psychosis and this is a good example. You knew what you were writing wasn't real so you kept it away from Quincy."

"She said she talked to you about it."

"Yes, she told me a little about it but it wasn't relative to her therapy so I never asked to see it. Are you afraid that reading it might pull you back to the place of psychosis?"

"I know you said it was a one-time thing but…yes, I'm afraid. I really can't go back there, Denise. I can't."

"Remember, it's just words and drawings and they don't have the power to hurt you unless you let them. Let's move to the sofa and read it together. We can stop anytime you want."

They sat side by side. Lindy retrieved the book from the bag and opened to the first page. Lindy read the entries, studied the drawings, and from time to time, glanced at Denise, as if trying to gauge her reaction. When they had read the last page, Lindy closed the book. "I remember a lot of this." She ran her fingers down the page. "Thinking Quincy was cheating, thinking she had cameras around the house, the voices. The drawings are scary but I guess they show what I was feeling. Poor Quincy, stumbling across this. She must have been out of her mind with worry about the girls." She glanced at Denise. "And about me."

Denise nodded. "How do you feel?"

"Sad." A tear escaped. "I just don't know how I'll ever make it up to Quincy, how I'll ever erase the pain I caused her."

"You can't undo the past. You need to focus on the future, on being happy and living the life you want. Any reaction to what you read and saw in the notebook?"

Lindy stared out the window, then turned to Denise with a smile. "The idea of the notebook was scarier than the reality. I remember the feelings. I lived it and we've been talking about it since I came back from Arizona. But I no longer have those feelings or thoughts. I'm no longer the person who wrote those things and drew those pictures. I felt like I was reading a novel, that some creative author filled the notebook with those crazy sentences full of horror and pain." Lindy looked down at the notebook in her lap. "In a way, I feel free."

Denise waited but Lindy didn't go on. "Is there anything more about the notebook you want to discuss? She moved back to her chair.

Lindy considered the question. "No. Something may come up later but right now I'm done with it."

Denise smiled. "So how did Thanksgiving go?"

Lindy's grin lit up her face. "Really well. I talked to everyone and I felt so welcomed and so loved. I'm sorry I waited, but who knows how I would have faced everyone when I was still so unsure and needy? I feel whole again."

"And how are you feeling about Quincy? About your relationship?"

Lindy reached for the bag and slipped the book in, then placed it on the table. She moved off the sofa, back to the chair she always sat in. She felt Denise's eyes on her but she couldn't answer when her mind was scrolling through her thoughts quicker than a computer search. What did she feel for Quincy? It was as scary as the thought of the notebook had been.

Lindy raised her eyes and locked onto Denise's kind gray eyes. "I love Quincy with all my heart. Through all of my craziness, even in the darkest days that I remember, I always loved her. But whenever I thought of her and yearned to be with her, to have her hold me, to make me feel safe, God's voice would scream that she was Satan and that my love was evil and Michaela and Emma and I would burn in hell with her."

"And now?" Denise's question was simple enough but Lindy hesitated. Her eyes went to the bag holding the notebook. She thought about Quincy rescuing her without hesitation or recriminations. How she'd stuck by her without any guarantee of restarting their relationship. How she'd let Lindy proceed at her own pace in her recovery. How she was taking care of her every day in every way without asking for anything.

"Are you afraid to love her?"

Lindy nodded. "I know she's not Satan but what if loving her causes me to...go there again?"

"I understand your fear but love doesn't cause postpartum psychosis. As we've discussed, it's a biochemical imbalance that can happen after childbirth and in your case probably facilitated by thyroid disease. It's been what, eight, nine or more months since you've hallucinated or heard voices?" She didn't wait for an answer. "You are a very strong, resilient woman, Lindy. When you confronted that scary notebook, you ended up feeling free from the psychosis. When you confronted a room full of people expecting hate and got love and respect instead, you ended up feeling whole again. Who do you trust most in the world?"

Lindy's eyebrows shot up. "Quincy?"

"Are you asking or telling me?"

Lindy chewed her thumb. "Telling you." Her voice was strong. "I trust Quincy more than anyone else in the world."

"Is there anyone else you trust?"

Lindy considered the question, then ticked off her fingers as she listed names. "Um, you, Babs, Amelia, Grace and—" She smiled at Denise. "I get it. I trust Quincy and you and most of our friends to be there for me if I relapse."

"Sounds like a really strong safety net. So why not risk loving Quincy, telling her you're in love with her? I assume you are, in love with her."

Lindy's smile was shy. "I am. I've been trying to be neutral until I'm sure but once in a while I slip and flirt. We sleep together and she holds me every night and I feel her heartbeat and her warm breath on my neck and sometimes when she thinks I'm asleep, she touches my face and my hair so gently I want to cry because I know what she's feeling. I want to touch her, to make love with her, to reassure her that I love her and want to be with her. But I've been afraid."

"And now?"

Lindy blushed. "I'm sure and I think it's time."

CHAPTER FORTY-TWO

Quincy

With Megan and Emma at school, Michaela at nursery school, and Dorothy at the physical therapy center for the day, Quincy left work at noon to pick up Lindy and take her out to lunch, something they'd been doing recently to have some private time. She checked the kitchen, the living and dining rooms, then called out but got no response. Had Lindy gone to the store? Maybe she left a note. She went back to the kitchen to check and caught the strains of Marvin Gaye's "I Heard it Through the Grapevine" drifting softly in the background. Quincy took a deep breath. Of course, she was in the sunroom. She loved to sit there and read and now that it was getting warm, she'd open some of the windows and sit quietly listening to the birds at the feeders they'd hung in the trees. She didn't know that Lindy was listening to music again.

Quincy strode through the hall, and always careful about surprising Lindy, slowly opened the door. Lindy faced the windows and the sunshine, her back to Quincy. The music played softly and Lindy was...Lindy was dancing to Percy Sledge's

"When a Man Loves a Woman," her hips and arms and legs moving as gracefully and as sensually as the first time Quincy had watched her dance in the mirror at Maggie's Bar. Tears filled Quincy's eyes. It had been so long since she'd seen Lindy dancing sensually. Lindy swung around, her smile wide and beautiful, and her eyes, pain-free and sparkling, met Quincy's. Like a match meeting flint, sparks flew between them. Quincy's heart filled with love and a surge of heat traveled through her. Lindy extended both hands, fingers snapping to the beat, and beckoned Quincy to her. "Come dance with me, love."

They danced facing each other, not touching but maintaining eye contact as they moved to the music. The music changed to "Let's Get it On," another Marvin Gaye song and Quincy realized Lindy was playing the CD she'd made for her when they first got together. It had all Lindy's favorite dance numbers on it. Before Quincy took in what was happening, Lindy stepped into her arms. They fit together perfectly, as they always had. Lindy pulled Quincy close, her breath warming Quincy's neck as they moved together to the music. It had been so long since they'd danced, but they slipped effortlessly into Smokey Robinson's "Cruisin'" then, Al Green's "Let's Stay Together." When Aretha Franklin's "Natural Woman" came on, Lindy breathed into Quincy's ear. "I want to come home to you, Quincy. I want to spend my life making up for the hurt I caused you. I love you. I hope it's not too late for us to start over."

Quincy was overcome with emotion and couldn't speak. She felt Lindy tense. She cleared her throat. "I'd like nothing better than to start over." Lindy looked up at her with teary eyes, then Quincy leaned in and kissed her. They kissed and danced for another song. "Will you marry me, Quincy?"

"I would, but we've already done that. Nothing's changed for me."

Lindy reached up and caressed Quincy's face. "I want to recommit to you in front of all our friends. I want them to know I'm better and we're a couple again. I want them to celebrate with us. Denise said she'd officiate if you agreed to it."

"I'd love to marry you again. All the love in my heart belongs to you, Lindy."

"And all the love in my heart is yours, Quincy."

Bella Books, Inc.

Women. Books. Even Better Together.

P.O. Box 10543
Tallahassee, FL 32302

Phone: 800-729-4992
www.bellabooks.com

CPSIA information can be obtained
at www.ICGtesting.com
Printed in the USA
LVHW021940181021
700737LV00002B/2